THE DANCE OF DEATH

SAVANNAH JAMES

The Dance of Death
Copyright © 2023 Savannah James

All rights reserved. Without limiting the rights under copyright reserved above, no part of this publication may be reproduced, stored in or introduced into retrieval system, or transmitted, in any form, or by any means (electronic, mechanical, photocopying, recording, or otherwise) without the prior written permission of both the copyright owner and the above publisher of this book.

This is a work of fiction. Names, characters, places, brands, media, and incidents are either the products of the author's imagination or are used fictitiously. The author acknowledges the trademarked status and trademark owners of various products referenced in this work of fiction, which have been used without permission. The publication/use of these trademarks is not authorized, associated with, or sponsored by the trademark owners.

Editing: Rebecca Scharpf
Cover/Map Design: Rena Violet
Interior Formatting: Champagne Book Design

To my brother,
thank you for being the Sokka to my Katara

Trigger Warnings

This book contains death, grief, language, sex, drinking, mentions of alcoholism, depictions of mental health struggles, depression, and mention of past suicidal ideation.

The Underworld

- Elysium
- Lethe
- Judges
- Aristaeus' House
- Asphodel Market
- Asphodel
- Charon's House
- Hecate's House
- Styx

Field of Mourning

Torture Fields

Phlegethon

Hades Castle

Dungeon

Tartarus

Cocytus

Acheren

Wall of Erebus

THE DANCE OF DEATH

I held it truth, with him who sings
To one clear harp in divers tones,
That men may rise on stepping-stones
Of their dead selves to higher things.

But who shall so forecast the years
And find in loss a gain to match?
Or reach a hand thro' time to catch
The far-off interest of tears?

Let Love clasp Grief lest both be drown'd,
Let darkness keep her raven gloss:
Ah, sweeter to be drunk with loss,
To dance with death, to beat the ground,

Than that the victor Hours should scorn
The long result of love, and boast,
'Behold the man that loved and lost,
But all he was is overworn.'

Verse I of *In Memoriam A.H.H*
by Alfred, Lord Tennyson

PROLOGUE

THANATOS

7854 OE *(Old Era)*

"You don't have to keep doing this, you know." Hades, the God of the Dead and King of the Underworld says. We are standing at the gated entrance, a small section of dirt and dying grass that forms only when new souls arrive. Otherwise it is just a large wall made of shadow and darkness; the ethereal form of my father, Erebus, the God of Darkness.

"What do you speak of?" I inquire.

"There is a place for you here, a place that you could call home." His voice is kind, and his words warm, but it is hard for me to trust them. Even though Hades has never given me a reason not to, what he's saying is too good to be true.

Though there have not been many souls I have had to cleave and collect, there have been enough where I find myself growing familiar with the Underworld and its inhabitants. It's a beautiful dimension, and at its center are three beautiful souls—all of whom have every reason to despise me, but instead have welcomed me at every turn. Hades, Hecate, and Charon knew about my brother and I long before they called the Underworld their home. Our reputation is known among the cosmos: we are the brothers that showed the universe that happiness is finite; the twins that were born from the fear of the end, and thus adopted those ideas as their purpose; the God of Death and the God of Fear, forever ruining the lives of every living creature because we serve as a reminder of everyone's inevitable end.

But despite this, Hades is offering me a place in his home, in the dark palace at the heart of the Underworld where he and the others have formed a bond deeper than I could have ever imagined. I've seen it firsthand. They depend on each other, not because they feel obligated to, but because they want to. They trust one another. They love one another.

I don't know what that feels like.

My brother and I travel the cosmos together because it is what we have always done. We are hated by everyone, including our own parents, so it made sense we would be together. In the first few years of our existence, Phobos and I had what Hades, Hecate, and Charon do, but those days are long gone. Phobos can feel the fear of every being alive, and this external input has twisted his heart into something dark and cruel. He now enjoys the fear and hatred we instill in others, and it has taken me a while to realize I don't. I don't want to be hated. I want what Hades has: friendship, trust, devotion.

Love.

"Why?" I ask him, tucking my feathers tightly against my back. I've always believed it makes me appear less threatening, though my scythe never leaves my side and that tool tends to put people on edge regardless of how I present myself. Hades has never given me the impression that he finds me threatening in any capacity, however, and this has been confirmed by Phobos. After one of my visits here, I asked him if Hades ever felt fear around me, and my brother responded, "You can't fear death if you yourself crave it."

Is that why Hades wishes for me to reside here? Does he think I will kill him and his friends?

Hades takes a step towards me, and the tendrils of shadow that emanate from the Wall of Erebus part further to make way for him. "I know what it means to be so lonely you no longer remember what it felt like to belong, if you ever did in the first place. In the Underworld, we're all outcasts in our own way, with our own darkness we try to fend off every day. But you don't have to do so alone. Not anymore."

His words stir an unknown emotion in my breast. "I'm not alone. I have my brother."

"Sometimes the loneliness we feel when among others is the worst kind. It's one thing to be physically alone, but to feel alone because none of the people around you see you? I know that feeling all too well. As do my friends. That is exactly why you should come live here with us. You have no obligation to your brother. You are free to do as you please, and I want you to know that there are options for you besides an eternity of fear and dread."

I consider his words, consider the potential future he proposes, and I'm hesitant to hope for such an outcome. "Even if I took you up on your offer, my brother would follow me here."

The King shakes his head, his smile one of youthful arrogance. "I control who enters, exits, and stays in the Underworld. Your brother will not be able to get near you while you're here, if that is what you wish."

"You may be powerful, but even you cannot keep him at bay. He is not just the God of Fear. He *is* fear, just as I'm death. Where fear grows in the heart, he is never too far away." He is like a plague, leaving nothing but destruction in his wake.

"That does not change the fact that this is my dimension, and even if he shows up on our doorstep, he cannot stay. After a few times of him being removed from the Underworld, he'll get the idea. He cannot take on Hecate, Charon, you, and I all at once. Soon he will realize he is unmatched, and he will slink away into the shadows where he belongs," Hades says reassuringly.

I cannot imagine my brother taking a defeat lightly. "While he waits in the shadows, he will plan his revenge upon all of us. All that lives in his heart is cruelty; he will bide his time until the slight against him has been repaid."

Unexpectedly, Hades grins, as if this is a challenge. "I've got nothing but time. Let him try."

The declaration is idiotic and naïve, but I find myself believing him anyways. Maybe that also makes me idiotic, but the future he's promising, one with comfort and joy instead of terror, seems worth the risk of my brother's wrath.

So I nod to the king standing before me, smiling for the first time since I was brought into this world. "I accept your offer."

Hades smiles, and I know without a shadow of a doubt that he is glad of my answer.

"Soon they will see you for who you are," a familiar voice whispers in my mind, as deep and foreboding as ever. *"With or without your brother, they will turn on you."*

Erebus.

"You're wrong, Father," I respond, never physically opening my lips.

"Perhaps, but one day they will all be dead, their souls having been cleaved and forced into an eternal prison by your hands, and you will still be alive." He says it matter-of-factly, without any of the malice or resentment that tend to be present in our every interaction. *"Don't you see? Love is not meant for beings like you. You were meant to be alone."*

Hades, having no idea that my father speaks to me, reaches forward and grabs onto my arm, giving me a look of affection and relief. "Welcome to your new home."

PART I

'You must begone,' said Death, 'these walks are mine.'
Love wept and spread his sheeny vans for flight;
Yet ere he parted said, 'This hour is thine:
Thou art the shadow of life, and as the tree
Stands in the sun and shadows all beneath,
So in the light of great eternity
Life eminent creates the shade of death.
The shadow passeth when the tree shall fall,
But I shall reign for ever over all.'
Alfred, Lord Tennyson

CHAPTER ONE

EURYDICE

***2023 NE** (New Era)*

I was eight years old the first time I saw death. My grandmother had been battling cancer for as long as I could remember, and it became obvious when I was eight years old that she didn't have much time left. My moms took me to see her in the hospital on the last day of her life, and even though I was only a child, I knew it was going to be the last time I would ever see her. She was so frail—so weak, so pale. When I grasped onto her hand, I was afraid even a squeeze from my tiny fingers would snap her bones like twigs. Thankfully it didn't, and my grandma complimented me on my pink glitter nail polish, which I had done myself the night before. I was proud of myself, and despite being on her deathbed, she listened to a little girl brag about what a great nail tech she would make.

As the day went on, my moms encouraged me to occupy myself with my toys, wanting to shield me from the depressing atmosphere that had fallen over the room. I did as they asked and sat in a chair near the window, counting how many red cars were in the car park, but I was still aware of my mothers' crying, of the soft-spoken goodbyes they exchanged with the dying woman. I wanted to say something to comfort my parents, or even my grandma, but knowing what to say has never been a talent I possess, so I just sat and tried to drown out the sounds of their grief.

At five in the afternoon, just as I was about to doze off, I heard one of my mothers scream.

"No! You can't take her! You can't take my mother! I won't let you." Mom shouted while my other mom held her by her shoulders. The person she had been yelling at was a man with black wings. He held a scythe in his hand, and I remember thinking that it looked like a hoe you'd use for farming, but it was about twice the size and had a pretty scary-looking blade.

The winged man had surveyed the room, and when his eyes landed on me for a second, an involuntary chill swept down my spine. His irises were stark white, like snow, and I knew immediately who it was. Thanatos, the God of Death.

Despite how unsettled I felt, I wasn't afraid or angry, unlike my moms. In his white eyes I saw a deep sorrow, and all I felt for him was pity. I couldn't understand the reaction from my parents and the nurses present; couldn't they see how much he hated doing this? Couldn't they see how sad he looked?

I approached the winged man, despite the protests of my parents, clutching my stuffed lamb tightly in my arms. "Are you here to take my grandma?"

The man seemed shocked by my question, but he nodded. "Yes, Eurydice, I am."

I tilted my head. "How do you know my name?"

He pointed to the necklace I wore, which spelled out my name in tiny purple beads.

I remember blushing in embarrassment.

"Won't Grandma be lonely in the Underworld?" I asked him.

He shook his head, his expression softening. "She will be around many souls, all of whom are kind and generous and very welcoming. She will be happy there."

I slowly nodded my head, stepping aside. "You have my permission then."

His lips tipped up slightly at that, but his expression resumed its depressed state as quickly as it had vanished. He glided across the hospital room floor towards my grandmother, ignoring the soft pleads and sobs from my parents, though I know he didn't do so apathetically. He ignored their sorrow because it pained him to hear it; I could tell from the stiffness of his shoulders and the way he seemed to cringe away from the noise.

He touched the tip of his scythe to my grandmother's forehead before gently pulling it away, and I watched in silent awe as my grandmother's eyes fluttered shut and her last breath left her chest. Though I couldn't see her, somehow, I knew my grandmother's soul was in this room, and that was confirmed when Thanatos stuck his arm out and seemingly grabbed onto air.

"Bye Grandma," I whispered, my eyes locked on Thanatos's visually empty arm.

The God of Death glanced down at me, and he solemnly inclined his head. "I promise she will be well taken care of."

I didn't know how, and I still don't know why to this day, but I believed him.

"Will I ever see you again?" I had asked him, and I remember thinking he could use a friend—someone to make that frown disappear.

"Yes, little one," Thanatos murmured, stretching his wings out behind him. "But I pray it will be a long time before you do."

My child mind thought this was his way of saying he did not want me as his friend, but it didn't take long for me to realize the true meaning of his words. And now, twenty years later, here he is again: The God of Death, standing over me with that sorrowful expression, only this time it's my soul that he has come to collect, and when I lock my gaze with his, I can see his last words to me floating through his mind.

It wasn't a long enough time.

Just like when I was a child, I trust Thanatos full-heartedly, and I don't feel any fear as he lifts that scythe and severs my soul from my body. I know he will take care of me. I know he will keep me safe.

"You deserve better than this fate," he murmurs to me as we travel to the Underworld, and though I cannot reply to him, I'm comforted by his kind words. As I learned throughout my life, we have no control over our fate. The universe is a tightly woven web, and we're all just strings waiting for the day we snap under the weight of what we manage to capture. Family, friends, careers, hopes, and dreams all fall with us into the void, and that's what is to become of all living people. We all grow up knowing this, I just thought my string could bear a bit more weight until it snapped.

I was wrong.

Just as I had learned in school, when Thanatos and I reach the Underworld, I'm pulled from my temporary trance and am met with the Wall of Erebus, where the infamous Cerberus guards the entrance to the Underworld. It's here I'm to be picked up by The Ferryman and led to the Judges, where my eternal fate will be decided. Years of studying the Underworld has made me far more comfortable with this sudden transition than I assume most are, and it's also allowed me to go into this more prepared. I know most of Mortals' fear of the Underworld and its inhabitants comes from a lack of knowledge, but I have it in spades.

But what Thanatos does goes completely against what I read about. He doesn't set me down; instead he flies through the wall, over the River Styx, and right to the bank where the Judges stand side by side, their glowing eyes flickering towards us in shock. Only now does Thanatos set me down, and I get the feeling he's never broken protocol before, and that makes my lips curl up into a smile.

I step out of his arms, and I'm surprised by how different everything feels; I can feel Thanatos's touch as he helps me steady myself, I can feel the ground beneath my feet, but it's different. Everything is lighter, like gravity isn't weighing me down the same way it used to. It's strange.

The Judges whisper to each other as they watch me, and their eyes are just as startling and unique as Thanatos's. I feel like they can already see inside my mind and heart even though they haven't touched me yet, that's how piercing their gazes are. I feel as if my soul is on display.

I guess it is.

I turn back to Thanatos, feeling nerves for the first time since my death. "In case I'm taken to the Field of Mourning and I forget, I wanted to thank you. Not just for looking after me, but for comforting Orpheus—"

I choke on the name of my husband, and my grief and regret for the future he and I have been robbed of hits me all at once. All the dreams we had, the plans we made—all gone within a few minutes. Now Orpheus will have to live out the rest of his life without me, mourning me like he's mourned all he's loved in his life, and no one will be there to comfort him. He's probably still in that street, cradling my dead body in his arms. I feel tears swell in my eyes, and though I try my best to stop them from falling, the mental image turns my tears into sobs.

I start to fall, but Thanatos grabs me before I hit the ground, and I'm once again swooped into his arms, but this time it's in the form of a hug. He lets me soak the chest of his suit with my tears, lets me clutch onto his sleeves like they're my lifeline, all the while gently rubbing my back, trying his best to comfort me.

"I'm so sorry." His wings fall forward and cocoon around me, adding an extra layer of comfort.

I burrow deeper into his chest, shaking my head. "I don't want to lose my memories. I don't want to forget him."

"There's no guarantee you will, but if you do, it will not be forever. You need time to heal, and once that healing is done, you will remember the beautiful life you shared together, and one day you will be reunited."

I lift my head slightly, peering into those stark white eyes. "Promise?"

Thanatos holds me a little tighter. "I promise."

Once again, I believe the reassurance he gives me, and it provides me the strength I need to leave his embrace and journey towards the Judges, to where my future will be decided. Two of the Judges smile at me as I approach, while another one stares, indifferent. Thankfully it's one of the smiling ones that reaches his hand out.

"There's nothing to be afraid of, my dear." He winks, and any lingering nerves fade away.

With a deep breath, I place my hand in his, and I watch in awe as the glowing eyes of the Judges fade away and I see my life play out before my eyes—all the good, bad, and everything in between. It's over after only a few minutes, and when the Judge drops my hand, I once again see them standing in front of me.

"Are you ready?" he asks me gently.

I look over my shoulder to where Thanatos still stands, and upon seeing the small nod he gives me, I respond, "I'm ready."

Chapter Two

Thanatos

Two weeks later...

Eurydice is sitting at the bank of the River Lethe again. In the weeks she has been in the Field of Mourning, she has spent nearly every afternoon in a patch of grass a few feet from the flowing water, writing in a leatherbound journal given to her when she was first taken here.

As with all souls before they drink from Lethe, Eurydice was asked if there were any items she would want in her house to make her more comfortable. We have seen that souls in Mourning heal faster when surrounded by comforting items from their lives, even if they cannot remember why they had been so special. It is better than having a market for the souls to purchase items at like in Asphodel—the crowded stalls and idle chatter would only cause anxiety and stress for those here.

Eurydice asked for only three things: a blank journal, a CD of classical music, and a subscription on her living room TV to National Geographic.

When the Judges informed me that these had been her requests—after I had awkwardly asked about her welfare—I found myself becoming more and more fascinated with her, which is a first for me. I have never been this involved in a soul's afterlife. I have never carried a soul directly to the judges or asked after them once they had been settled into their resting place. And I certainly have never watched a soul like a Mortal stalker.

It is mildly concerning.

I confessed this all to Persephone, the most recent addition to our family, last night after our library date. Ever since she married Hades and became queen, she's made an effort to spend time with each of us one on one, crafting a bond with us as strongly as we are bonded to one another. Her initial response to my confession was to throw her head back and laugh, as if I had told a good joke. When I had not shared in her laughter, Persephone placed her hand over mine and shook her head. "If I didn't know better, I would say you have a crush, Thanatos."

A few dozen denials flooded my brain, but I couldn't bring myself to voice them, because I think she might be right. I have been alive since the beginning of creation. I was here before the first blade of grass sprouted from the grounds of the Mortal World, before even the Fates themselves began to weave their prophecies and destinies. And yet I have never encountered anyone who treated me the way Eurydice has. From the time Eurydice was a child until her existence as a soul in the Underworld, she has treated me with kindness and respect. She has always seen me as a person.

I have no idea why this is, but it is as intriguing as it is intoxicating.

I know I should stop gazing at her from a distance; I know I should turn away and go about my life without paying her a second thought. But I also know I couldn't do either even if I tried.

I should probably go speak to her. Rip the Band-Aid off, as the Mortals say.

But what if she does not remember me?

Why do I care if she does?

With a deep breath, I make my way down towards the riverbank, keeping my wings tucked behind my back and my scythe dragging behind me. I don't want to hold it up and seem threatening. Eurydice has never been afraid of me before, but I have always written that off as childhood naivety sticking with her through adulthood. If she does not remember me, she may very well scream in terror like everyone else does. The idea makes my gut sink, a feeling I have never experienced before.

Eurydice must hear me approach her, because she turns her head towards me when I'm still several yards away from her. Without even a second of hesitation, her face breaks out in a smile, and the relief I feel flood through me is palpable.

"Thanatos," she says warmly, standing up from the kneeling position she had been in before. "What a surprise."

I close the distance between us and offer her a small smile, uncharacteristically unsure of myself. "I wanted to check on you and make sure you were settling into the Field of Mourning well."

Her smile turns playful, and she leans forward as if to share a secret. "Do you do that with every soul or am I just special?"

I attempt to laugh, but the noise I produce is more of a grunt. "I confess you are the first soul I have ever sought out after I cleaved them from their body. I hope you don't find this visit unwelcome."

She shakes her head, grabbing hold of the hand that still clutches my scythe. "Of course your visit is welcome. Why wouldn't it be?"

I'm still recovering from the shock of her touching me, so I'm unable to answer right away. She did it so naturally, and she did so to the hand holding my scythe! And now she wonders why my visiting her would be unwelcome? If she were not still touching my hand, I would swear she were a figment of my imagination.

"I'm the God of Death," I explain the obvious. "I'm not exactly seen by anyone in the best of light."

She waves that comment off with a roll of her eyes. "That's a bunch of bullshit. It's not like you chose to be the God of Death, and I know you don't enjoy your task. You shouldn't be punished for things you cannot control. Besides, death is natural and someone has to carry out the duty you perform or else we would all live in purgatory forever."

I stare at her, once again not knowing what to say.

She laughs. "Don't look so shocked. I told you I trusted you, did you think I was lying? I know you're a good person. It's not your fault that no one else can see past your job description."

Her statement makes me pause. "So you remember our last meeting? When you died?"

She sighs, glancing behind her at the river. "Yes and no. I remember you very clearly. I don't know how I died or what happened after you cleaved my soul, though. All I remember is you showing up, holding my hand, and telling me how everything would turn out alright."

This shouldn't please me as much as it does. "Is there anything else that you cannot remember? Not only from your death, but from your life?"

Do you remember the husband you left behind and wept in my arms over?

Eurydice's gaze grows distance as she thinks. "I remember living in Australia, I remember my job, school, friends…I don't remember my parents, though I know they aren't dead. I don't know if I was in a relationship either. I certainly hope not. My parents must be feeling unimaginable pain; I don't want anyone else to feel such loss on my behalf."

"How can anyone who knew you not feel such loss? The rays of sunlight from Helios fell away the moment your soul left the Mortal World, leaving it cold and dark in your absence."

The laugh that escapes her is breathy, almost sheepish. "You can say that after only having met me twice?"

I glance down at her hand, still covering mine. "One only needs a moment in your presence to see the beauty of your soul."

A soul cannot blush, but I have no doubt her cheeks would be red if she were alive. Her eyes light up at my compliment and she tears her gaze from me, as if unable to handle my stare.

"I'm really glad you came to check on me," she says, squeezing my hand once before letting it go. "I'm completely directionally challenged, so I probably will need more checking up on. For safety reasons, of course."

The bright smile she gives me warms me from my cheeks to my toes. "Of course. It's my duty to make sure all souls are safe and comfortable here in the Underworld."

"I'm in safe hands then." Her smile widens further, enjoying our banter.

"Most wouldn't think so," I point out.

She shrugs. "I'm not most people."

No, you certainly aren't.

She gestures towards the direction I came with a nod. "I was just about to head back to my house. Would you walk with me?"

I give her an incline of my head, extending my arm out as invitation for her to go first. Only when she is past me do I turn and begin walking, falling into step next to her. We're silent for the first few minutes, then she swivels her head towards me, making her brown ponytail sway.

"Could I ask you a few questions?" She leans close to me, like she's afraid she'll miss what I'll say otherwise.

I incline my head, holding my scythe behind my back. "If you wish."

"Do you sleep?" she begins.

I shake my head. "No, I don't."

"Do you eat?"

"Yes, but only because I enjoy it. I can survive without it."

Her eyes light up in excitement, and her tone conveys such joy and wonder. "If you ran around for an hour, would you sweat?"

What an odd question. "I have never tried, so I have no clue."

She gives me a sheepish look, then she begins to laugh at her own expense. "Sorry. I've always wanted to know more about you, but there aren't exactly books or artifacts available to answer my questions."

Did I mishear her? "You wanted to know more about me?"

She blinks, scrunching up her face as if bewildered by my question. "Yes."

Her reactions are quite confusing. "There's not much to know about me."

She laughs my comment off. "I doubt that very much. And you can tell me all about yourself when you come over tomorrow. That way you can fulfill your duties of checking up on my welfare and I can talk your ear off with all my questions."

An odd fluttering sensation starts in my chest, and I have no idea what to make of it. "I would like that. Thank you for the invitation."

She nods eagerly. "I'm glad to have someone to spend time with. It's always been hard for me to make friends, and now I'm dead, so any ounce of sociability I had is gone."

I chuckle at her self-deprecating comment. "I would disagree with that. You made friends with me easily enough."

She tilts her head slightly to the side, analyzing me with her brown eyes. "We're friends?"

"If you would like to be," I reply.

She gives a firm and decisive nod. "More than like."

"You look happy," Persephone says around a bite of steak, analyzing me from her seat at the dining room table. "Did something happen today?"

"Yeah you look practically smitten." Hermes, The Messenger God, bumps my shoulder, chuckling around the rim of his wine goblet.

I shake my head. "Nothing out of the ordinary."

"So it was a different man with white hair and wings I saw lurking around Lethe today?" Hecate, Goddess of Witchcraft, asks with a smirk, sharing a glance with Persephone.

I feel my cheeks heat, a mildly uncomfortable sensation. "What is it you want me to say?"

"That after all of these years you finally have a crush." Hermes bumps my shoulder again, sounding like a child in his excitement.

I narrow my eyes in his direction. "I don't have a crush, and even if I did, it wouldn't matter, nor would it be your business."

I turn away from him, and out the corner of my eye I see Hermes straighten his posture and proceed to mimic my movements. Thankfully Charon, The Ferryman of the Underworld, puts a stop to this by throwing his bread roll at his head. It hits him on the nose and then falls into his lap. He picks it up and begins to eat it, all the while glaring at Charon.

I live with children.

"In all seriousness, I'm glad you've found someone else to spend time with. Even if it's just as a friend," Persephone tells me, giving me a warm smile.

I return it in full measure. "Thank you, Seph."

Hades sends his wife a look of complete adoration from beside her, then he nods to me. "You're welcome to bring her here whenever you please. This is your home and I don't want you to feel like you have to hide anyone from us."

I resist the urge to bang my head into the table. "We've had a few conversations, that is all. You are getting ahead of yourselves."

"When was the last time you had 'a few conversations' with someone other than us?" Hecate asks in that knowing tone she often uses.

I fall silent.

She smirks. "Exactly, so we are going to tease you. It is what family does."

I cast a glance at the far end of the table where Charon glowers silently. "No input from you?"

Charon glances up from his plate and shrugs. "As pathetic as you stalking a soul by a river is, I'm not in the mood."

Persephone's jovial expression falls. "What's wrong? Did something happen?"

Charon's hard expression softens ever so slightly. "Just once again reflected on my monotonous task and my insignificance to the universe at large."

"Ugh, I hate when that happens," Hermes exaggerates, shaking his head.

Charon just glares at him.

"You're not insignificant, Charon." Hades's tone leaves no room for disagreement. "Without you, souls wouldn't be able to reach their place of rest. You are a vital part of the Underworld, even if those in the Mortal World don't know it."

Charon shakes his head, aggressively throwing down his cloth napkin onto the table. "You may be hated and feared by all who know you"—his eyes flicker between Hades and me—"but at least you are known. I would welcome hatred and fear if it was offered to me, because the alternative is being a ghost—a shadow you forget follows behind you under the light of the sun."

Hades and I lock eyes, and I know he and I are thinking the same thing. Charon believes he would rather have the hatred and fear because he's never had it. I would give anything to be forgotten by the world. I would rather be a ghost than be a demon. I know Hades feels the same way.

"No one knows who I am either," Persephone points out. "For most of my life I lived in captivity, and only a handful of Mortals and the Gods have knowledge of my existence. I don't know if I'll ever reach the acclaim or acknowledgment of other Gods, and I don't give a fuck. Every Mortal in every dimension is only known by a handful of people. They're known by their friends and family, by the people who love them and support them. Why can't that be enough for you?"

Charon has no answer for Persephone. He just quietly excuses himself and exits the dining room, not even bothering to teleport away. Persephone moves to go after him, but Hades covers her hand with his and stops her. They share a conversation with only a glance, and she settles back in her seat, her expression filled with concern.

"He'll be fine," Hecate assures her, taking another sip of wine. "Just give him some time."

"He's had nothing but time and yet here he is still sulking," Hermes comments.

Hecate ignores him. "I went from being a welcomed resident of Olympus, to being unknown, to being as hated as the two of you, and now to being a celebrated figure amongst the Mortals. I learned long ago that people, both Mortal and Immortal, are fickle. If you spend your life judging yourself how others do, you will never be happy."

Hecate pushes out her chair and stands, glancing around at each of us. "Just like Persephone said: As long as you have people who love you, everything will be alright. Even if you don't have statues or temples or people worshipping at your feet, you are made immortal through the hearts you occupy. Love—real and unyielding love—is stronger than any hate. It's even stronger than time itself."

And with that, Hecate teleports away too, leaving all of us to silently soak in her words.

Chapter Three

Eurydice

BEING DEAD IS QUITE STRANGE. You don't get hungry, you don't get thirsty, you don't get tired. You can still feel emotion, but it's as if there is a wall separating you from it, or that you're feeling it at a lower concentration. It's definitely been something to adjust to.

I don't know if this transition is made easier or worse because of how my house in the Field of Mourning is designed. It has a working kitchen, bathroom, and bedroom, all of which I have no use for. It's strange opening the fridge only to see no food and feel no hunger, or realizing you haven't had to pee in two weeks when you pass by the toilet. I'll sometimes lie in bed to watch TV or write in my journal, but it feels wrong to lie there without being lulled to sleep by the soft mattress and warm blankets. I wonder how long it will take for me to forget what it felt like to be hungry or tired. Will I eventually forget what it felt like to be alive altogether?

I hope that won't be the case.

Besides TV and journaling, I like to take quite a few walks around the Field of Mourning. I like to study Lethe's water, wanting to uncover why it has the ability to wipe someone's memories, but I also enjoy it so I can get out of my head, so to speak. When I'm in my house, I'm reminded about being dead at every turn. When I'm outside, it's easier to let my mind grow silent of questions and existential contemplations. But even then, things are noticeably different. I feel the wind, but not the chill that usually follows. I can walk for hours without breaking a sweat or raising my heartrate. There is no pull on my muscles or ache in my joints when I tried to go for a run. It's unnerving.

I wonder if other souls here go through the same motions that I am, or maybe my analytical brain just can't let things go. Both are entirely possible, but I can't ask anyone this question. Logically I know there are other souls here, but there's no one around for miles. There's only a grassy field that stretches endlessly, only broken up by the River Lethe.

It's as disturbing as it is fascinating.

As I have done every morning since my death, I get out of bed—after lying there with my eyes closed for a few hours with a documentary about the Amazon Rainforest playing in the background, pretending to sleep—and sit at the kitchen table to write in my journal and check on my samples from Lethe. I only get a few words written down before a knock sounds at my door.

I shut my journal and walk across my minimally decorated house to the door, finding Thanatos on the other side. I swear I feel the phantom sensation of my heart racing, but that's probably just in my imagination. "Hi."

He smiles, and I feel dumbstruck at the sight of it. "Hi. I hope I'm not intruding."

"No, not at all. Want to come in?" Gods I feel breathless. How is that possible?

Thanatos nods, tucking his wings in as he enters my home. As I shut the door and lock it, Thanatos looks around my living room and kitchen, both of which are in one open floor plan, with a staircase leading to the second floor in front of the door. A TV sits on a stone coffee table in front of a stiff-cushioned couch, there are wooden benches in the kitchen, and the rug covering a large portion of the floor is grey.

"I know it's not great," I start rambling, heading back towards the kitchen. "The Judges explained to me that this house is only temporary and I'll be able to decorate my home in the Asphodel Meadows once I've fully healed, so for now I'm stuck with the impersonal décor."

Thanatos shakes his head, his wings relaxing behind him, his feathers dragging against the floor. "It is lovely."

I only now see that Thanatos has something in his hands, and I feel even more like an idiot. "What did you bring?"

Thanatos appears to have forgotten the items as well. "Oh, these. Yes, well, I saw that you have already made a dent in your current journal, so I retrieved you a few more from Hecate. I hope they are to your liking."

I take the three journals from his hands, admiring their leather binding and thick yellowing pages. They're perfect. "Thank you. That was very thoughtful of you."

His smile is small, kind of bashful. "It was no trouble. May I ask what you are using the journals for?"

I take a seat at the kitchen bench, gesturing for him to do the same. "When I was alive, I was a theological biologist at the Immortal Medicinal Research Association. We studied the biology and DNA of Immortals to see if we could solve medical conditions and diseases among Mortals."

His eyebrows rise, bewildered by this information. "How come I've never heard of this organization?"

"Not many have," I admit. "It was kept secret on purpose, with only one office and lab in Australia. It was founded by Prometheus a little over thirty years ago after he grew tired of the Gods not being more proactive with Mortal issues. In his own words, the Gods have the power to cure every illness and choose not to because they can only 'meddle' with our affairs so much. An answered prayer is one thing, but getting rid of the common cold is another. At least according to Apollo."

Thanatos nods in understanding. "How did you come across the association if it's so secret?"

"I was born and raised in Australia and made my interest in studying the Gods well known. I was a theology major in university and was working to become a professor, but Prometheus recruited me into the organization after I was recommended by a teacher of mine. I changed my major to biological and environmental studies, got my PHD, and worked as a lab technician for the IMRA. So to answer your original question, I'm using the journals to study the Underworld and see if there are any hidden secrets it can tell me. Maybe I can find something that can help the souls who live here."

Thanatos looks impressed, and that makes me glow from within. It's not every day you get to brag about your achievements to your idol, to the person who started you on the path to achieve all that you have.

Ever since I met him as a child, I've been fascinated with the Gods. I borrowed every book on them ever written throughout my adolescence, I took classes in school that filled in the gaps the books left, and through it all, I harbored an unhealthy obsession with the God of Death. For most people my age, they had pictures of Aphrodite or Apollo on their walls, they prayed to Dionysus every night to give them a chance, and they swooned over the actors portraying the God they fancied in movies. But my walls were bare, my prayers were nonexistent, and my heart was full of longing I knew was pointless. I couldn't help it though; Thanatos's kind eyes, beautiful face, and somber expression have haunted me for the past twenty years.

And now he's sitting in my kitchen smiling at me.

"Are there any more materials you need for your studies?" he asks. "I would be happy to retrieve whatever you require."

I can't help but feel giddy. "Well I've been using wineglasses to hold samples of Lethe." I gesture to said glasses to my right. "So some test tubes and beakers would be great. Some syringe needles, a microscope, a dropper, a Bunsen burner…I could use some tubs as well to store samples and tools."

Thanatos looks amused by my excitement, and he gently laughs. I've never heard it before now, but I'm addicted to it already. "Hecate will have all of those items. I will retrieve them and deliver them to you tomorrow."

"Careful, other souls might accuse you of favoritism," I tease, not expecting him to take my comment seriously.

But he does. "Anyone who makes those accusations would be correct."

I'm his favorite. "Can I ask you something?"

"Anything."

I tilt my head to the side and flutter my lashes. "Could I study you?"

He blinks at me. "Study me?"

I nod, explaining, "At the IMRA, we got to study Olympians, Titans, and Divine Creatures…but no one has ever studied a Primordial Deity. Most of them are in their ethereal forms permanently and that makes it impossible for them to be given the thorough examination the other species are. I would love to be the first to research how you differ from the others and what aspects of your biology may benefit Mortals, even if this knowledge will never go beyond the Underworld."

Thanatos contemplates this for a moment, then he nods. "You may study me. And once you are done, I will give your research to Hermes to deliver to your former organization if that is your wish."

I barely contain a squeal of glee. "You would do that for me?"

"Yes, Eurydice. That and more." He says it so simply, like it's a given fact.

I thought I had gotten over my silly crush on him, but it appears I was wrong.

"Can we start tomorrow after you drop off my equipment?" I ask, already planning out the tests and exams I want to conduct.

He reaches forward to grasp onto my hand. His skin is soft and cool to the touch, and his grip is firm but gentle. He leans down and presses a kiss to my knuckles, and I'm taken aback by how warm his lips are, and even more so by the shiver that races through my body. I don't think the dead are supposed to shiver.

"Until tomorrow, Eurydice." I can feel his words brush against my hand where his lips still hover.

Yep. Definitely not over it.

"You don't have to go right now, do you?" My voice sounds so breathy and aroused, it's kind of embarrassing. I hope he doesn't notice.

Predictably, Thanatos seems shocked by my question. "I don't wish to overstay my welcome."

When will he realize that's impossible? "Nonsense. Being dead is quite boring; I can't find enough things to do to fill up my time. I would love some more company."

"What have you done to fill your time so far?"

"Well, I obviously do my experiments. I sometimes listen to music. Sometimes I watch some National Geographic—"

"What is that?"

I blink. "You don't know what National Geographic is?"

He shakes his head, and I swear my heart would have stopped in that moment if it wasn't already silent. I grab onto his hand and march him up my stairs and towards my bedroom, where in front of my bed lies a large flat-screen TV that only plays the National Geographic channel. When I was first assigned to the Field of Mourning, the Judges asked me what I could have in my house to make me more comfortable, and I felt so flustered by talking to *the fucking Judges of the Underworld* that I said the first three things that came to mind.

Journals. Classical music CDs. The National Geographic channel.

Don't get me wrong, I love all three of those things, but why couldn't I have asked for a bundle pack of subscriptions? Why couldn't I have asked for a premium Spotify subscription? Classical music is one of my favorite genres, but I can't listen to Adele or Sam Smith or Ruth B?

I gotta have my Adele.

But it's too late now, and I refuse to make Thanatos my errand boy, constantly fetching things for me. I don't want him to think I'm using him.

I sit him down on my bed, making sure to avoid his wings, then I point to the screen. "I love documentaries, and this channel has the best of the best. They have docs about nature, animals, the ocean, the Gods, and history. Personally, the history ones are my favorites, but I have never watched a documentary through them I didn't like."

I give him the remote, and he looks down at it like I've given him a diamond. "Pick one."

He scrolls through a few rows of documentaries before clicking on one about the *Titanic*, and I can't help but grin.

"I love the *Titanic*," I gush.

Thanatos looks confused by this comment. "You love a ship that hit an iceberg and sunk?"

I bump his shoulder. "No. I like the history behind the *Titanic* and the mysteries it holds within the wreckage. And there's a movie called *Titanic* that is probably my favorite movie of all time. It tells the story of the ship sinking but focuses on the relationship of a rich heiress and a scrappy artist."

"I have never seen this film, but if you enjoy it so much, I would like to watch it."

"I would love to show it to you, but I don't have it here—"

"I can retrieve it for you," he offers, placing the remote in his lap.

I give a little whine in protest. "You don't have to do that."

"I want to provide the things you like so you'll be more comfortable."

"But I don't want you to spend all your free time running out to get me things."

"Why not?"

Is it not obvious? "Because you have so many other responsibilities and souls to look after. I can't hog all of your time."

Thanatos hesitates for a moment, then he tells me, "This is where I want to spend my time."

Maybe I'm not dead and I'm just in a coma. That's the only explanation that makes sense as to why someone like Thanatos would prefer to spend his time with me. This all has to be a dream or hallucination. "I don't understand why."

The corners of his lips perk up, almost forming a smile, but not quite. "Neither do I. But I would very much like to find out."

I try to quell my outward reaction, but on the inside, I'm melting. "Well alright then."

I take the remote from his grasp, turn of the volume, and settle in next to him to watch. "I have a rule where no one is allowed to talk during a documentary, so hold all questions or comments until the end," I instruct as the prologue begins.

"I'll be as silent as the dead," he replies.

I glance at him, discovering a smirk on his lips, and I find myself laughing. It was a corny joke, but something tells me Thanatos rarely, if ever, jokes around with someone. It makes me feel all the more privileged to see him this relaxed and authentic.

If this is a coma-induced hallucination I hope I never wake up.

CHAPTER FOUR
Thanatos

*"With gnashing teeth, the Demon rages,
Cursing the hopes his fancy wove,
Alone! Alone! Through all the ages,
No gleam of hope—no hope of love!"*

"WHAT ARE YOU READING?" A QUIET VOICE ASKS, STARTLING me.

I look up from my spot on the library sofa to find Persephone, her hair tied up in a braid and her body wrapped in a black robe. She and the others went to bed hours ago, but she must not have slept. She looks wide awake despite it being nearly two in the morning.

I show her the cover of the book, *The Complete Collection of Mikhail Lermontov.* "He is one of my favorite poets."

She sits down beside me, her legs tucked under her, and takes the book from my grasp. She briefly skims over the page I'm on, and I watch her eyebrows furrow. "What is this poem about?"

I lean back, stretching my wings out behind the back of the couch. "Me."

This does not ease her confusion. "Really?"

I nod. "Mortals are often afraid to use mine and Hades's names, so they created the terms 'demon' and 'devil' to refer to us. This poem is about 'the demon,' whose duty is to travel the earth and take Mortal souls. But one day he comes across a woman named Tamara, whom he instantly falls in love with. She had just gotten married to her husband, but the Demon killed him and tried to woo Tamara. Despite what he had done, she saw what a tortured soul he was and gave in to his affections. She kissed him, and his kiss killed her, leaving him alone again."

"That's very depressing."

I smirk, liking her bluntness. "Tales about me tend not to be joyful."

"Why would Lermontov write this? Do you know?"

"When his time came, I asked him that same question, and he gave me an honest answer. He said he wrote a poem about me because I'm the only being that can escape death, and therefore I will always be alone. He called me the ultimate tragic character, which is perfect for a poem."

Persephone sets the book aside and scooches closer to me, then I feel her head rest against my shoulder. "You know that's not true, right?"

"Which part?"

"All of it." She curls up against my side, her arm looped through mine. "Is this about Eurydice?"

I sigh, glancing down at the poem lying open-faced on Persephone's lap. "I don't know. I have never been drawn to someone like this before. I don't have the experience to recognize how I feel," I tell her honestly.

"That's how it was with Hades when we first met," she admits. "It took me a while to figure out that what I felt for Hades was love."

"And you are lucky that he feels the same way, but I have little hope of Eurydice reciprocating whatever it is I am. Ignoring who I am and what I do, she has a husband in the Mortal World whom she loves. When she gets her memories back, which I suspect will be soon, her love for him will return full force...and that will be it."

"You don't know that," she argues. "None of us know what the future holds, not even Death." She gently elbows me. "If you have feelings for her, I say go for it. Thousands of souls find love in the Underworld while they still have living partners, and some do even after they've been reunited. You've said yourself that the afterlife feels totally separate to the souls from Mortal life. Eurydice could very well feel as you do and be battling with the same insecurities. You will never know unless you try things out, and I learned that the hard way with Hades."

I say nothing, and instead contemplate the advice she has given me. Could it really be possible? Could Eurydice feel as I do? That's not a question I can contemplate the answer to until I decide what exactly I do feel. I have known love before, though only the familial kind. I would venture to guess that romantic love is different, but it is not something I have experienced, nor lust. There are those like Hecate or Hestia that don't feel attraction, but I don't believe I'm one of them. For years, I couldn't experience any emotion, and it is has only been through interacting with others, mainly my family, that I have known emotions like joy, sorrow, humor, and love. I think romantic and sexual attraction have escaped me because I have not had an interaction of that nature before, mostly by others' resolve.

Who wants to go on a date with Death?

As if hearing my thoughts, Persephone snuggles closer against me. "I love you. So does Hades, and so do Hecate, Charon, and Hermes. And if Eurydice is as wonderful as you say, she won't be able to help but love you too."

I place a kiss on the top of her head, wrapping a wing around her shoulders.

"Does that Lermontov guy have any poems that aren't so depressing?"

I nod, watching her shut her eyes, and tuck my wing around her like a blanket.

"Will you read to me?" she asks through a yawn.

Trying to hide a smirk, I pick up the book and flip it to a random poem. I murmur it to her until she is snoring quietly against my shoulder, my wing still tucked tightly around her.

"This is amazing!" Eurydice exclaims, eyeing the box I have in my arms like it's a giftwrapped present. "Hecate really had everything on my list?"

More or less.

When I showed up at Hecate's house this morning with the list Eurydice had written for me, Hecate said she could only help me out with the test tubes and beakers. In order to get the syringe needles, microscope, dropper, Bunsen burner, and bins, I had to have Hermes go to a Mortal store and buy them. He said he got everything 80% off because the manager happened to be a worshipper of his. He's apparently quite popular in Boston, Massachusetts.

I keep that information to myself, opting to give a simple answer. "It was no problem."

Eurydice takes the bins from my arms, where all the other supplies rest inside of, and runs into the kitchen, unpacking all of the tools and equipment with a giddy smile. I cannot help but form a smile of my own as I watch her. Her joy is infectious.

"Where do you want me for this study of yours?" I ask, standing just outside the kitchen, watching her organize her new tools.

She pulls out a stool from underneath the kitchen counter, patting the wooden top. "Come sit."

I do as she instructs, sitting down on the wooden stool, then I begin the painstaking process of shedding my suit jacket. There are slits for my wings to slip in and out of easier, but to prevent rips and tears, I still have to shrug it off slowly. Thankfully, Eurydice sees my plight and assists me. She then drapes my jacket over the back of her couch while I roll up my dress shirt sleeve.

She retrieves the syringe needle as well as a rubber band, then I watch as she meticulously ties the band around my arm and then searches my skin for a vein.

She pokes and prods my inner arm with a gloved finger. "I'm going to make the assumption that you're not afraid of needles."

I chuckle at that. "No. I'm not afraid of needles."

She instructs me to ball up my hand, which I do, then she places the needle in the crook of my arm. "Alright, so I'm not going to count down like I do for some of my other patients."

True to her word, she sticks the needle in my arm without any lead-up, and my illuminating blood fills the small syringe within seconds. Eurydice gazes down at my blood with awe, giving an audible gasp. "I've never seen a God have blood like this before. Usually it appears the same as Mortal blood. But yours…it's like your blood is made of starlight."

"It probably is," I respond, pressing the cloth she hands me against my bleeding arm. "I'm the child of Nyx and Erebus, the personifications of Night and Darkness. My birth was not of the usual sort. I appeared out of the night sky as you see me now."

Eurydice sets my blood aside, then she turns back to me with rapt attention, sitting down on the stool next to me. "Can you tell me more?"

I've never had anyone, especially a Mortal, take such an interest in my past. It's as strange as it is wonderful, and I can hardly refuse her. "It is said that Uranus, the primordial deity of the universe, became sentient one day, millions of years ago. He soon grew lonely, so he made the primordial deities Gaia, Chaos, Nyx, and Erebus gain consciousness as well. Uranus and Gaia fell in love, as did Nyx and Erebus. Chaos, having grown jealous of the others' happiness, started to plant the seeds of fear in their hearts, telling them that nothing can last forever and their happiness would one day end. And thus, me and my brother Phobos, the God of Fear, were born from the fear of death my parents harbored."

"Did your parents resent you?"

"Yes. Our birth had a profound change on all the Gods; they realized that their happiness was finite, and in response, they created more deities to ensure that after they died, there would still be Gods traveling the cosmos. Gaia gave birth to Helios, Selene, and Eos; she created the Titans as well as the Goddess Aphrodite; Uranus created the Judges of the Underworld; my mother, Nyx, created the Furies; and Chaos created Charon, The Ferryman of the Underworld."

She rests an elbow on the kitchen counter, using her palm to support her head. "What was it like? Living back then?"

I contemplate for a few moments how to articulate the experience, my wings twitching awkwardly as I do. "It was as if I were a lion's cub in an unknown jungle, trying to figure out what it means to be alive, all the while surrounded by gazelles that resent me for being a carnivore, even though I have never eaten a single hunk of flesh."

She nods, pursing her lips. "I'm sorry you had to go through all of that. May I ask how you ended up living here in the Underworld?"

Eurydice seems to have remembered that she's supposed to be working, so with a glare at her work station, she takes my blood and deposits it into a test tube, never moving from her seat. She takes a dropper and places a single drop of blood for observation under the microscope. She examines that drop of blood as she listens to me talk, her brows creased in concentration.

"After Cronus overthrew Uranus as leader of the Gods, most of the primordial deities permanently took on their ethereal forms, including my parents. My brother and I, however, did not. We roamed the surface of the newly-transformed Gaia and spread chaos to all the Gods and Divine Creatures that roamed alongside us. My brother fed off the fear he and I caused; I on the other hand never took pleasure in other beings' suffering, and it took a great toll on me having a front-row seat to our causing it. Hades saw the pain I was in every time I delivered him a soul, which was a far rarer occurrence back then. After a few decades, he offered me a place to live in the palace, as well as food from his table and his ear if I ever wanted to discuss what had happened to me. I took him up on his offer, and I abandoned my brother to feed off of others' fear alone."

Eurydice lifts her head from the microscope, her expression troubled. "I'm so sorry, Thanatos. That's awful—I didn't mean to pry so much. Forgive me if I asked too many questions about a tough subject. I've just wanted to learn more about you ever since I was eight."

This admission warms my slow-beating heart. "I wanted to tell you about my past. You are the first person I have wanted to speak about it to since I permanently moved to the Underworld."

She gives me a large grin, one that lights up her whole face. "Really?"

I nod, forcing myself to admit, "You are the first Mortal to not look on me in fear and hatred, to instead smile at me and treat me with kindness."

Despite the compliment, her lips tighten in a line, and her eyes grow livid. I begin to wonder if I somehow overstepped a boundary, and I open my mouth to apologize when Eurydice says something that silences me.

"The Fates have dealt you such a cruel hand." She glares down at the microscope, and instinct tells me she is venting to herself rather than to me. "Can no one use their critical thinking ability to understand that you didn't ask to be the God of Death? That you take no pleasure in your job and you are in fact one of the kindest people to grace the cosmos? Everyone's lack of intelligence infuriates me."

She is angry on my behalf? On *my* behalf?

Eurydice shakes her head and takes a deep breath, gesturing to the microscope she has been glaring at as if it spurned her. "Your blood will need some more analysis. It looks almost nothing like regular DNA." She bites her lip, tapping her fingers on the kitchen counter's surface. "Would you be willing to get me a few more items? Having *Lewis Lynn's Dissection of the Immortal Anatomy* and *Ryan James's A Study in the Stars* would be a great help. I'm so used to having a wall of reference textbooks in my office at the IMRA, it's strange being without them. Any kind of scientist can tell you that we rely on outside information a lot. If we memorized every fact in our field, our brains would explode."

What an odd image. "Yes, of course. Is there anything else I can retrieve for you?"

She hesitates for a moment. "I don't want to take advantage—"

"It's not taking advantage if the service is freely offered."

She gives me a small, shy smile. "Could I write you a list?"

"I would appreciate it if you did."

She rips a piece of paper out of her journal and begins scribbling down supplies, her dark brows furrowed in thought. Her brown hair is pulled back into a ponytail with a few pieces dangling out, gently sliding across her cheeks. Without taking her eyes off the piece of paper, she tucks those loose strands behind her small ear, her long, elegant fingers brushing the side of her neck. I have been alive since before the formation of language and thought, and in all that time, I have never seen someone as beautiful as Eurydice Martin. I doubt I ever will again.

"I feel like I'm keeping you from more important things," she comments as she hands me the list. "You're bending over backwards helping me with my projects when you have a duty to the Underworld and all the incoming souls. I don't deserve this special attention."

"I believe you do."

She gives an annoyed huff. "Because I treat you like a person instead of a leech? You shouldn't reward me for doing the bare minimum."

Her kindness towards me was the start of my fascination with her, yes, but my reasoning for helping her now has grown far beyond that. Eurydice is missing the ethereal beauty and wisdom that comes with being immortal, as well as the pride and hubris the Gods tend to conflate with perfection. She is flawed, authentic, and perfect in her imperfections. She has more spirit in her than any being—Mortal, Immortal, alive, or dead. She has more beauty than any artist could hope to capture on a canvas. Not to mention her undying curiosity, ambition, intelligence, and her compassion. In my few interactions with her, she has awakened a part of me I did not realize was dormant.

"Perhaps I'm helping you because I like you."

"You like me?" She stretches the words out as if still processing them.

I give a firm nod, feeling my wings tense up behind me. "Very much, and I would like the honor of getting to know you better."

"There's not much else to me other than my projects, my love for documentaries, and my obsession with Adele," she says in an attempt at humility.

"I doubt that very much," I argue.

"Well...as long as I'm not keeping you from your duties, it would be *my* honor to get to know *you* better." She smiles, her expression so soft and warm it reminds me of sitting in the library in front of the fireplace with a book in my lap.

I open my mouth to say more, but a whisper from the void has me pausing.

"A Satyr is dying from starvation in Paris; he has minutes before his soul must be cleaved..." the Fates inform me.

"Thanatos?" Eurydice waves her hand in front of my face, her voice growing wary.

I must have zoned out when the Fates started speaking to me. "I'm afraid I have to leave. I have just been informed that I must go collect a soul."

Her eyebrows furrow. "What do you—oh my Gods, do the Fates speak to you directly? Like in your mind?" She looks around the room, thinking they are about to make a physical appearance.

I stand up from the stool, giving her a simple nod. "Yes. Only I can hear them."

"What do the Fates sound like?" she asks as I stretch out my wings, grabbing onto my scythe.

I ponder her question for a moment, then I give her an honest answer. "They sound as harsh as the destinies they weave."

CHARON

I think my favorite invention of the modern age is headphones.

When I'm in my little boat, ferrying crying souls across the Styx, hating myself and my life, headphones are my one safe haven. They drown out the sobs and cries of the dead, allowing me to lose myself in the motion of the oars and the dips and curves of the water beneath me. For a few minutes, I feel at peace. I feel like I can leave my body and become the music surrounding me.

That is, until I reach the bank where the Judges await incoming souls. Then I'm reminded about the miserable monotony of my existence. Rachmaninoff and Borodin can only keep me from reality for so long.

I once again reach the Wall of Erebus, where the gateway to the Underworld lies and new souls wait to be ferried by me. Thanatos currently stands there with a Satyr and a Mortal child, both of whom are cowering in fear in the face of the God of Death. Thanatos does a good job of acting indifferent to their fear, but I know better.

My boat hits the bank of the river, and Thanatos gently tries to usher the new souls towards it, but they instead back away towards the gate, only to be stopped by Cerberus, who gives them both a stare that reads "don't test me." Having more fear of the three-headed dog than either of us, the Satyr and Mortal child practically fling themselves into my boat, making it teeter from side to side in the water. I grip hold of the oars to make sure they don't fall into the depths below, trying to ignore the cowering souls on the other side of my boat.

"I must go," Thanatos informs me. "There are more souls to be collected in France."

"We've been getting a lot of souls from there lately. Did Demeter's storm hit there hard?"

A few weeks ago, Demeter, Goddess of the Harvest and mother of Persephone, created a catastrophic snow storm that, despite being over, still effects the entire northern hemisphere. The chaos this storm has caused is paramount, not just with all the Mortal casualties, but in the faith once held for the Gods on Olympus.

My friend nods gravely. "France, Ireland, and America are struggling the most as of now. They relied so heavily on their farms and livestock, which Demeter has now almost completely destroyed. Even with much of the snow and ice now melted, the effects of this storm will last years."

I grunt in acknowledgment, not knowing what to say to that. "Well I won't keep you. Try to be back for dinner though, will you? I'm making some stew, and if he has his way, Hermes will devour it all in a single helping."

Thanatos gives me a small smile. "I will be there."

His black wings stretch out behind him, then he vanishes into nothing, leaving me with the terrified souls.

Alright, let's get this over with.

"In case you haven't figured it out yet, you are dead," I tell them, putting my headphones back on, ready to start playing music the second I'm done with this infernal speech. "As a soul in the Underworld, you will live out your afterlife in either the Asphodel Meadows, the Field of Mourning, Elysium, or Tartarus, depending on how you chose to live your Mortal or Immortal lives. The Judges of the Underworld will view your memories and decide where you belong, then they will escort you to your new home. On our way to the Judges, please keep your hands inside the boat at all times, and don't try to escape once we reach shore. If you thought Cerberus was scary, you don't want to meet the Furies. Any questions?"

The two souls just gawk at me with wide eyes.

"Great." And with that, I fish out my phone to find a song to listen to while I row, but a growl from Cerberus makes me pause. I glance over my shoulder at the three-headed beast, finding him snarling at a Mortal standing a few feet from the Underworld gate.

A *living* Mortal.

"Don't move," I order my passengers, quickly exiting the boat to assess the situation and make sure Cerberus doesn't have an early dinner. As I move closer towards the gate, I notice a few things about our unexpected visitor. One, he doesn't seem afraid of Cerberus, despite the beast still snarling at him. Two, he's carrying a satchel on his shoulder, so this was clearly planned. And third, he is ridiculously attractive.

Obviously, that's not what I should be focusing on right now, but it's hard to ignore.

"I have to say, I'm impressed," I begin, stopping by Cerberus's side, petting his soft pelt of fur. "The last person to find the secret passage to the Underworld from the Mortal World did so five centuries ago. How did you find it?"

The Mortal turns his gaze to me, his determined expression never wavering. "I knew someone who had a fascination with the Underworld. She told me about it."

Vague, but okay.

"State your business, Mortal. You're trespassing in this realm."

"I've come for my wife," he says, his dark brown hands clutching onto the strap of his satchel as if it were his lifeline.

"I'm going to take a wild guess that your wife died."

The Mortal nods, his chiseled chin wobbling. "A few weeks ago—hit by a car that slid on the icy roads."

Another victim of this cursed storm. "I'm very sorry for your loss, but you aren't the only one who has lost someone they love because of Demeter's storm. Nor are you the only person to want their loved one back, but you have to accept that it is impossible. Once a soul is cleaved from flesh, it can never be bound to it again."

His bottom lip quivers ever so slightly, but he tightens his jaw to keep his sorrow at bay. "Nothing is impossible."

"The best I can do for you is tell you how your wife fares, but the living are forbidden from entering the Underworld, just as the dead are forbidden from exiting."

"I know how she is," he grits out. "She had a traumatic death, so she's in the Field of Mourning right now, probably having little to no memory of what happened to her. She may not even remember me. But that fact will not stop me from trying to bring her home, and neither will anything you say, Lord Charon."

What did he just say?

"Y-you know who I am?" I ask dumbly.

The Mortal seems taken aback by my question. "Yes. Like I said, I knew someone who knew a lot about the Underworld."

His wife, no doubt. "Unless you want to become Cerberus's new chew toy, I suggest you go back where you came from."

"Please," he whispers, so brokenly and with such pleading in his voice it actually makes my heart ache, which is quite the feat. After a millennia of ferrying souls, I thought I had gotten used to the tears, pleas, and regrets of the dead or grieving. But there is something about this Mortal that's different, in more ways than one.

"Go home," I say again, making sure nothing gets lost in translation. "Or you will discover the consequences of trespassing in the Underworld."

To my surprise, the Mortal man does what I say, slowly beginning to back away from the gate. But there is a flare of something in his eyes that gives me pause. The pain and grief is still there, but now there is resolve too. I know this parting is only temporary—that he will return to the Underworld despite my warning.

Handsome, determined, and stubborn. A lethal combination.

CHAPTER FIVE

ORPHEUS

HEARTBREAK IS A FUNNY TERM.

You say you're heartbroken when you lose someone you love, whether by death or by Mortal error, but it in no way describes how you feel when something like that happens to you. You don't feel as if your heart has physical cracks running along its surface, or that it no longer works the way it used to. In fact, you don't feel pain in your heart at all.

Your heart still pumps blood, your lungs still consume air, your legs still move under you, but you aren't *alive*. You're living, but you feel dead. Loss is not the breaking of the heart, it is the breaking of the spirit. It is damage done irrevocably to your soul.

This is how I have felt for weeks now. It's how I felt when I called an ambulance to take my wife's body away, when the police took my statement about the hit-and-run that killed her, when I had to return to our hotel room covered in her blood. The only semblance of emotion I've felt since the life left her eyes was when I called her moms. The snow and ice from Demeter's storm wouldn't allow any of us to bury her, so I had her cremated, with her parents on the phone with me when it happened. I listened to their piercing sobs as I waited to take home Eurydice's remains, none of us uttering a single word to each other and instead just sharing in our grief.

The only person who was able to be there physically for the cremation was the God of Forethought himself, Prometheus. He was Eurydice's boss, and I know the two of them worked closely together for many years. From a single look in his eyes, I could see that the God mourned her as more than an employee, but a friend.

"I will not ask you how you are doing or say I'm sorry for your loss, because I know you have been told that too many times as of late," Prometheus said to me, placing his hands in the pockets of his suit jacket as we sat in a dimly lit waiting area. "But I hope you will take comfort knowing that Eurydice is at peace in the Underworld. I contacted my friend Hecate and asked if she would look in on her, and Eurydice is comfortable and thriving in the Field of Mourning. According to Hecate, she's been going by the River Lethe and writing in a journal each day."

I stared at the God for several moments, dumbstruck by this incredible act of kindness. "You have no idea how much that means to me."

Prometheus shook his head. "Think nothing of it. Eurydice was my friend, and I will do anything in my power to help make this dark period a little lighter."

The only thing that would help ease my suffering is having my wife back. But I didn't say that to him. He might be a God, but that task is beyond his capabilities, or anyone else's.

As if he read my mind, Prometheus said to me quietly, "I have lived for thousands of years, and in that time, I have lost many loved ones. The feeling of loss will never leave you, but in time, you will be able to think of Eurydice and feel joy. You will look back on your years together as a blessing and not dwell on how it was cut short. And if you ever want an update on how she fares in the Underworld, only ask."

Prometheus left me with that final offer, and it filled me with a determination that flooded my entire being.

Instead of having him check up on my wife, I'll do it myself.

Eurydice told me where the entrance to the Underworld is in the

Mortal World, as well as every detail known about that dimension to Mortals. *I think I have a chance of getting down there. I could see her, make sure she's actually okay and not just take someone else's word for it—*

Maybe I could bring her back home.

It's never been done before, at least not to my knowledge. But if Lord Hades had found some way to bring people back from the dead, I doubt he would have actually gone through with it. I believed my wife when she had said Thanatos is a good person, especially after meeting him, but I've heard too many horrible things about the God of the Dead to give him the benefit of the doubt. It's entirely possible that there is a way to bring souls back from the dead and we just aren't privy as to how. And even if that's not the case, if anyone could discover the secret of how to cheat death, it would be Eurydice. All I have to do is find her, and then we can figure out the rest together.

Is it crazy? *Yes.* Will I succeed? *No idea.* Is this a good idea? *Absolutely not.* But what other alternatives did I have? Sit here in a foreign country while I wait out the melting ice, confined to my hotel room with only my wife's urn for comfort? No. I refused to sit and wallow while I knew she's in the Underworld, either feeling as trapped and miserable as me or having no memory of her former life.

I didn't know which is worse. Still don't.

And so began my two weeks' long trip to Greece, where the entrance to the Underworld lies. Without access to a plane and with only being able to go low speeds in a car, the journey took far longer than usual, but the long stretches on the road were put to good use. I had time to plan, and plan I did. By the time I reached Athens, with nothing but my satchel and my wife's urn, I was ready to make the journey of retrieving her.

Unfortunately I had forgotten that Cerberus, the mighty three-headed dog, guards the gates to the Underworld. I never stood a chance getting past the beast, especially after Lord Charon caught me. Eurydice had told me about Charon several times, but the man himself did not meet my expectations. I thought Charon would be an emotionless husk, with no more life than the vessel he captains. But instead I found myself met with a sad, angry, frustrated man.

He seemed to genuinely pity my situation, and I think if he could have helped, he would have. But I have no intention of heeding his warning. He'd said bringing someone back from the dead is impossible, but all I'd heard was that it had never been done yet, and that's plenty enough for me to work off of.

So here I'm now, shovel in hand, wandering through a fog-covered graveyard, preparing to enact plan B.

Thanatos

After I collected the latest soul, I return to Eurydice's house, where I find her absent from her makeshift workstation in the kitchen. It is around eleven o'clock in the evening, and while she is usually still working at this hour, maybe she decided to go upstairs and watch TV in her room. She told me I was welcome to visit when I had free time, but I'm still hesitant as I walk up her stairs and towards her bedroom. I knock a couple times before looking inside, but she is nowhere to be seen.

Then I hear someone singing.

It's coming from the toilet a couple feet away, and in the background of the voice, I can hear water running, so she must be in the shower. I don't recognize the song Eurydice sings, but the lyrics describe wanting to run away to the lakes—which I infer is in reference to the Lake District in England—where the great romantic poets lived and died. It is a beautiful song, and Eurydice sings it gracefully. Her voice is slightly off-key and she struggles a bit when she tries to sing at too high a note, but as with everything about her, her imperfection makes her all the more perfect in my eyes.

After she is done with that song, she moves onto another one, then another. I don't know how long I stand outside her door listening to her singing; I feel as if I have been caught in the thralls of a siren's song and am unable to move away from it. What finally breaks the spell, however, is Eurydice opening her bathroom door, wearing nothing but a towel, and letting out a startled gasp. Her eyes are wide as they lock onto mine; her hair hangs wet around her shoulders; her skin is so hot that she emits steam as she's exposed to the cooler climate of her home. Her chest rises a bit unevenly, like she's been exercising, and there's a certain spark in her eyes that makes my stomach tense up, though I have no clue why.

"You have a beautiful voice, unlike any I have ever heard. Forgive me." I teleport away before she can respond, appearing moments later in the library, which, thankfully, is vacant. I sit down on the couch in front of the fireplace, as I usually do at this time of night, but I'm overwhelmed with emotions I'm unused to and unsure of—a common occurrence as of late.

I regret my actions tonight. I startled her and made her uncomfortable, two things I tend to instill in those I encounter, but I hope never to make those emotions present in Eurydice again. I don't wish for her to start viewing me as others do. I couldn't bear it if she did.

Mingled with my embarrassment is something akin to joy? Excitement maybe? Thrill? I cannot pinpoint the emotion, but I feel my heartbeat speed up to nearly a normal rate, and there is a tingling sensation spreading throughout my body, as if I were struck with an electric current.

I haven't a clue what to make of this.

What is this soul doing to me?

I don't know how you make this look so easy." Persephone slams her fingers on the keys angrily. "I sound like a toddler."

"From your playing or your tantrum?"

She glares at Charon. "Not funny."

"It's kinda funny." He squeezes her shoulders from where he stands behind her. "Don't worry, it just takes practice. You'll get it."

"I thought you were playing wonderfully," I compliment from where I sit a few feet away. The three of us are in the library, where I'm catching up on some reading while Persephone attends her daily piano lesson from Charon. For all of his teasing, I agree with Charon's assessment of her skill. With practice, she will play beautifully.

Persephone starts the song Charon picked for her over again—"Für Elise" by Beethoven—and she once again fumbles with her key transitions, but she is getting better with each attempt. Most people would take years to achieve the progress she's made in weeks. She should be proud.

Now she directs a glare at me. "Liar."

I smile, refocusing on the book in front of me. "I would never."

"How are you doing?" she asks Charon over her shoulder, and I watch their interaction from the corner of my eye.

"I'm fine."

She gives him a look of skepticism.

"What? I am," he says defensively.

"So you're no longer concerned with your 'insignificance to the universe at large'?"

He shrugs. "I'm used to it by now."

Seph shakes her head. "Your problem is that you can't appreciate what you have, and instead you dwell on what you can't and shouldn't want."

"You don't—"

"You can't tell me you actually want other people's attention, Charon. You hate people."

Fair point. Charon gives an indignant huff. "Maybe I hate people because none of them know who I am or what I do."

"Or maybe you hate people, yet for some reason want their approval, which is a common theme in this family." She grumbles that last part, and I don't have to look up to see Persephone direct a pointed stare towards me.

"Seph, can you not lecture me right now?" Charon begs.

She sighs, giving a reluctant shrug. "Fine. But you'll think about what I've said, yes?"

He rolls his eyes. "Yes, *Mom*."

She smirks. "Now who's throwing a tantrum?"

That earns a chuckle from me, and Charon responds by chucking the sheet music at my head. It hits me square in the nose, and I hear a cheer of victory from my friend.

"What the hell did I just walk into?" a new voice says, and we all turn to see Hecate carrying a tray of tea.

Persephone continues on playing. "Just some early morning fun."

Hecate huffs a laugh. "Oh I'm sure. How about you all stop roughhousing and drink some tea?"

"Is it Earl Grey?" I ask, rubbing my nose.

"Yes, it is."

"Did you bring lemon?" Persephone asks.

"And sugar?" Charon inquires.

"I swear I live with children" is her only reply to their inquiries, and then she turns her attention directly to me. "Shouldn't you be going to see Eurydice? I thought she was still doing experiments on you."

I shift in my seat, suddenly feeling like the feathers on my wings have been ruffled. "I'm not sure she wants to see me."

"Why not?"

"Because I waited outside her bathroom and listened to her sing in the shower," I reply bluntly, electing to leave out the fact that the library has acted as my hideout for the last twelve hours.

My three friends stare at me in mixtures of shock and bewilderment, and of course Charon starts to laugh. "You've become a stalker," he says, gripping his stomach from how hard he is laughing.

Hecate hands me a cup of tea. "Ignore him. You can't hide away forever, Thanatos. Communication is important in every kind of relationship, even friendships. Go explain to her what happened before she starts filling in the gaps herself and actually thinks of you as her stalker."

Wise advice.

I take a brief sip of my tea, then I hand it back to her. "Thank you."

She shrugs. "It's what I do. Don't stay long with her today, though. I had another conversation with Prometheus and we are concerned about a famine starting in Western Europe and the Americas. The visions we have received are bleak."

Persephone's jaw clenches as she aggressively prods the keys. "We need to have another meeting with the Olympic council. This is such bullshit and I'm going to give them a piece of my mind."

Charon gives her shoulder a comforting squeeze while I send a small nod to Hecate. "I will be ready to leave when the Fates require me."

Charon gives an exaggerated sigh. "I will too. My job is never done."

Nor is mine.

EURYDICE

Mortals often complain about not having enough hours in the day to do all the activities they wish to do, but now that I have all the time in the world, I'm struggling to find ways to fill that time.

I don't sleep or eat, and the way the Field of Mourning is designed is that you are separate from other residents. Every soul is grouped around others that experienced the same end as they did, and I've been told I'm on the east side of Mourning, but I have no idea what that means. I've wandered around in an attempt to find other souls, but I've found none. When I asked Thanatos why, he said that the Field of Mourning changes depending on a soul's need. Some soul's need the interaction of other souls to heal, and for others it could only bring them harm. Since I have no memory of how I died, I could learn about my death, or at least the kind of death I experienced, from talking to other souls in this area. If souls on the eastern side of Mourning all died from illnesses or accidents or murder—someone who has their memories back could tell me about the manner in which they, and by extension me, died.

I really hope it wasn't murder. I don't want to be the subject of a true crime podcast where two women eat chicken wings and discuss my gruesome demise.

A soul isn't supposed to be told anything about their life that they've forgotten; you have to let their memories come back naturally. So once I remember how I died, I'll be able to speak with other souls. But for now, the only company I have is Thanatos.

Though he's been noticeably absent today.

He got me the other supplies and textbooks I wanted and dropped them off at some point while I was either upstairs or on a walk, and it has allowed me to dive deep into my research of his biology. His DNA is unlike anything I've ever seen, even among other Gods. Not only does it look completely different, but it has elements never seen in a genetic code and elements not even on the periodic table. He also has some DNA commonly found in Gods and Mortals, but it only makes up about 20% of his overall genetic makeup. I don't think his blood could be used for medicinal purposes, not like the other Gods, at least. With the Gods, Titans, and Divine Creatures, only one or two genes separates them from Mortals. Thanatos isn't even in the same football field as everyone else.

This discovery would be more exciting if he were here for me to share it with him.

As if I manifested him into existence, Thanatos appears in my living room, his expression schooled and his posture stiff. His wings are firmly pressed together behind him, and his scythe is in a death grip between his fist.

I open my mouth to speak, but he holds up a hand, making me pause.

"I apologize for last night. I came to see you, and once I realized you were indisposed, I was about to leave. But then I heard you sing, and I physically couldn't step away. In every way, not just through song, you have me caught in a spell that I cannot understand and cannot escape. But if you don't wish for me to visit anymore, I will respect that wish and stay away," he solemnly explains, shame etched into his handsome features.

You have me caught in a spell that I cannot understand and cannot escape. How is it he manages to sound so eloquent all the time?

"There's nothing to apologize for," I assure him. "You didn't upset me or frighten me. In fact I…" I trail off, contemplating whether to finish my thought or not.

"Yes?"

"I'm glad you heard me. I never sing in front of anyone; it feels far too vulnerable. But that doesn't matter with you."

He takes in a deep breath, then his eyes dart away, landing on the open textbooks on my counter. "Have you found anything?"

When I lead him into my kitchen and tell him my findings, he looks unsurprised. "I told you: I was born from the sky and darkness. I would expect nothing less."

As I write down a couple notes, I comment, "I'd have to study other Primordial deities to be sure, but I think you're the most inhuman being to exist."

"Does that unsettle you?"

I glance up from my notebook towards his hesitant expression, and I immediately put his mind at ease. "It makes me even more fascinated with you."

His shoulders relax at that, and I try to hide my smile.

"Could you explain to me the process of your research?" He clasps his hands in his lap and rests them on his knee, which he has bent over his leg. "Once a God or Divine Creature donates their blood, what do you do?"

"Well, I analyze it under a microscope like I've been doing. I write down any surface level similarities and differences I see between other blood samples I've studied; I test the cells by the process of chemical lysis, which is adding water, bacteria, and enzymes to break open the cell and study it. I disrupt cell membranes and structure through harsh environments like excessive cold or pressure; extract DNA, nucleotides, lipids, and proteins to analyze them; and then purify those components, which can allow us to create advanced forms of artificial enzymes, nutrients, fatty acids, amino acids, and biopharmaceuticals for Mortals, since Gods share an almost identical genetic structure. That's when I move on to testing with medications or other artificial molecular components. But your DNA is far too different to be beneficial medically. I actually hesitate even calling it DNA."

"Well I apologize you didn't make a groundbreaking discovery with my blood."

"On the contrary, Thanatos." I drop my pen and straighten in my stool, crossing my arms over my chest. "I'm the first scientist to study a primordial deity, to discover how vastly different our genetics are, and the first to discover several new elements. I would say that's pretty groundbreaking."

He smiles at me. "So what will you do now?"

"After I've done a little experimenting, I want to send all my notes to Prometheus. I'm limited by what I have access to in the Underworld, but he could build off of what I discovered and reach somewhere truly extraordinary."

Thanatos leans forward in his stool a little, his white eyes filled with curiosity. "Who have you and your institution studied in the past?"

"Prometheus obviously, Epimetheus, Hephaestus, Dionysus, Rhea, Hermes, and Hecate."

His eyebrows furrow. "Neither Hermes nor Hecate have ever said anything."

"They signed non-disclosure agreements. If the wrong person was to learn of what we do…"

He cocks his head to the side. "You mean Zeus?"

"Not just Zeus, but yes."

"Should I sign one of these documents as well?"

I chuckle. "I don't have one on hand, but I don't think it would matter even if I did. I technically don't work for the institute now that I'm dead. What do paper agreements mean anymore?"

"I promise to keep your secrets all the same."

The sincerity of his statement is so adorable. "I know you will."

He looks simultaneously off guard and bashful like he always does when I show basic decency to him, and he predictably changes the subject. "Have any of their blood samples actually improved Mortal lives?"

I nod, going over to my kitchen sink to wash my hands. "Just one example is how Hephaestus's blood has allowed us to create a more advanced treatment for burns. Not only does Hephaestus have the standard DDNA genes, but he also has a gene that we dubbed EFGG—it stands for Elemental-Fourth-Generation-God—that allows him to withstand the fire he can create."

I can see the confusion on Thanatos's face, so I explain further.

"When we first started our research, we learned a great many things. The biggest of which is that not much separates the Immortal from the Mortal. When it comes to Gods and Titans, there are only two real differences: the presence of DDNA and genes pertaining to their abilities. DDNA stands for Divine Deoxyribonucleic Acid, because it has the same basic structure as regular DNA, but it has an extra base that Mortals don't have, which we just named 'divinity.' This base allows for immortality, teleportation, and the enhanced speed, strength, and agility all Gods possess. You take out that extra base and you have a regular Mortal.

"As far as the genes retaining to a God's powers go, they depend on many factors. Hephaestus, for example, is a fourth generation God. Primordial deities created the Titans, who then created the Gods, who then had children, so Hephaestus's genetics will be more diluted in power than previous generations. His powers are also elemental, and we have seen similar genetic markers amongst Gods and Divine Creatures with similar powers. But as to why Hephaestus is the only one of his siblings with an elemental power when not even his parents have them…I think it has to do with the Fates. I think they have a large hand in what powers a God does and does not have."

Thanatos nods along, giving me all of his focus. "That makes sense."

"It would explain why Zeus, Poseidon, and Hades have their powers. They're the only three Gods ever to inherit their role after birth, at least that we know of. My suspicion is that some positions can't be replaced, so the Fates bestow them instead of having them be inherited. There has to be a ruler of the Underworld, so the fates won't allow that title to die with whichever God claims it."

"That is brilliant." The wonder in his voice sends the echoes of a flutter through my silent heart. "You are brilliant."

I wave off the compliment. "I'm really not. I was just one worker bee in a giant hive. Prometheus is the real genius."

"I think you sell yourself too short, Doctor."

"Doctor?" I repeat with a laugh.

"You said you received a doctoral degree in biological and environmental sciences, which makes you a doctor. You earned that title ten times over, so I'm simply referring to you by your appropriate title."

Why does he make that sound so hot? "But that's so formal."

"To most yes, but to us it would be a nickname. Friends give each other nicknames, do they not?"

And now he's referring to us as friends. "What nickname should I give you then? It's only fair."

He ponders this for a second before shrugging. "I have never had a nickname before."

Thanatos is a pretty hard name to condense into a nickname. Thana? Than? Tos? They all suck.

"How about *Amiciel*?" It means "friend" in the language of the Gods.

For the first time today, he looks genuinely speechless. "You know the language of the Gods?"

I feel a little embarrassed, but I nod. "*I cogniec a maguus zex a teskt I zaloven ni…university.*"

I know a little from a text I found in university.

"You never cease to impress me," he says with a shake of his head.

It's like he knows just what to say to make a dead girl blush.

"I think I would prefer you call me by my actual name," he says after a moment. "You're one of the only people to say it without hatred or fear."

"Thanatos it is then."

He glances down at the test tube of his blood I have on the counter.

"If you cannot test my blood with products on the Mortal Market, will you do chemical lysis as you usually do in this circumstance?"

I don't even try to contain my excitement. "Yes, want to watch?"

He gives me a small, shy smile. "I would love nothing more."

I move to pick up the test tube to do just that, but then I hear a soft whisper.

"Help them," the whisper says, and at first, I think it's Thanatos, but the voice is feminine, so it couldn't be.

"Help them," the voice pleads, but there's no one around but me and Thanatos, who is starting to look at me in concern.

"Is everything alright?"

I nod, still looking around for the source of the voice. "It's nothing. I'm fine."

"Are you certain?"

I want to ask him if hearing voices when you're dead is normal, but I somehow know the answer is the same whether you're alive or not. So I nod to him again.

Hopefully it's nothing.

CHAPTER SIX

CHARON

I KNEW IT WAS ONLY A MATTER OF TIME BEFORE THE HANDSOME Mortal showed up again, and he did so far sooner than I would have expected. It hasn't even been two days since he first arrived here. I'm as impressed as I'm annoyed.

His genius plan to sneak into the Underworld was to wear the clothes of a corpse. No doubt he thought that would be enough to get past Cerberus, but I think he's learning that nothing can. I find him once again at the end of Cerberus's snarling snout, though this time he looks far less unsteady. There's a confidence and determination that's been enhanced in him since last time.

"I can't decide whether you're brave or stupid," I say as I stuff my headphones into my pocket.

The Mortal shrugs. "Let me know when you make your decision."

I roll my eyes. "I told you not to come back here. Do you have no sense of self-preservation? I could have you thrown into Tartarus for this."

"Then do it. You will be making my job easier since Tartarus is right next to the Field of Mourning, where my wife is."

Stupid. Definitely stupid. "What's your name, Mortal?"

"Orpheus Martin."

"Well, Orpheus, all I can do is tell you about your wife's well-being, and I can assure you she's fine. I've never met an unhappy soul outside of Tartarus."

"And how often do you actually talk to the souls you ferry?"

I feel my eye twitch at that. "Watch it. I'm the one keeping you from torture, so I would mind the tone."

He doesn't back down though. "I'm not going to stop trying. Torture me, kill me, imprison me. I don't care. Nothing matters except getting Eurydice back."

Eurydice? "Is that your wife's name?"

"Yes. Eurydice Martin. She died a few weeks ago in a car accident."

Son of a fucking bitch.

I dig out my phone and press on Thanatos's number, and he thankfully picks up on the second ring. "Yes?"

"There's a situation at the gate," I inform him.

"What sort of situation?" my friend asks calmly.

"Orpheus Martin is here. Alive."

There's a long pause, then Thanatos is by my side with his thumb on the "end call" button. Orpheus jumps when Thanatos suddenly appears, not being used to teleporting, but he quickly recovers. Despite the situation, he gives Thanatos a look of respect, which is returned in kind.

"What are you doing here, Orpheus?" Thanatos's tone is strained, taut like a violin string.

"You know why I'm here. I want my wife back," Orpheus replies defiantly.

Thanatos's wings tense behind him—a small reaction that no one ordinary would notice, but to those that know him? It's clear as day that Orpheus being here has him on edge, which is an emotion he is unused to.

"You know that is not possible. I told you before I cleaved her soul, there is no way to restore a soul once their thread is cut. I'm sorry." He looks genuinely regretful, but I have to question how deeply Thanatos laments this situation.

"No way that you are aware of," Orpheus argues. "How do you know your lord hasn't kept secret how to restore a soul's thread? How do you know you've tried every option? And even if you have, I know Eurydice could figure it out. No one understands the ethereal and divine like she does."

"Death is a natural part of life," Thanatos says calmly. "One cannot exist without the other."

"That's easy for death himself to say."

"It is because I'm death that I can say that. I'm a slave to the Fates as much as anyone else. I do as they bid. I was created by them to end lives because that is how the natural order works. To disrupt it would be to destroy the fabric of reality."

Like a child, Orpheus crosses his arms and gives us a snark-filled shrug. "That's your opinion."

"Holy Gods you cannot be this stubborn." I groan.

"You have no idea how stubborn I can be," Orpheus says as a fact and as a threat.

I glance at the hulking dog beside me. "Escort Orpheus out of the Underworld. He's overstayed his welcome."

Cerberus resumes his growl and starts walking towards Orpheus, forcing him to start backing up, much to his chagrin. "This isn't over," he warns.

"No, I suspect it isn't," I mumble, watching Cerberus herd him towards the passage.

Once Cerberus and Orpheus are out of sight, I turn to my friend with concern. "You okay?"

Thanatos flexes his wings and nods. "Why would I be otherwise?"

I glare his way. "Don't bullshit me. You know why."

Thanatos stares straight ahead, his wings starting to droop, the dark feathers brushing the black tendrils emanating from the Wall of Erebus.

"She doesn't remember him now, but one day she will. All of their history, all of their…their love, will return."

I reach out and squeeze his shoulder. "Plenty of souls find new partners in the Underworld. I think you are selling yourself too short—a bad habit you and Hades can't shake."

That gets a smile out of him. "You do the same."

I ignore that. "Yes, one day her memories and feelings for him will return, but that won't erase what she experiences and feels for you. You act as if she'll forget you."

"Who would choose death over a man who defied death to save her?" he asks quietly, and the defeat in his tone pierces my heart.

"I may not have met her, but I know Eurydice sees you for who you really are, just as Persephone sees Hades. If it can happen for him, it can for you."

"Hades is not as hated as I am," he argues.

"No, but he's feared more than you. I would argue fear is harder to overcome than anger."

Thanatos doesn't disagree with that. "Still. I shouldn't raise my hopes too high."

"I'm all for being pessimistic, but I don't think you need to be."

Now Thanatos turns his face fully towards me. "Neither do you. You always lament on how no one knows you, that you are forgotten to the worlds beyond the Underworld, but Orpheus knew who you were."

He did. "Only because of Eurydice."

"That is two people that knew you, and both have not had a negative reaction to you. I think you are the one that shouldn't be pessimistic."

"I'm still forgotten by the world."

"Why does this matter to you so much? Why do you need acknowledgement from Mortals? Do you want to be worshipped alongside Hecate and Hermes, or do you wish to be condemned like Hades and I?"

"Why does your reputation matter to you so much? Why do you

care if Mortals hate you? You and Hades care about being acknowledged by Mortals just as much as I do."

Thanatos shakes his head, an emotion akin to pity in his gaze. "We have to be true to ourselves and to the ones we love, Charon. Everybody else does not matter. You are right that Eurydice sees me for who I really am, and maybe you are right that she will still feel something for me once her memories of Orpheus return, whether it be friendship or something more. But I must be realistic. No one would pick death over life, regardless of my reputation. It is in the nature of Mortals to fight against death, not to embrace it."

"And you would just let her go?"

He gives the shallowest of nods. "She is not mine to release. I'm still unsure of my feelings towards her, but I know I don't want to force her to be by my side if that is not where she wishes to be. That goes for all others too. If I show myself to Mortals, my true self, and am still hated and shunned for it, why would I waste energy caring about their opinions when it is clear they don't care about mine?"

I hate how much sense he's making. "Easier said than done."

"That is the nature of life, alas." He gives me a reassuring smile. "Nothing is ever easy, but that does not make it any less worth doing."

EURYDICE

When did I become so pathetic?

Thanatos left suddenly to take care of an issue at the gate of the Underworld, and though he said it wouldn't take long, he's been gone for three hours now. While I've tried my hardest to focus on my project, my mind has been too consumed with unhelpful thoughts. It's like I'm in high school again, wondering why the person I like hasn't reached out to me. I feel like a child.

He probably had to go take care of some souls. Besides, he can't dedicate all of his free time to me. He has other friends, other responsibilities…I'm being silly.

After another twenty minutes of trying—and failing—to be productive, I put my work aside for the day and decide to go take a shower. When I was alive, they always helped me relax and clear my head, though now the whole experience is ten times better. The shower I have in this house has water rain down from the ceiling and has an additional nozzle that I can detach from the wall. There's also a jacuzzi bathtub with three jet settings.

Safe to say that I've bathed a lot since I died.

It's honestly sad. Since I can't talk with any other souls yet and there's no place where I can buy things to entertain myself, I'm stuck with taking showers and going on walks when I'm bored. Yes, I have my documentaries and the few other things I asked for when I arrived, but they can get repetitive quickly.

Thanatos has told me that I won't have this problem once I move to the Asphodel Meadows. The Field of Mourning isn't designed to be a permanent living space, nor is it meant to bring the souls who live here entertainment. Mourning gives the soul what they need to heal from their trauma, not to stave off their boredom. It makes sense but it doesn't make it any less annoying. I'm so used to action. I was a workaholic to the max before I died. Even on weekends I would go out shopping or go to the movies or go over to a friend's house. I was constantly moving. Being forced to exist in a plain that's designed to give me infinite time to reflect and relax? It's my own personal hell.

So I'm off to take a shower, because it's either I do that or go for a walk, and I'm not feeling up to physical activity.

I turn on the water and make sure the temperature is scalding hot, then I undress and slip inside, welcoming the downpour consuming my body. I lean back and shut my eyes, focusing only on the feeling of the droplets hitting my face. For all I had complained about relaxing, I do enjoy this immensely.

I don't know how long I stand there under the water, but eventually I start washing myself and belt out one of my favorite ballads—which are objectively the best kind of music. This time I sing "Stone Cold" by Demi Lovato, and I'm just as off-key as usual. But just when I'm getting to the last chorus, a shiver races down my spine, and I feel goosebumps prickle my skin.

It feels like someone is watching me.

I shut off the water and look around my toilet, but no one is in sight. There's not a creek or whisper of another being besides myself. All I can see is the fog from the shower and all I hear is my own shallow breaths.

"They need you," a cold, gravelly voice whispers. It doesn't sound like it's coming from any direction, more like it's being spoken directly into both ears.

"Who's there?" My words sounds strained and uneven. It's the same voice from last time, and I'm utterly convinced that someone has broken into my home.

"You must help them," the voice says next, and I can't help the whimper that escapes my lips.

"W-who?" I've started shaking now, and it's only partially because I'm wet and naked.

Instead of telling me, the voice shows me.

Images flash inside my mind. Images of people—souls, but they look different…wrong. Their eyes are wide in pain and sorrow, their faces gaunt and their bodies brittle. They scream out for help, they cry and wail, but no one can hear them. They're trapped without any way of being heard. Their torture goes on forever, their spirits unable to rest.

I can feel their pain as if it were my own. I feel their fear, their sorrow, their anger.

Who are these people?

"Help them," the voice repeats, and I swear I feel something brush my face.

Unable to take it anymore, my knees buckle under me and I hit the floor of my shower, my eyes suddenly falling shut.

Thanatos

After my conversation with Charon, I needed to get out of the Underworld. The place that is usually my respite suddenly became claustrophobic. It was as if my worrying thoughts and feelings started to suffocate me, and only now that I have had some distance can I recognize that the sensation I'm feeling is not one I've experienced before.

Fear.

I'm afraid that if I grow too attached to Eurydice, I will get hurt when she inevitably remembers Orpheus. I don't think I have ever been afraid of anything before. Oh, how my brother must be pleased. He always enjoyed the fear he instilled in others, and no doubt he is enjoying mine now. The irony that his power should plague me now, after all my years of berating him for taking his power for granted, for exercising it cruelly. What cosmic karma is it that death is being tortured by his twin, fear.

I refuse to bow to my brother's influence or to my own worries. I'm far above hiding away from my problems like a coward, and it's not fair to Eurydice to avoid her. She has done nothing wrong, and I have no wish to punish her. I'm the only friend she has in the Underworld, and the idea of her being locked away in that house alone makes me ache. Eurydice deserves all the good that the afterlife has to offer, and I refuse to take part in sullying that.

So, after a few hours of hiding away, I teleport back to the Underworld, appearing right in front of her door. She and I have passed the point of knocking, so I just walk in and start searching around for her, though she's nowhere in sight. Once I've searched the living room, kitchen, and bedroom, I start to get concerned.

She is usually working on her experiments at this time of day, but maybe she went for a walk? I'm just about to head back downstairs when

I hear a whimper come from inside the bathroom. It's faint, but I know right away that the sound came from Eurydice. I rap my knuckle against the door, but there is no answer.

Worry turns my gut into knots as I open up the door, finding Eurydice on the floor of her shower, seemingly passed out. I rush over towards her and turn off the water, then I wrap her up in a towel and carry her towards her bedroom. The whole time, she is limp and unresponsive, and in all my years I have never seen a soul like this. They don't sleep, they don't faint, but Eurydice seems to have done both.

Once I get her to her bed, I dry her off and cover her in blankets, remembering a passage in a Jane Austen novel I read where the sick should be kept under blankets and avoid being wet. I don't know if this advice applies here, but I feel it's better to be safe than sorry. Once I'm sure she is comfortable, I call Hecate, who thankfully isn't busy and promises to teleport over in a few moments.

Before I've even slipped my phone back into my pocket, Hecate is at my side, her brows knit in confusion. "You found her like this?"

"Yes. I dried her off and covered her, but she hasn't moved."

Hecate inspects Eurydice delicately, her palms glowing green as she uses her magic. She whispers a few words under her breath, most likely a spell, and Eurydice slowly starts to stir. The second her eyes open and a little groan escapes her, I fall to my knees by her side, relief flooding every cell of my being.

"She had a vision," Hecate informs me, her eyes glued to a disoriented Eurydice.

Without looking away from the soul in front of me, I say to Hecate, "That's not possible." She's a Mortal. Mortals don't have the ability to use magic.

"It should be," she agrees. "but it couldn't be anything else. I looked into her mind and heard the voices of the Fates."

I look back at Eurydice, who is staring at Hecate with growing concern. "What does this mean for me?"

"I don't know, but until we do, I think you should stay at the palace so we can watch over you," Hecate suggests, clasping her hands in front of her. "Who knows what the Fates are up to, and I'd rather you not be alone the next time they decide to enter your mind."

"You think there will be a next time?" Her voice starts to waver, and without thought, I grip onto her hand, squeezing it tightly.

"They appear to be trying to tell you something, and I promise that all of us will help you discover what it is. We will ensure that you stay safe," I vow.

She gives me a weak smile, and it warms my heart to see it. "Thank you, Thanatos."

A smile back. "Anything for you, Doctor."

CHAPTER SEVEN

ORPHEUS

There are temples for almost every God in Greece. It's just my luck that the one temple I'm looking for is on the other side of the country, forcing me to drive three hours to get there.

Since my plan to wear clothing from a corpse didn't work, I'm now resorting to plan C, which is visiting the temple of Hecate and convincing one of the priestesses to aid me in entering the Underworld. The priestesses of Hecate have a reputation of being fiercely loyal to their goddess, which is odd because that wasn't always the case. According to Eurydice, Hecate was as hated by the public as Hades and Thanatos, but something happened around a hundred years ago that changed that. A temple suddenly appeared in Greece and a large number of priestesses started praising and worshipping Hecate. Eurydice searched in vain for a long time to find out how Hecate's reputation suddenly changed. I think this is by design. Hecate strikes me as a person who values secrecy. And I'll bet her followers are no different.

Traveling from Britain to Greece was long and difficult because of Demeter's Storm, but somehow traveling to another city in Greece is even harder. Everywhere in the Northern hemisphere is dealing with lingering ice and snow, power outages, famine, and economic recessions; but in Greece there are riots that have sprung up, and I'm sure in time they will spread to other countries as well.

People are angry that Demeter was allowed to make an apocalyptic storm without any consequences from the other Gods. According to King Pieros and Queen Jia—who have a God as a son-in-law—Demeter has been exiled from Olympus as punishment for her storm. But that has only made the masses angrier, and I'm right there with them. That's like punishing a thief by locking them in the house they tried to rob. Demeter could inflict her will upon us again whenever she chose. And us powerless Mortals would be forced to endure it. This goes for all other Gods as well, most of whom have taken their wrath out on us Mortals at some time or another. Yet here they still are, worshipped and beloved.

As I cross the street to where Hecate's Temple lies, I see a crowd of Mortals gathering around a woman with white skin and bright red hair. She's speaking into a megaphone, her gloved hands and jacket-wrapped body shuddering from the cold. But the freezing temperature only seems to strengthen her resolve, as her voice is firm and clear as she shouts. "Demeter is only one in a long list of Gods that has treated us like toys for their amusement," she says, wrapping the scarf around her neck even tighter. "And she won't be the last until we let our voices be heard."

"The Gods don't care about what we have to say," someone from the crowd shouts to her.

"Without worshippers, what real power does a God have? If we take that power away from them then—" she argues.

"If we step out of line, then it won't be Demeter who punishes us. It will be a God far worse!" another shouts.

"Yeah, what's stopping Lord Hades from killing us all should we anger the Gods enough?" says the person next to the last.

A young girl from the crowd steps onto a nearby bus bench and starts screaming, "Don't say his name! We barely survived Demeter's wrath; do you want to incur the wrath of the King of the Dead?"

"That coward has hidden away for centuries. I say let him come up here and give us a taste of his power," an old man shouts from nearby.

The crowd goes ballistic at that, and I force my legs to walk a bit faster to the temple. If things get violent, I don't want to be anywhere near them.

When I reach the stairs leading up to the main entrance, I see more people rushing towards the crowd, and the voices have become so loud that I can no longer hear the girl with the megaphone. I watch as she desperately tries to regain control of her audience, but it's to no avail.

"It is truly astonishing what the unknown and unpredictable does to the mind," a familiar voice says to my right.

I turn towards the sound, but I see nobody there. Part of me wants to just continue up the stairs and ignore that deep, lyrical voice, but before I can truly decide, I'm already walking down the stairs and around the side of the temple. The crowd gets quieter the farther I walk, and the sound of my own heartbeat increases exponentially. It's as if drums are beating next to my ears, and my skin prickles in awareness, like I'm being watched.

"There's no need to be afraid, Orpheus," the voice says again, but there still isn't anyone here. "I come as a friend."

Suddenly, a figure made of smoke appears in front of me, and their features slowly sharpen until it becomes a face I recognize, and all I'm left with is shock.

"Thanatos?"

He chuckles, shaking his head. "Not exactly."

I'm about to ask what he means, but my eyes catch his arms and it makes me pause. They're covered in tattoos, most of which are comprised of words I assume are written in the language of the Gods. I've never seen Thanatos without a suit jacket on, but something tells me he doesn't have tattoos. The man standing before me also has no wings, and his attire is more akin to a lead singer of a rock band than a God. Everything else about this man is undoubtedly Thanatos, though. Besides those few differences, they look identical.

Wait a minute.

"You're Phobos," I deduct. "The God of Fear and Thanatos's twin brother."

Phobos gives a little bow. "Guilty as charged."

"How do you know who I am?"

Phobos smiles, and it's filled with far more malice than I would ever find from Thanatos. The God of Death always has a soft, kind look in his eyes, but in his brother I only find anger and hatred. "I've been following you for a few days now, ever since you dug up that corpse and wore its clothes to retrieve your wife. I admire your dedication."

Phobos begins circling me as he talks, and every time he goes out of my line of sight, the hair on the back of my neck sticks up. "You see, as the Primordial God of Fear, I can feel whenever any being in any dimension experiences fear. Sometimes the Fates dictate that I instill fear within someone, but even without my meddling, fear spreads regardless. My very being creates it. You can imagine my shock when I sensed it within someone who had never felt fear before, whom I thought was immune to my powers."

"I'm guessing that someone is Thanatos."

The God nods his head, his expression turning into faux contemplation. "Out of curiosity, I observed the Underworld for a few days, trying to discover the reason behind my brother's sudden fear. What I found was you and your wife."

"I don't understand."

Phobos stops in front of me, excitement gleaming in his white eyes. It's a startling change. "My brother and your wife have become very close in the last week. So close, in fact, that my brother dreads the day she will remember her life with you. He fears that, even if you don't succeed with your mission of retrieving Eurydice, that he will lose her in his life regardless."

No, no that can't be right. Absolutely not.

"You're telling me that Thanatos and my wife are seeing each other?" I can barely get the words out.

He nods, still smiling. "I cannot sense how one feels other than their fears, but it sure looks that way."

"Eurydice wouldn't do that to me," I grate out, bile rising in my throat.

Phobos holds up his pointer finger. "Ah, but she has no memories of you. As far as she knows, she died without a significant other and is otherwise free to date whomever she sets her eyes on. It just so happens that her eyes are on my brother."

I ball my fists at my side, trying to stop myself from strangling the God before me, an action that would definitely lead to my death. "Why would you tell me this?"

"To further your resolve."

I narrow my eyes his way. "Why do you care if I succeed or not? What's in it for you?"

He takes a step closer to me, his jovial mask slipping ever so slightly. "That's my business. All you need to know is that our interests currently align, so I'm going to help you."

Phobos produces a vile from his pocket and holds it up between us. It's black-tinted glass that contains a glowing liquid inside. "Take this and you will be able to enter the Underworld undetected. As far as that dog and The Ferryman are concerned, you will be like every other soul. You must be cautious though; it only lasts five hours and it will not render you invisible. I would recommend buying a big coat with a large hood to hide your face."

I eye the vile and then him. "Where did you get this?"

Phobos nods his head to the temple next to us. "Those priestesses would have never helped you. They're too loyal, too strict when it comes to the rules. Thankfully they have a storage room filled with items such as these."

Hesitantly, I take the vile from him, and I'm shocked by how cold it is to the touch.

"Good luck to you, Orpheus Martin. I do hope you're successful, for your sake as much as your wife's," Phobos says with a grin, then I watch with wide eyes as he seemingly vanishes into nothing, though I can still feel his presence. It chills me to the bones in a way that the lingering storm hasn't accomplished.

The God of Fear indeed.

Thanatos

Are you sure this is okay?" Eurydice whispers to me, worry evident in her voice.

I give her an encouraging smile as I lead her towards the thick throne room doors. "I know what Hades's reputation is, but I assure you that he will have no problem with you staying in the palace. He is the most generous man I've ever known."

That seems to put her more at ease, and I'm humbled that she trusts my judgment so much. I take it a step further and gently stroke my fingers against the back of her hand, and I swear I see her shiver. "I would never put you in a position where you would face any level of danger. I hope you know that."

Eurydice surprises me by linking her fingers with mine. "I know."

Not trusting myself to say any more, I push open one of the doors, still clutching her hand in mine. Hades and Persephone are sitting in their respective thrones, chatting quietly to one another, but they pause when their eyes land on the two of us. Hades looks curious and a little amused as he takes us in, but Persephone lacks all subtlety, breaking into a wide grin and immediately getting to her feet, closing the distance between us.

"You must be Eurydice," she says brightly, grabbing hold of her free hand. "I'm Persephone, Hades's wife."

The way Eurydice's eyes widen is almost comical. "I didn't know Lord Hades had a spouse."

"You wouldn't know. We only got married a short while ago, and our relationship hasn't been made public outside of the Underworld."

I lean closer to Eurydice to say, "It's a long story. I'll explain later."

Hades strides to his wife's side and offers Eurydice a smile, then he extends his hand out. "We are honored to host you in our home, Ms.

Martin. If there is anything we can provide for you or if you require any help, just ask. It is our duty to help the souls in any way we can."

I know how difficult Hades finds putting himself out there like this, and I feel a wave of pride that's mirrored in Persephone's eyes. That pride is still there when her gaze lands on me, and I have to fight off a blush, unused to such affection.

"Th-thank you, My Lord," Eurydice stutters, unlinking our fingers so she can accept Hades's hand. She holds it as if she were about to grab onto a coiling snake.

Hades brings the back of her hand up to his lips gently. "There's no need for the formalities. Hades is fine."

Eurydice gives a shaky nod. "I'm sorry. I didn't—"

"Don't worry about it," Hades interrupts, squeezing her hand. "I know what my reputation is. Your reaction is normal."

Eurydice glances down bashfully. "I'm sorry all the same. Thank you for being so welcoming, Hades. And it is wonderful to meet you both."

"Hecate and Hermes are gathering your belongings and will put them in the first door on the left of the third floor. It's right next to where Hecate will be staying, in case you need her," Persephone can hardly contain her glee. "It's also right next to the stairwell that leads to the library, where Thanatos spends most of his free time."

Persephone gives me a knowing look, and I have to refrain from openly glaring.

"I'm going to show Eurydice around the palace," I announce, ignoring the teasing glances and expressions of my friends. "We'll see you both for dinner."

"We will?" Eurydice asks, still looking unsure.

"We have dinner together every night, and I think you'll enjoy it even though you cannot eat anything. You can finally have a conversation with more than just me."

She wraps her arm around mine. "You say that as if that's a bad thing. You are more than enough company for me."

"Aww," Persephone gushes, though she tries to cover it up with a cough.

I don't hide my glare. "We'll see you at dinner."

I lead her out of the throne room by foot and take her through each level of the palace, stopping in every room to explain its purpose and history, but I admit I rush through the rooms leading up to the library. I don't know why, but I want her to appreciate my place of respite as much as I do, and once she sets her eyes on it, she gives me the reaction I was hoping for, one of complete and utter awe.

"Holy shit," she gasps, spinning around to take it all in. "This is incredible. How many books are in here?"

"I have not counted, but there are books that date back to a time before Mortals existed. I would guess the number reaches the hundreds of thousands."

She gapes at me, her jaw hanging open. "You're kidding."

I shake my head, barely containing a smile. "I don't kid."

Eurydice returns to admiring the library, lightly caressing the spines of books as she passes them by, smiling wider and wider as she reads the titles of some of our collection. I follow behind her as she explores, and I find myself admiring her rather than the novels that usually hold all of my attention.

"I spend most of my spare time here," I tell her, linking my hands behind my back as I follow her. "Besides a few meetings with Hades and dinner every night, every second I can spare is spent here."

"I can see why." She pulls out a first edition copy of *Darwin's Theory of Evolution*, and she holds it with the delicacy that one would handle a diamond. "I take it you like to read?"

I take a wistful glance at the bookshelf next to us, answering honestly, "As the personification of death, it can be so easy to feel void of life, and books are what keep me from losing myself."

Eurydice's smile grows melancholic. "I loved to read as a kid, but once I got to university I just couldn't find the time. Things only got worse once I started working."

"Well, now you have eternity to rediscover your love for it."

She looks excited at the prospect. "Do you have any recommendations?"

I oddly begin to feel subconscious. "You probably wouldn't enjoy the books I read. Hermes has described them as 'stuffy and boring.'"

Eurydice only rolls her eyes. "I highly doubt anything you enjoy is stuffy and boring. In fact, I want you to give me a full reading list."

She wants to read my favorite books? I didn't think such a person existed. "You may regret asking for one."

She waves me off. "Nonsense. It will give you another excuse to come hang out with me. After I finish each book, we can discuss them."

As if I need an excuse.

I gesture for her to wait, then I proceed searching around the library for all the books I want her to read, and after a few minutes of collecting, I return to her with a tall stack in my arms.

She eyes the stack thoughtfully. "These all your favorites?"

I nod. In my arms are *Frankenstein*, *The Book Thief*, *The Phantom of the Opera*, *The Metamorphosis*, and about five different poetry books.

"Is one above the others?"

I ponder her question for a moment—never having done so myself—then decide, "Probably *The Metamorphosis*."

"Any reason why?"

I hesitate for a moment, not wanting to unload all my thoughts and feelings onto her. "I'll tell you after you've read it. I think you'll understand it better then."

She smiles and nods, grabbing the book from the stack in my arms. "I'll get started on it right away."

"There is no rush. Between your project and these visions, you have a lot on your plate."

She shakes off my comment. "You've helped me with my experiments and listened to me drone on and on about my studies. It's only fair I take part in your interests too. Besides, I want to read more now that I have the time, so it's hardly a chore."

I'm about to speak when I hear the Fates inform me of a new soul to collect.

"You must cleave the soul of Liz Henry in Athens, Greece. They have minutes left."

I heave a sigh, giving Eurydice an apologetic look. Without having to explain, she nods in understanding. "Duty calls." She shrugs.

"Duty calls," I agree. "I will see you at dinner in a few hours. I'm assuming you'll be in your room studying my blood in the meantime?"

A spark of excitement lights inside her eyes. "I'm in the process of exposing your cells to extreme conditions, and nothing can harm them. Not the harshest chemicals, environmental factors, or other means. Now, it's still too early to say definitively, but I think it's safe to say you are completely indestructible."

"Yes, it is a truth I have known for a long time."

She gives me an odd look. "Most would be thrilled to know that, yet you seem sad."

I can understand why Mortals and other Gods would crave the certainty of forever, but they have no idea the true toll it forces you to endure. I tell her as much. "I'm the only indestructible being alive. Even the other primordial deities can experience a sort of death by losing their consciousness. But I'm destined to roam the realms of creation even after all else has vanished from them. The fate of Death is to never die. My fate is to be alone."

Eurydice stares at me in silence, her gaze filled with empathetic sadness. It's unbearable to witness. I don't want to see her pity. I don't want to see the truth of what I said be reflected in her eyes. So, with a diverted gaze, I spread my wings and teleport away, off to fulfill my duty to the dying, as will be my duty until there is nothing left but me.

Chapter Eight

Charon

I stare at Eurydice as she sits across from me at the dining room table, and all I can think about is the husband she doesn't know she has that's become a sharp pain in my ass.

I've become paranoid since his second attempt to break into the Underworld. Each time a soul would be delivered at the gates, I would do a thorough examination of them to make certain Orpheus wasn't disguising himself. He's made it clear his determination is unending and my threats mean shit to him, so I had no doubt he would be very crafty for his third attempt.

I was proven right.

Just before dinner, on my last boatload of souls for the day, I noticed a hooded figure in the back of my boat wearing a ski mask. Though I couldn't sense a Mortal, my instinct told me that something was off. Before I even pushed away from the bank, I ripped away the hood and mask, finding a scowling Orpheus staring up at me. This time, instead of making him go back to the Mortal World, I teleported him to my house, where he is currently tied down spread-eagle on my kitchen table. I told him I would decide what to do with him when I returned in a few hours, and little did I know I would spend those few hours in the company of the woman he's trying to rescue.

I really hate my life.

Eurydice leans forward and breaths in deep, barely suppressing a moan. "This steak smells fantastic! Who cooked it?"

"Charon cooks all our meals," Hecate answers, bumping me with her shoulder.

"You're incredibly talented, my Lord," she says sincerely.

I feel a blush creeping up my neck, and I hear myself mumble, "Charon is fine."

"Thank you for inviting me to dinner," she directs to Hades and Persephone, then she turns to Hecate and Hermes. "And thank you both for moving all of my items. I know you are busy, I hope it wasn't an inconvenience—"

Hermes shakes his head, assuring her with a mouth full of potatoes, "No problem, beautiful."

Eurydice smiles. "I thought I told you that using such pet names is inappropriate?"

Hermes winks. "We're not in a professional setting at the moment."

Thanatos looks between them, simultaneously confused and uncomfortable. "You have met before?"

Eurydice nods. "I worked with him at the IMRA a couple years ago. Lord Hermes has made the most blood donations out of every God other than Prometheus, so everyone at the IMRA knows him to some capacity. It's lovely to see you again." She nods his way.

The smile he gives her is rakish. "And you, Ma'am."

"I regret that I had the flu the last time you came in, I was really bummed I couldn't meet you," she says to Hecate.

The Goddess beside me shrugs, taking a sip of wine. "I regret that our paths didn't cross, but the Fates have control over these things, not any of us."

"What's the IMRA?" Persephone inquires, asking the question on everyone else's mind.

Eurydice then goes on to explain the secret organization founded by Prometheus, as well as their goal of finding solutions to Mortal health issues through the study of Immortals. It doesn't surprise me in the least that Prometheus would create something like that, and he was smart to keep it secret. If Zeus were to find out, I have no doubt in my mind that Prometheus would be punished, regardless of their bond. And I cannot even fathom how the Mortals a part of the IMRA would be punished if discovered.

I respect Eurydice's willingness to risk her life in order to help her people.

"If you'd like, you could analyze the rest of our blood, as well as Thanatos's. Anything you discover we will have Hermes deliver to Prometheus," Hades offers.

Persephone covers one of Hades's hands with hers and nods. "And if you ever need assistance, I'd be happy to lend a hand. I'm an artist, so I have a very steady hand."

"My lady, you don't—"

"Oh none of that." Persephone waves her off. "And it's no problem. I'm always happy to leave all the prayers and meetings to my husband."

"Wow, thanks" is his reply.

She winks at him. "I'll make it up to you."

His lips stretch into a grin. "And how exactly would you do that?"

Hermes makes several gagging motions. "Please, not while I'm eating. You two are becoming insufferable."

Persephone and Hades just ignore him, sharing a brief kiss filled with a tenderness and love that makes my heart ache with longing. What I would give to have someone love me the way those two love each other.

The way Orpheus loves Eurydice.

I heave a sigh, wiping my mouth with my napkin. "I'm gonna get going. I had a long day and I'm absolutely exhausted."

"Then why don't you stay in your room here at the palace? It would be easier than exerting yourself to teleport." Persephone's eyes are filled with concern, and I hate that I have to lie to her.

I shake my head, giving her a weak smile. "I'm fine, Seph. I'll see you tomorrow."

"It was nice meeting you!" Eurydice says with a sweet smile, and I can easily see now why Orpheus would risk so much to get her back. She's lovely.

I nod gently to her. "You too."

I vanish from the dining room and appear in my home within seconds, and I'm relieved to find Orpheus right where I left him, still tied down to my table. My captive lifts his head and glares at me, pulling against the ropes. "Was this really necessary?"

I cross my arms, leaning my shoulder against the wall closest to him. "You're the one who keeps trespassing despite my warnings, so how am I supposed to trust you to behave unless I force you to?"

Orpheus pouts. "Oh I'm sorry, am I becoming a bother?"

I don't think I've ever had the urge to strangle someone before now, but the idea is truly tempting. And what I would give to bite that pouting lip.

"Yes, you are becoming a pain in my fucking ass, so here's your options: I take you to Tartarus and let you sit in the dungeons for a week or you leave the Underworld and don't come back until you're dead."

His arms flex beneath the restraints. "Fine, put me in Tartarus, but you have to know that won't stop me. Once I'm released, I'll try to break in again and again and again until I get my wife back. Nothing you could throw at me could stop me."

Gods how dense is this guy? "Have you no sense of self-preservation? And what about your family? Your friends? Would you put them through the torture of not knowing what's happened to you while they are still grieving Eurydice?"

His eyes darken a bit, his jaw tensing. "I don't have anyone but Eurydice. My mom died, my dad stopped being a father a long time ago, I've never been much of a people person, and Eurydice's parents are too focused on their grief to give a shit about what I do. I think they could stomach a couple months of worry if at the end of all this I bring them their daughter back."

I pinch the bridge of my nose, my frustration giving way to pity. "I told you, there's no way a soul can return. It's been tried before, and the consequences and damage done were irreversible."

"All I'm hearing is that it was only tried once and that's not enough times to claim something is scientifically impossible. And I doubt the King of the Dead truly did all he could."

Anger flares within me. "I know what Hades's reputation is, but he's a good man. He did everything he could and the fact that he failed haunts him every day."

"I want to hear that from him."

I blink. "What?"

"You say bringing a soul back to life is impossible? That it's been attempted before? I want to hear that from Hades himself."

I want to tell him that he's crazy, but maybe this will be what finally puts some sense inside his thick head. "Fine. I'll take you to Hades. But when he tells you exactly what I have, I want you to leave the Underworld and stay away. Deal?"

Without hesitation, Orpheus nods. "Deal."

I approach him slowly, reaching for the ropes binding him to my table, and I don't stop myself from staring at him, and he stares right back. He really is beautiful, in a way that I haven't seen in Mortals before. Their species was designed to look like the Gods, but without the immortality that keeps their beauty flawless and timeless. Orpheus comes pretty close to that perfection, however. Every part of him is sculpted as if by an artist, and it takes all my willpower not to run my hand down the tendons of his sculpted brown arms and his long fingers as I untie him.

Once both of his wrists are freed, I leave him to take care of his ankles. As he pulls apart the knot, I tell him, "There's some food in my kitchen if you are hungry, as well as fresh water. The bathroom is down the hall, you're welcome to use the shower if you wish, and the couch is all yours. Don't touch anything or go snooping around, and if I find you trying to escape, I will lock you up in Tartarus without a second thought. Do I make myself clear?"

Orpheus plants his feet on the ground and stands, giving me a firm nod. "Crystal, my lord."

I cringe at that. "I'm not a lord. Charon is fine."

Surprisingly, he sticks out his hand for me to shake. "Charon, then. And you can call me Orpheus, if you'd like."

My blood heats at hearing him say my name. I grab onto his hand, finding his fingers nimble and calloused. A musician's hands. "You just might be the strangest being I have ever met," I tell him.

He gives me a small smile. "I'll take that as a compliment."

"I don't know if I intended it to be one, but whatever floats your boat, as you Mortals like the say."

That gets a laugh out of him, though it's rough, like he had a hard time making the sound. "Thank you for agreeing to help me."

I slip my hand out of his grip, curling my fingers at my sides. "You're welcome, Orpheus. Now, go get some rest. We'll leave first thing tomorrow."

And with that, I leave the Mortal to his own devices, my palm still tingling from where my hand met his.

ORPHEUS

Charon's house is not what I would have expected a God's house to look like. I expected extravagance, wealth, and gaudy décor. But his house looks more like an English cottage you'd find on Pinterest. It has stone walls and roof, dark wood floors, vintage-style furniture from the 19th century, and virtually no decorations. On the walls there are only a few pictures, all of which contain the same people: Charon, Hecate, Hermes, Thanatos, and whom I'm guessing is Hades. The only images of Hades known to the Mortal World are in ancient statues, and those don't really give you an accurate depiction of what someone looks like, especially after thousands of years.

He's very attractive, and the smile he gives his friends is a genuine one. Perhaps Charon is right and Hades's reputation does not align with his character. After all, that turned out to be true for Thanatos once I met him, but I had already been made biased in his favor. Eurydice has always been fascinated with him, ever since they met when she was a girl. She swore up and down that Thanatos was a good person, and would defend him to complete strangers if they dared to speak ill of him in her presence. Of course I believed her, though sometimes I did wonder if she was just blinded by the crush she always harbored for him.

I used to tease her relentlessly about it, but I always knew it was harmless. My celebrity crush was Chris Evans, hers was Thanatos. Though if Phobos is right, then maybe that crush isn't so innocent anymore. I try not to think about that though. I have to be focused on the task at hand and not get swept up in my emotions.

After Charon left me alone, I searched through his kitchen to find something to eat, and I ended up devouring an entire tub of ice cream, as well as half a bottle of wine. I then took a shower, and distracted myself by contemplating how the Underworld has running water. I couldn't come up with any logical answer by the time I finished, and now that I'm spread out on the couch, I have nothing to occupy my thoughts with save for what's to come tomorrow.

I should be worrying about possible imprisonment and/or torture, but when I think about that possibility, all I feel is apathy. If I'm punished, it means that I failed in trying to rescue Eurydice, and there's no torture greater than a life without her. I'd rather rot in the dungeons of Tartarus than return to the Mortal World alone; at least then I would be close to her, even if she was out of reach.

Even if she didn't remember me.

That knowledge has been a hard pill to swallow. Knowing that my wife has no memory of me or our life together adds to the already suffocating grief. If I manage to find a way to bring her back, how do I restore her memories? If I came to her now, would she even want to leave the Underworld?

I take a couple deep breaths, urging myself to calm down. There's no point in worrying about the 'what if's.' The minute I start accepting the possibility of defeat is the minute I'm defeated. I won't let myself be consumed. I won't let grief swallow me whole.

Like how it swallowed my father.

My mother died of breast cancer when I was ten. She had been sick most of my life, so the day she finally passed was a day of relief as much as grief. I had witnessed her suffer for so long, and I was glad she could finally be at peace. My dad, however, felt no relief. His grief festered and twisted him into an absent father and a raging alcoholic. I was forced to spend my teenage years wondering what bar he was passed out at, hoping it wouldn't be the time he didn't return home. And as I got older, I had to be the one to search for him and make sure he returned home safely, even after I moved out.

He let his grief consume him until there was nothing left. He let his life, his relationships, and his family fall apart. I refuse to do the same.

I'm going to fix everything.

The sound of a piano playing pulls me from my thoughts, and at first, I think it's all in my head. It's happened before. But the longer I listen, the surer I am that it's coming from the direction of Charon's room. I wonder for a second if it's a recording, but there's no way it could be. After all these years, I can recognize the difference, and what's flowing through the crack in the doorway is real, raw, and without any mistakes.

Despite being told not to enter his room, I feel lulled into a trance by his music, and I suddenly find myself pushing the door open slightly— just enough to see Charon with his eyes closed, his fingers flying over the keys in pure muscle memory. He's played this piece a thousand times and doesn't even need to think to do so. It's an intoxicating feeling. You become the music in those moments.

I recognize the piece immediately. It's "Moonlight Sonata" by Beethoven. A deeply moving yet sad piece about lost love and regret.

I've listened to this song a thousand times, but it's only this time that I feel tears well in my eyes. The music flows through and around me, piercing my heart in a way that's as visceral as it is unexpected. It's as if Beethoven composed the feelings inside my heart, and hearing them delivered back to me is torturous. All I can see in my mind's eye is my wife dying in my arms while I'm helpless to do anything to stop her death, and all I feel is the grief of my own lost love and regrets told through the notes of Beethoven's work.

I openly weep as I stand in the doorway, and no doubt Charon knows of my presence, but he says nothing. He finishes the last few stanzas of the song, and only then does he open his eyes and lock his gaze onto me.

"You play beautifully," I whisper, my cheeks stained with tears.

Charon nods in acknowledgment, rubbing his palms on his pants. "Do you play?"

I nod, wiping my eyes. "Yes. I also play trumpet, flute, trombone, cello, violin, viola, harp, and lyre."

His eyes widen, and I feel a little spout of pride at impressing someone who's been alive for so long.

"I didn't know anyone in this millennium knew how to play the lyre. Are you one of those child prodigies?"

I shrug. "Ever since I was a kid, music was the only thing that made sense to me. I could understand it in a way I couldn't understand people, and it could understand me. That must sound crazy—"

"No," he says firmly. "I know exactly what you mean."

After hearing him play, I have no doubt he does.

"Is that what you do for a living? You're a musician?" he asks, gently caressing the keys in the beginning notes of "Clair de Lune."

I take a few steps towards him, admiring the beautiful instrument in front of me. It's a sleek black grand piano, polished to the point where my reflection is visible in its opaque surface. "I'm the concertmaster of the Sydney Symphony Orchestra."

He stops playing abruptly. "You're lying."

He sounds so accusatory, I have to laugh. "I started when I was eighteen as principal flute. I practiced hard and worked my way up over the last ten years, and it's paid off. We were going on tour when Demeter's storm hit. Our last stop had been England, and that's where—"

A lump forms in my throat, preventing me from speaking. My silence seems to speak for itself though, because Charon nods in understanding.

"I truly am sorry for your loss. Please don't mistake me fulfilling my duties as having a lack of sympathy."

I never thought that but hearing it from him is nice all the same. "The fact that you can still feel sympathy says loads about your character. After all these centuries of transporting the dead, I don't think anyone would blame you for becoming numb to it all."

He continues to strum the keys, and all the while his eyes stare at me with an intensity that roots me in place.

"I have my friends to thank for that. Before they arrived, I was as you describe."

"You were here alone before the fall of the Titans?"

A single nod. "Yes. Back then, death was uncommon, and only a few beings were sent down here to the Underworld. The Judges and Furies had not been created yet, none of my friends were alive…No one would have known if I lived or died, and no one would have cared. Not much has changed, honestly."

"What do you mean?"

I forget sometimes how old these Immortal beings are because of their youthful appearances. Charon looks no older than I am, but in his gaze, I see the pain and loneliness that comes with immortality. I see a broken spirit hidden behind those amethyst eyes.

"Before you met your wife, did you have any idea who I was?"

I ponder this for a second, then shake my head.

"Very few do. My entire existence, I have been ignored, left forgotten by the Mortals and Immortals. The living and the dead. Hades and Thanatos insist that being hated and feared are a worse fate, but they forget I have a point of reference. Back when Mortals had to pay a toll to me to exist in the Underworld, I was known as a figure to fear. I was the cursed ferryman of the dead."

"And you preferred it that way?"

Charon shrugs. "No one wants to be hated, but if no one knows you exist, do you even matter?"

I lean my side against the instrument, crossing my arms. "So you want to be worshipped amongst others of your kind."

He shakes his head, playing the last few keys of the song. "I want to be seen. Isn't that what anyone wants?"

I don't know how to reply to that, so I don't. I let the silence speak for itself.

Charon glances at the half-open door of his room, the vulnerability I saw only moments ago vanishing without a trace. "You should rest. We have a big day tomorrow."

He begins playing the keys of the piano at random, and I know this is a clear message to leave him alone. As I'm about to exit his room, my eyes catch on a glimmering object behind a glass cabinet door. Its metal frame is solid gold, its strings are drawn tight, and the craftsmanship of the entire instrument could rival ones showcased in museums.

It's a lyre.

"Could I ask a favor of you?" I hear myself say.

His fingers pause on the keys. "What is it?"

A single flicker of hope lights in my chest. "Could I borrow your lyre?"

Chapter Nine

Eurydice

When you don't sleep or eat, it can be hard to stick to a schedule. That is why I've devised a way to have some structure in my afterlife: daytime is for working on my projects and experiments, while nighttime is for leisure activities like catching up on reading or watching a movie.

It's currently three o'clock in the morning and I'm propped up in my bed at Hades's palace, with *The Metamorphosis* resting on my lap, and my body wrapped in what must be the softest blanket ever made. If I have it my way, I will spend an eternity of nights just like this.

Thanatos is currently taking care of a soul, and all the other inhabitants of this castle have long since gone to bed, so there's no one I can talk to about this book at the moment, and I'm getting antsy from all of the questions and comments I have. I actually end up crawling out of bed to grab one of my notebooks. I spend about half an hour writing down everything going through my head so I can tell Thanatos later.

This book is deeply depressing. It tells the story of Gregor, who lives a normal life until he wakes up one day as a roach. He is secluded into his bedroom by his family, who are terrified of him and what he's become, and he slowly loses touch with humanity and the monotony of life he once wanted to escape. As I read Gregor's thoughts and feelings during this tragedy, I can't help but draw a comparison to Thanatos.

He told me that he and his brother had been born because the other primordial deities feared the end of their happiness. Thanatos must felt as Gregor did: isolated from his family and forced to become the subject of their resentment. Gregor was the cause for his family's lives altering forever, falling into poverty and hiding from society and their judgment. Thanatos's birth probably did the same. Gone was the idea of eternal bliss and unending pleasure for Uranus, Gaia, Chaos, Nyx, and Erebus. Now they were faced with the looming threat of becoming what they once were, just unconscious entities holding the fabric of the universe together. And Thanatos was the personification of that harsh new reality.

I know his father, Erebus, acts as the gate to the Underworld…I wonder if he ever visits his son. And what of his mother? Does the Goddess of the Night ever check in to make sure her son is happy?

I can see why Thanatos loves this book. There's something extremely powerful about reading a story that reflects the secrets of your soul, and within these pages I feel like I'm seeing straight into his.

"Souls, the souls. You must help the souls," a harsh voice whispers to me.

A shiver runs down my spine and dread fills my chest. I had hoped that the Fates speaking to me would stop on its own, but I knew my hopes were unrealistic. They want something from me, and they won't shut up until I decipher their message.

I close my book and fling myself towards the door, making a direct beeline for Hecate's room. She answers after only a few knocks, wearing a dark purple robe and a grey silk scarf wrapped around her hair. She was clearly sleeping, but she's alert as she asks me, "Is it the Fates?"

I nod, cringing as I hear their voices again.

"They need you."

Hecate gestures for me to enter her room. "Let's see what we can find."

I walk past her and sit down on the edge of her bed, watching her pull up the sleeves of her robe and roll her shoulders.

"Here's what we're going to do," she begins. "I'm going to look into your mind again, but this time I'm going to open up a pathway of communication. Theoretically, you'll be able to talk back to the Fates."

"Theoretically?"

Hecate shrugs. "Usually, only Immortals have been able to receive visions, and even then, it's rare. The only Mortal in history to ever have visions from the Fates was Princess Cassandra of Troy. The Fates warned her about the Trojan War and what it would cost her family, and everyone paid the price of not listening to her. I think it's worth a shot trying to talk to them now, even if it's never been done before."

I stare at Hecate for a long time, listening to the quiet whispers of the Fates, dread curling in my gut. What if it doesn't work and the Fates keep sending me these visions? What if I end up hurt from this, forced to spend even longer in the Field of Mourning without all of my memories?

"Trust me, Eurydice. I won't let any harm come to you." She gives me a warm smile, offering me her hands, palms facing up.

I slowly nod, reaching out my hands towards her. She grasps them tightly, and right away I feel a subtle heat caress my skin. The dark room becomes illuminated with green as Hecate starts the spell, her voice becoming a murmur as she recites words in the language of the Gods, and I'm so nervous I don't manage to catch any of its meaning. Like when I first had a vision, I feel a chill course down my body, and I get the prickling feeling like I'm being watched, so it must be working.

As I expected, the view of Hecate fades away and all I can see is where the River Acheron meets the River Cocytus, and more specifically, the souls trapped beneath their surface. The rivers are a pale pink, making the translucent souls all flowing with the current tinted slightly. Their faces are locked in a wail of anguish that never reaches my ears, their eyes wide and their jaws unnaturally open. They remind me of the ghosts in the Dead Marshes in *The Lord of the Rings*, except this isn't fictional. These were real people once. They probably had family, friends, things they were passionate about...

And now they're prisoners.

"Why do you keep showing me this?" I ask aloud, hoping Hecate's spell has done its job.

"The souls need your help," the Fates reply. I look around, expecting to see them standing somewhere beside me, but just like usual, they appear in no physical form, and only their voices, cold and menacing, surround me.

"Why me?"

"Many have tried, all have failed. Only you can discover the key to their eternal salvation," they explain, as if that answers all my questions.

"I'm not special," I argue. "If Hades or Thanatos or Hecate couldn't figure it out, I certainly can't."

"Only you can discover the key to their eternal salvation," they repeat.

"How do you know that?"

What a dumb question. They're the fucking *Fates*.

If I didn't know any better, I would say there is humor in their voices when they reply, *"What don't we know?"*

Yeah, I walked right into that one. "Can you at least tell me how?"

"You study the biology of living things. Acheron and Cocytus are no different than your former subjects. Use your knowledge. It will be what guides you."

As if waking from a dream, my body jolts and I suddenly find myself back in Hecate's room, with the goddess herself standing before me, her glowing palms beginning to fade.

"Did you hear all that?" I ask, rubbing my shaking hands together.

She nods. "Looks like you have a job to do."

"I don't know what the Fates see in me," I repeat. "I have no power; I don't have nearly as much knowledge as Thanatos or Hades or you... What makes them think I can do this?"

Hecate sits down beside me, her expression filled with as many questions as mine is. "We're about to find out."

Thanatos

"Please. Please, I don't want to die," the Mortal begs before they're overtaken with a thick, wet cough.

Starvation, hypothermia, pneumonia, injury, and heartbreak. This is what Demeter's storm has caused, even though most of it has dissipated. The weather is cold and travel is still difficult, but other than that, it's as if it never happened. But it did, and every Mortal and Immortal on this plane are paying for it.

Hades and Persephone have gone to three meetings with the Olympian council these past couple weeks, begging Zeus and the other Gods to help those suffering in the Mortal World, but they can't seem bothered to care. Immortal beings are suffering from this storm as well—Nymphs, Satyrs, Centaurs, and Cyclops, all of whom live here and are treated just as poorly as the Mortals. It's as if they have all been disowned since they chose not to live on Olympus, but none of the Gods have stopped to wonder why that is.

And this willful ignorance has led to the current state of this world.

I kneel down next to Mariah Jennings, a thirty-nine year-old single parent of two, whose children were lucky enough to have been visiting their father in Egypt when the storm hit, so they weren't affected as hard. They're safe.

But Mariah wasn't so lucky, and now those children will be without a parent.

"I'm so sorry," I tell them genuinely, placing the tip of my scythe against their forehead, then pulling until their translucent soul falls forward into my arms. I'm about to teleport away when I hear a siren from outside, and curiosity propels me towards the window a couple feet from me, and the scene I am met with reinforces my already strong feelings of disgust towards the Gods and this cursed storm.

There's a riot outside. Mortals and Divine Creatures are taking to the streets of Greece, holding up signs, throwing items of worship, and shouting the same thing over and over again.

"Free us from the Gods! Free us from the Gods!"

I can only imagine what Dionysus and the Kallis family are going through right now. His marriage to Princess Ariadne was once seen as a binding between the Mortals and Immortals, but now all the people see is a God in a position of power amongst the Mortals. Public opinion of the Gods has soiled, and now even the ones who genuinely care about Mortal affairs are looped in with the likes of Zeus and Demeter. They are all becoming as hated as Hades and I are, and I don't know how to feel about that.

Turning my back to the window, I stretch out my wings and teleport away from the chaos before me, but the voices of the rioters still haunt me.

"Free us from the Gods! Free us from the Gods!"

CHAPTER TEN

CHARON

Before I took Orpheus to the palace, I knew I needed to give everyone fair warning, especially with Eurydice living here temporarily. So I called an emergency meeting in Hades and Persephone's office, where they, Hecate, Thanatos, and Hermes await to hear whatever I have to say.

"I'm just going to cut to the chase." I press my hands together in front of my face, then I twist my wrists until my combined fingers are pointing towards my friends like the head of an arrow. "Orpheus Martin is being held captive in my house and he seeks an audience with you, Hades."

Everyone but Thanatos balks at my revelation. He stands there silently, casting his gaze down to the floor. I hate that I catch a glimpse of hurt in his expression.

"Are you telling me you have a *living* Mortal in your house?" Hecate repeats for clarification, placing her hands on her hips like an angry mother.

I wince at her tone. "He kept showing up no matter what I did or what I threatened," I defend myself. "Nothing will deter him. I think if he talks to you and hears the truth from your lips, he might finally stay away."

"The truth of what?" Hades asks calmly, his hands clasped together on top of the desk.

"He wants to bring Eurydice back from the dead, and he doesn't believe me when I say that there is no way to achieve that."

Hades looks to Persephone, who's sitting by his side, his eyes questioning. She responds with a small nod, as well as a slight raise of her brow, to which Hades sighs.

Is this a thing married couples are able to do? Just communicate without words?

"Alright," Hades concedes. "You can bring him here. But first, can you tell me why neither you nor Thanatos told me about this?"

Thanatos's eyes widen at the accusation, but Hades gives him a look as scolding as Hecate's tone was. "Don't lie to me."

His shoulders sag a bit, and his eyes fill with shame. "I should have said something."

"Why didn't you?" Hades directs the question to both of us, and I hate the hurt in his expression too. I hate knowing that the people I consider my brothers are now in pain by my actions.

"I-I don't know," Thanatos replies, looking frazzled, which is a word I would never use to describe my friend.

Hades seems to know what has Thanatos in this state, so he just leaves it at that. He then directs his attention back to me. "Bring Orpheus here, but I insist on talking with him alone."

Persephone's eyebrows knit. "What about me?"

"The word 'alone' will always mean you too," he assures her. "While he's here, we need Eurydice out of the palace. I won't risk her running into him. Thanatos, why don't you take her to the Acheron. Given what Hecate told me this morning, I think she's most needed there."

"What the fuck are you talking about?" I ask, looking between all of them. I seem to be the only one out of the loop.

Hermes, who's been watching this conversation like one would a reality TV show, tells me in a gossipy tone, "The Fates want Eurydice to save the souls trapped in the Acheron and Cocytus."

"Are we sure?" I direct the question to Hecate, who is still glowering at me disapprovingly.

"Yes. Apparently, the answer to their freedom lies in science, not magic."

That's hard to believe, but who am I to question what the Fates think?

Refocusing on the task at hand, I look between Hades and Persephone, murmuring, "I'm sorry I kept this from you both. I thought I could handle him myself, but I was wrong. Forgive me?"

Hades gives me a nod, his face never softening, but his tone does. "Always, my friend."

Persephone takes it a step further and wraps me in a hug, something I'm still not used to. I pat her shoulder a couple times and then pull back, teleporting to my house before anyone else has the chance to hug me. I give the others a ten-minute grace period, because I agree with Hades that Eurydice must not be allowed to see Orpheus. It could trigger her memories coming back before she's ready, something detrimental to a soul's healing process.

Once I'm sure she's out of the palace, I grab onto Orpheus's arm and teleport him to the office, where both Hades and Persephone still sit side by side. Hades looks over the Mortal before sliding his gaze to me, giving me a clear signal to go, but I hesitate.

"I would like to stay, my lord, if you don't mind." I hate calling my friends their titles, but in settings like these it's necessary. We have to all play our rolls and be professional.

Hades considers me for a moment before nodding. "Very well."

Persephone takes a step forward and smiles at Orpheus, placing her hand on Hades's shoulder. "You're Orpheus?"

"Yes, and you are?"

"Persephone. I'm the Goddess of Spring and Queen of the Underworld."

Orpheus double takes. "Since when is there a Queen of the Underworld?"

"Since a few weeks ago. It's a complicated story."

Orpheus studies Persephone for a second, then he says, "And it must be a coincidence that Demeter's storm started around the same time you became queen."

Persephone blushes, the guilt in her eyes giving her away. "Demeter is my mother. But blood is where our similarities end. If I could change the state of the Mortal World, I would."

I fully expect things to start rapidly going downhill, but Orpheus surprises me by saying, "We can't control who our parents are or what mistakes they make. I know that better than most."

Persephone gives him a sorrowful nod, and I notice her slip her hand into Hades's. "Charon said you wanted to speak with us?"

Orpheus takes an uneven breath. "Yes, I do."

"And what is it you have in your hands?" Hades asks, eyeing the lyre Orpheus has borrowed.

"Well, my lord, I've never been good with words. I can't give moving speeches or eloquent prose. I can't convey how I feel or what I'm thinking by telling you. Instead, I express myself through music. And so, I ask if I can make my case to you about my wife by playing for you. I only ask you to let me finish before you throw me into Tartarus."

Hades gives a curt nod, then Persephone gestures with her hand for him to commence playing. I step away from Orpheus's side, going over to sit on the edge of Hades's desk so I can give the Mortal my apt attention.

Orpheus closes his eyes and starts to play. His fingers strum each cord expertly, starting an instrumental narrative that grabs everyone's attention from the first few verses. I don't recognize the piece he's playing, and I have a sneaking suspicion that's because it's original. I have no idea if this is something he's been working on, but from the raw pain in each chord strum and each note, I would guess he's composing this on the spot. His eyes are shut, but tears slowly leak out from his lashes, dripping down his beautiful face. His expression and body language convey every emotion he puts into the song.

I had joked earlier that he was a child prodigy, but it couldn't be a joke. I have heard Gods play the lyre and they couldn't do it with such grace, raw emotion, and expertise.

By the time Orpheus drops his fingers from the chords and opens his eyes, I'm speechless. I feel as if I were the one going through grief, like he ripped those emotions out of his heart and shoved them into mine.

Persephone gives a little sniffle, and I glance over at her to find sobs beginning to shake her frame. Her hand clutches onto her chest like her heart might burst from it. Hades is in no better shape. Tears stream down his face, and after one look at Persephone, I watch my friend openly weep.

I haven't seen Hades cry in centuries.

Orpheus, with tears in his eyes, falls to his knees, clutching the lyre to his chest. "I've been told that returning someone from the dead is impossible, that it's been tried before, but I beg you. Please give me back my wife. I will do anything. Carve out my heart and keep it as a trophy, because it hasn't beaten once since the light left her eyes."

Hades wipes his cheeks with his jacket sleeve and clears his throat, though his voice is still hoarse with emotion as he begins to speak. "The very thought of something happening to my wife—" His voice breaks on the word, and I catch his lip wobbling. "It is unbearable. Don't think I can't fathom your pain or that I don't know what it's like to be lost to grief. I understand it all too well. But that doesn't change the fact that bringing someone back from the dead is impossible. I tried once, and the result was catastrophic. There is a soul of a child that hasn't found rest in thousands of years and likely never will because I tried to bring her back. I refuse to sentence anyone else to that fate."

"But you only tried once. Maybe there's some other method, some missing information that could—"

"I'm not willing to risk the afterlives of souls," Hades interrupts, finality to his tone. "I refuse to experiment on them and jeopardize their happiness by getting their hopes up or by harming them. I'm king; I have the responsibility to keep all those in my kingdom safe."

"I can't give up. You said I'm lost to grief, but that would only happen if I cannot succeed in saving her," Orpheus whispers, body shaking with the effort not to fall apart.

"The fact you cannot accept the reality of the situation proves you are lost to grief. I'm as much of a slave to the Fates as the rest of the universe. When they decide someone's time is up and their thread is cut, no one has the power to bring them back. If I knew of a way, this realm would be empty. I would return Eurydice to you in a heartbeat. But I'm as helpless as you are."

A chocked cry bursts from Orpheus, and I watch him crumble in on himself. "I can't live without her. I don't know who I am without her."

"You have to let yourself grieve," Persephone says softly. "You're not doing yourself or Eurydice any good by letting your pain consume you. She wouldn't want that for you. She would want you to keep living your life until you can be reunited. You must accept she's gone so you both can move on."

Orpheus continues to sob, my lyre still clutched to his now heaving chest. He holds onto it like it's the only thing keeping him from physically breaking, and it's in that moment that something inside me shifts.

It's in that moment I know I'm well and truly fucked.

ORPHEUS

I feel nothing as Charon takes hold of my arm, preparing to teleport us away from Hades's office. All of the pain, sorrow, anger, and grief vanishes as a numbness overtakes me. I don't feel Charon's hand on me, nor the ground falling beneath my feet. I don't even hear the sound of the River Styx rushing downstream, even though we now stand right at the riverbank. Right by Charon's house.

I failed. Those words repeat in my head over and over again.

I failed I failed I failed I failed—

"Come on." Charon gestures towards his front door, which sits ajar.

Confusion breaks through some of the numbness. "What are you talking about?"

Charon gives a growl of frustration before grabbing onto my arm again, dragging me towards his front door. He grumbles to himself the entire journey, and he only stops when he's shut the door behind us. He looks skyward, seems to give a little prayer—which is an odd sight to see an Immortal do—then finally looks at me.

"I'm going to help you."

Okay now I'm really confused. "But Hades—"

"He's never tried again. Not after the soul of that little girl, and I don't blame him. But maybe there is some hidden answer we're missing. Something that's evaded us..."

Charon trails off, beginning to pace the length of his living room. I just stand there watching him, unable to comprehend what he's telling me.

"Y-you're going to help me?" A glimmer of hope rises in my chest, but I try to tamp it down.

Charon gives me a distracted wave of his hand. "Thought that was obvious."

"But why?"

Charon licks his lips before making a *pop* sound with them. "Because evidently I've lost my fucking mind."

A hysterical laugh breaks from my lips, and I feel myself smile so wide my cheeks hurt. "How?"

"That is the million-dollar question, isn't it?" Charon briefly pauses his pacing, rubbing a hand down his face. "We can't ask anyone else for help, so we're on our own. There are no texts or books that would hold the answer because they were all written way after Hades and Thanatos attempted resurrection. Usually, in a situation like this, I would go to someone like Hecate or even Circe, but Hecate wouldn't aid us and Circe's magic—"

Charon cuts himself off, his eyes widening.

"What?" I take a step forward, wringing my hangs together.

"The answer lies in science, not magic," Charon whispers, reaching forward to grip my shoulders. "The Fates have been giving Eurydice visions of the River Acheron. They think she can help free the souls trapped there and in the River Cocytus because of her skills as a theological biologist. She could be the key to discovering the answer to resurrecting a soul."

This information should shock me a lot more than it does, but if anyone could free those souls, it would be Eurydice. Even Prometheus called her a genius in their field. She's the perfect choice, and I have no doubt if she put her mind to it, she could solve this problem too.

"So what do we do?"

He lets go of my shoulders and begins to pace again. "You can't interact with Eurydice under any circumstances. She doesn't remember you, and any interactions with you could mess with her healing process. She also can't know we are seeking the key to resurrection for her sake. If, and that's a big if, we manage to uncover the secret, we have to wait until she has her memories back and can make the decision for herself."

"I agree."

"Good. Now, she will be working on freeing the souls in Acheron and Cocytus. Thanatos will be by her side while she works on this task, so the only time I'll have to question her will be at dinner at the palace—after she started having visions, we moved her and all of her equipment to a room there where she can conduct experiments. I can interrogate her each night on her findings and maybe that will give us some answers about how science differs from magic."

"And if it doesn't?"

"Then we wait until she's done with the souls and I'll give her this as a project under the guise of aiding that poor girl Hades and Thanatos tried to bring back to life."

I nod, backing up until I reach his couch. I sink down to it gently, emotion making my chest clench painfully. "Thank you, Charon. I know now what helping me could cost you. You have no idea how grateful I am."

His gaze softens a bit, and I get a firm nod. "Don't thank me yet. I make no promises this will work."

"You don't have to. But thank you all the same."

I see his jaw flex, his expression unreadable, then he murmurs, "You're welcome."

"What am I supposed to do with myself?" I give a halfhearted chuckle, finally feeling the weight of all these thoughts and emotions crashing down on me. "I'll lose my mind if I just sit here."

Charon checks his phone for the time, then he gives me a resolute nod. "Well, I guess you'll be ferrying souls with me. Because there's no way in fuck I'm leaving you here by yourself."

I smirk at that. "I'm up for anything."

Charon goes into his contacts, of which there are five, and presses on one, though from the angle I'm sitting at, I can't tell who.

He notices me staring at his phone, and he explains through a sigh, "We're gonna need some help."

EURYDICE

"How long have these souls been trapped?"

Thanatos, who is standing a few feet behind me, answers in a melancholic tone. "Six thousand nine hundred and forty-eight years."

Holy fuck.

The Rivers Acheron and Cocytus start at the ends of the Field of Mourning and the Asphodel Meadow before merging together within Tartarus. We are currently at the spot where the two rivers intersect, and I must say that I'm really glad I didn't end up in Tartarus. Between the looming dungeon in the distance, the endless field of dying grass, the red tint to the cloudy skyline, and the distant screams of tortured souls… this place is truly a punishment.

"There isn't a lot of information about the Underworld in the Mortal World, but from what little I've heard, the toll that needed to be paid for passage by Charon was started by Hades because he hated the idea of anyone living in his domain," I tell him, my eyes glued to the soul of a little boy floating beneath the surface. "But now that I've met Hades, I know that's not true. Will you tell me what really happened?"

Thanatos shakes his head gently, his jaw tense with unease. "It was Zeus that enforced the toll. He didn't like the idea of Mortals living in an ethereal plane like the Underworld, so he felt that they should pay to be here. We all tried to stop this practice, but the boundaries of Zeus's and Hades's powers had not been established yet. It took decades for those boundaries to be worked out, and for Prometheus to convince Zeus to stop the toll."

"How could the boundaries have not already been in place?"

"Remember, it was Cronus that ruled over Olympus, the Mortal World, and the Underworld. His three sons inherited the roles after his imprisonment, but for the first few years, their powers were unstable because these domains weren't used to acting separately. Hades had been trapped in the Underworld for thousands of years because the Underworld had never sustained itself before. It used Hades as a battery to power it. Poseidon, too, had to deal with nearly catastrophic storms and perilous sea conditions in the beginning. Zeus was the least affected, but even he came into his powers slowly over time."

A small smile brushes my lips at the thought of Prometheus arguing with Zeus on behalf of Mortals, and I feel an ache spread throughout my chest because of it. "You know when I first met Prometheus, I bowed to him and called him 'my lord.' He begged me to never call him that again. He said it made him feel like an uptight asshole."

A brief chuckle leaves Thanatos's lips. "That sounds like him."

"I can't imagine how painful it must have been for him knowing that so many Mortals were being trapped in these waters. He told me once that he views all Mortals as his children. He said he risks the wrath of Zeus and all the other Gods by helping us evolve because he's never loved anything like he loves us. I never viewed him as a parental figure in my life, he was always a friend…but now I wonder…I have no memory of my family; is someone else besides Prometheus mourning me as a parent would their child?"

Thanatos takes a step forward until we are just a foot apart, and I feel his free hand not holding his scythe rest on my shoulder. "I can't answer that question for you. All of your memories will return in time."

I heave a heavy sigh, turning around until I'm facing him directly. "Yeah yeah I know, my soul needs time to heal. But what am I healing from? How come I have most of my memories but only a few escape me? How come I'm being tasked with helping to fix these souls when my soul is still broken?"

His expression grows serious, his eyebrows furrowing as if in anger. The hand that had been on my shoulder now gently cups my jaw, and I feel my lips part from the cold press of his fingers, half in surprise and half in secret joy.

"Your soul is trying to process the fact that your life was ripped away from you. You don't remember your loved ones because you are coming to terms with being parted from them and grieving the life you shared with them. This does not make you broken. We all have things we're trying to heal from, whether we remember them or not."

"And what are you trying to heal from, Thanatos?"

He doesn't hesitate. "I'm healing from a wound that has not even made its mark yet."

I lean slightly into his hand, loving how his thumb strokes my skin. "I finished reading *The Metamorphosis*. And I know why it's your favorite story."

"Why?"

"Because you think of yourself as Gregor—a burden to your family, a living reminder of the end of luxury and happiness, and a creature destined to be alone. That's why you stay away from everyone, why their comments and snide remarks pain you. You don't believe you're a demon, but you know that because everyone else thinks you are, you'll always be alone."

His whole body grows stiff, and my heart breaks at the pain in his gaze, the resignation to the fate I have described. "I am death, Eurydice. I cannot die. Even when every soul has joined the ranks of the Underworld, even when eternity fades away and there is nothing left besides the very deities that started everything, even when the Fates stop weaving the webs of the future, I will still be here. I know this as assuredly as I know the sun will rise and set. I may have my family now, my friends…but it is only temporary. Everything is temporary but death, and that's what terrifies people. I will always be hated for what I am, and the very few who don't share that sentiment will one day be gone too."

I gather the courage to grab onto his hand, and I place a hesitant, gentle kiss on his palm, making him go rigid. His wings rustle behind him. "As powerful as you are, you can't tell the future. No one but the Fates can. Your destiny is not set in stone. You being misunderstood by Mortals and feared by Immortals isn't proof of that destiny. All it proves is that people are judgmental assholes and they are too blind to see how wonderful you are. I've known that from the second I met you."

Thanatos starts pulling away from me. "Eurydice—"

I grip onto his wrist to keep him still. "I used to get in fights at school over you. Anyone who claimed you were evil, I would yell at them and make sure they knew how kind, intelligent, and gentle you were. Everyone thought I was a freak, but I didn't care. I knew the truth about you, and I've grown up secretly hoping for the day I would get to see you again. I've been half in love with you since I was eight."

His expression crumbles, as if my words hurt him, and I desperately want to know why. Thankfully, Thanatos isn't one to shy away from hard discussions, and he doesn't leave me wondering long. "You don't have all of your memories, Eurydice. You say these things now, but what if you have someone in the Mortal World? What if you have a partner or—or a spouse that you have forgotten?" I've never heard Thanatos stumble over his words, nor have I seen him appear so unsettled.

"But we don't know that I had someone," I argue. "All I know is that my feelings for you have only grown since I was a child, and I think you feel the same way for me. I've never felt for anyone what I feel for you."

"That you remember," he replies quietly, avoiding my gaze.

I eye him suspiciously, and something occurs to me. "You know, don't you? You know I had a significant other in the Mortal World."

Thanatos says nothing, but he doesn't have to.

What does it say about me that I don't care? I still want Thanatos despite knowing there is someone in the Mortal World mourning my loss. But he's right, I don't remember how I felt for this mystery partner. Maybe I grew out of my crush for Thanatos and fell in love for real. But if that's the case, then why does it feel like the opposite? I don't remember a time not having feelings for him, and I doubt that will change when I regain all my memories. It's entirely possible I fell for this person while secretly harboring this flame, and that immediately fills me with guilt.

This whole situation just got a lot more complicated.

Thanatos leans forward until our foreheads are pressed together, and I feel like melting into a puddle at being so close to him. His warm breath skates over my cheeks, I can smell a faint trace of vanilla emitting off of his skin, and I can see the longing in his eyes as they bore into mine. "You will get your memories back soon enough, and once you have them, decide for yourself what you want to do."

"You say 'soon,' but it could be years until I get my memories back." I sound so whiny, but I can't help it. I want him so badly I physically ache.

He brushes his nose with mine, his lips just centimeters away. "I only want your happiness, and I will do whatever is within my power to ensure it."

Gods I want to kiss him so badly, but I know that would only upset him, so I refrain. But if it isn't the hardest thing I've ever done…that I can remember.

"I guess I should start working on this." I nod to the rivers behind us. "Will you help me take samples? Or is there somewhere you have to be?"

He pulls his face away from mine, his hand falling to his side, leaving my skin cold in his absence. "There's nowhere else I'd rather be."

PART II

Hark! death is calling,
While I speak to ye,
The jaw is falling,
The red cheek paling,
The strong limbs failing;
Ice with the warm blood mixing;
The eyeballs fixing.
Nine times goes the passing bell:
Ye merry souls, farewell.

Alfred Lord Tennyson

Chapter Eleven

Charon

"You really do this day and night?" Orpheus asks as he leans against the side of the boat, his arms acting as a cushion for his head.

I shake my head as I row us closer to the gate of the Underworld. "I have an hour off in the morning, and I sleep for little bits at a time during the night until Thanatos brings another soul. He always alerts me when he will be retrieving one, so I can plan accordingly."

"Sounds tedious."

I bark out a laugh. "Understatement of the fucking century."

"How do you pass the time?" he asks.

"I listen to music mostly. Beethoven, Schubert, Borodin, Rachmaninoff."

Orpheus's lips quirk up slightly. "Borodin has always been a favorite of mine. 'Notturno' might be my favorite piece to play on the violin. Only second to Vivaldi's 'The Four Seasons.'"

"Why are those two your favorite?"

"Well, 'Notturno' is slower paced but builds to a climax that moves me to tears each time I play it. The song is so enchanting, like it's trying to whisk you off to some far-off land. I've just always loved the majestic nature of it. And 'The Four Seasons' is just so energetic, it's like

I'm providing the music for an action scene in a movie. That's actually what I picture in my head. I think it helps me stay on tempo better."

I smile at the image his description conjures, finding this side of Orpheus endearing. He is clearly in love with music. It's in his eyes as he speaks off how the songs transport him, how they move through and around him. It's in his body language, which is never more relaxed and at ease than when he's discussing his craft. There's a boyish, almost childlike love of music in his heart. It's pure.

"How did you get into playing?" I ask.

Orpheus's smile takes on a sorrowful edge. "My mom. She always loved classical music. I can't remember a time when it wasn't a part of my life, honestly. It was always playing in the background of the house, in the car…then one day I begged her to let me take piano lessons, and things took off from there. Within a year of starting my lessons, I was being offered music scholarships to prestigious universities around the world and knew how to play several instruments. My mom had been so excited and so proud…but then she got sick. I stopped everything to focus on her, to help make sure she got better. But she didn't."

"How old were you?"

"Ten."

Shit. "I'm so sorry."

He shrugs. "I couldn't bring myself to play for a long time after she died. It was like she took my love of music with her. It was painful to even pick up one of my instruments. But when I was fifteen, I met Eurydice, and it was her who convinced me that I could keep the memory of my mom alive by playing again. So I did."

"I'm assuming you met Eurydice at school?"

He nods, his eyebrows bunching in distress. "She was in my high school math class. She tutored me throughout sophomore year, and we eventually started dating in our eleventh. I proposed before I left to study at the Royal Academy of Music in the UK, and we were married right after I graduated when we were eighteen."

It's very strange hearing about Eurydice before she died, about the life she lived with Orpheus by her side. Ever since she arrived in the Underworld, she's adapted and changed so seamlessly, like she moved apartments, not entire dimensions. She's been here a few weeks, and yet it seems like she's been here for years. I think a large part of that has to do with Thanatos. The two of them are attached to the other's hip, and though I don't know Eurydice all that well, I can attest that I've never seen my friend so happy. It makes me feel guilty, knowing that I'm helping to ruin Thanatos's happiness. But if Eurydice would rather go back to her husband, I know Thanatos would want that for her. There isn't a selfish bone in his body. He would give up his happiness if it meant ensuring the happiness of someone else.

Unfortunately, I'm not that selfless.

"When we were at the palace, you said you understood what Persephone had been through with her mother, but given how you spoke of your own mom, I doubt you were referring to her," I surmise.

Orpheus shakes his head, his jaw clenching. "My dad. He didn't cope well with my mom's death. He shut down and turned to drinking. I spent my teenage years taking care of him and making sure he didn't get himself killed. He let my mother's death consume him."

"And you don't want Eurydice's death to consume you the same way?" I guess.

He gives me a single nod.

We make it to the gates of the Underworld, where Hermes is waiting with a new group of souls for me to ferry.

"Well well well, this must be the infamous Orpheus," Hermes greets us with a grin. "Nice to meet you."

Orpheus gives me the side-eye, and I send a glare Hermes's way. "I told Hermes our plan because if I'm going to keep an eye on you and perform my duties, I'm going to need an accomplice to ensure Thanatos stays away."

"Yep." Hermes puts emphasis on the "P." "He's letting me choose the dinner he cooks for a month as payment."

"Which I still think is stupid because I'm bribing you to do the job you are supposed to do and choose to neglect."

Hermes's smile turns sly, though I don't know why. "I don't neglect my job. I just have something more important to do."

Alright, I'll bite. "Pray tell."

Hermes only shrugs. "You'll see eventually."

With a roll of my eyes, I turn my attention to the souls trembling in fear. "Please enter the boat one at a time and try not to rock it too aggressively."

With a little push from Hermes, the three souls begin venturing towards us, though they once again grow still when they reach the edge of the bank. Just when I'm about to speak again, Orpheus stands up and offers the first soul a hand. They're a water nymph, if the webbing on their tawny hand is anything to go by. Orpheus doesn't even bat an eye by the soul obviously being Immortal, he just smiles at them and carefully leads them onto the boat. He then does the same for the Mortal man with pale freckled skin and the child with brown skin and green eyes.

With everyone now on the boat, I give my stupid little speech. "In case you haven't figured it out yet, you are dead. As a soul in the Underworld, you will live out your afterlife in either the Asphodel Meadows, the Field of Mourning, Elysium, or Tartarus, depending on how you chose to live your Mortal or Immortal lives. The Judges of the Underworld will view your memories and decide where you belong, then they will escort you to your new home. On our way to the Judges, please keep your hands inside the boat at all times and don't try to escape once we reach shore. Any questions?"

All three of them shake their heads, so I begin rowing back towards where the Judges await. The three souls stay huddled together in the back, while Orpheus takes a seat across from me, a weird look on his face. "You give that speech each time?"

"Like clockwork."

"No wonder you're so cranky."

I glower at him. "You are a very vexing person. Has anyone ever told you that?"

Orpheus chuckles, and the sound is as smooth as honey. "Every day of my life."

CHAPTER TWELVE
THANATOS

Eurydice has worked two days without rest. I have had to leave a few times to cleave souls, but thankfully Hermes has decided to do his job so I don't have to be apart from her long. More than ever, I feel compelled to be by her side. She's entered into a hyper-focused state, one that would alarm me far more if she were alive. I have no doubt she would forget to sleep or eat if those were still biological urges she felt for her survival.

It is around three in the morning, and Eurydice has not looked away from her makeshift workstation for five hours. Her head is turned down, reading through her notes, looking through samples, and scribbling down any thoughts or theories she comes up with.

She has not said a word since yesterday.

"Eurydice."

If she hears me, she does not acknowledge it.

"Eurydice," I say again.

Still nothing.

I had been sitting on her bed observing her for some time, but now I cross her room to where she works on top of two desks pushed together to make a counter. I grab her shoulder, squeezing it gently, and this finally gets her attention. She looks up to me, dazed, like she had been in a trance.

"What is it?" Her words are slurred, exhaustion weighing down on her.

"We're going to take a break."

"But—"

"No," I say firmly, guiding her away from her workstation. "You need to take breaks. You won't be able to solve anything when you're exhausted."

"I'm dead. I'm not supposed to get tired."

"Yes, but as we are all learning, you are no ordinary soul. You have earned some time to recuperate. How about you go take a shower? Or we could go for a walk?"

She shakes her head. "I don't feel like moving right now."

An idea pops into my head, and I extend a hand out towards her. "You won't have to move."

"What are you talking about?"

"Do you trust me?" I ask.

She nods without hesitation, placing her hand in mine. I guide it to rest on my shoulder, then I bend down and wrap an arm around her legs, picking her up bridal-style.

She lets out an incredulous laugh. "What are we doing?"

"Just hold onto me," I tell her, then I teleport us outside the palace. Without prior warning, I launch myself into the air, making Eurydice wrap her arms tightly around my neck, pressing the side of her face to mine.

I flap my wings at a rapid speed, bringing us up higher and higher into the sky. The Underworld expands underneath us, and when Eurydice gathers the courage to look down, she is met with a full view of each sector. From here, the brightly-colored island of Elysium, with its multicolored leaves, gilded mansions, and lush grassy fields are clear and bright. The serenity of Asphodel and Mourning, with their cozy cottages and sprawling hills of asphodels, poppies, and narcissus flowers is a sight to behold. The dark atmosphere of Tartarus—a deep red now that the sun has set, making the foggy torture fields and the looming dungeon even more terrifying than usual. We pass right over the pit of fire, and I love how the flickering flames makes Eurydice's brown eyes glow, giving them an amber hue.

The moon's light reflects in the different rivers, but it does so most brilliantly in the Styx. I fly us down towards its surface, and the light allows for us to see our silhouette in the water. I can see the grin on Eurydice's face, the utter joy in her eyes. I watch from the reflection as she extends a hand out and runs her fingers through the current, giggling in glee.

"Do you do this often?" she asks.

I shake my head, still soaring over the water. "No. It has been a while since I flew."

"Could we do this more often?" She's smiling from ear to ear, and it's far more beautiful than any of the scenery we pass over.

"Whatever you want, Doctor."

She turns her face towards me, and to my surprise, she places a kiss on my cheek. She then nuzzles her head into my shoulder, and I feel her body let out a sigh. "Thank you."

I hold her a little tighter. "It's my pleasure."

I flap my wings harder, lifting us away from the water, and then we soar into the dazzling night's sky.

CHARON

"Dionysus called for another meeting in Olympus, so I'll have to raincheck our piano lesson," Persephone says to me over the phone, having already teleported with Hades to Olympus.

I try my hardest to hide my relief. I would have no idea what to do with Orpheus if she hadn't canceled. Over the last few days, I've come up with so many excuses to my friends. From headaches, to indigestion, to a paranoia that the Furies are playing a prank on me—I've had to come up with ways to cancel Persephone's piano lessons, meetings with Hades, and tea with Hecate. I have no idea what excuse I would have given today.

Part of me worries if I leave Orpheus for too long he'll do something stupid—which is entirely possible—but I have no problem leaving him to attend dinner at the palace. I think the real reason I don't want to leave him is because he's expressed a need to stay occupied. Without a distraction, his grief will overwhelm him, and I want to do what I can to help him. I know all too well what it feels like to not be able to stomach your own thoughts. Sometimes our minds are more of a prison than a safe haven.

"It's totally fine. Knock Zeus down a peg for me, will you?"

She chuckles. "You bet. After the meeting, we're going to check on my shop and visit Psyche and Ami, so we may be a little late for dinner."

"No problem, I'm sure the others will want to eat late anyways."

"You're the best."

"I know." I hang up after that, refocusing on the Mortal in front of me, who's humming to himself on his side of the boat.

Once I slip my phone in my pocket, Orpheus asks, "What did she want?"

"During my hour off each morning, I give her piano lessons in the palace library. She had to cancel because she and Hades had to attend a meeting in Olympus."

"If you only get one hour off, why do you spend it giving her lessons?"

I shrug, continuing to row. "Persephone asked me to give her lessons so I could get to know her better. I was a little hostile towards her when she arrived. I was worried Hades would get his feelings hurt, but I was wrong about her. She's a part of our family now. So what started as an obligation is now a chance to spend time with her, and the others tend to join in as well."

"You refer to them as your family often, but what about your biological family? Don't you have parents?"

I shake my head. "I was created by the primordial God of Chaos to ferry the souls in the Underworld. I was not born, nor did I grow. I came into existence as you see me now, then Chaos explained my purpose to me, and I have been in the Underworld ever since."

"When was this?"

"When the Titans were first created."

His eyes widen. "You were alone for all those years down here?"

I don't answer that, but I think my silence speaks for itself.

"What did you do back then?"

"Well, there weren't many others in the Underworld, and only a couple souls actually needed ferrying. The Underworld came with the palace, so I lived there by myself. I spent most of my time inside sleeping. Sometimes I would play the lyre. But I mostly just slept."

"I don't know how I would have coped with that."

"I didn't cope. I simply just existed because I had to. I thought about—" I pause for a moment, feeling tears prickle in my eyes. "I thought about ending things several times. But I would have still been stuck in the Underworld. I was basically already dead."

"Charon." Orpheus shakes his head, his expression unreadable. "I'm so sorry."

I shrug, taking a couple of deep breaths. "Things got better when Hades and Hecate showed up. Then again when Thanatos and Hermes came here. I no longer hate my existence and wish for it to end—though sometimes it may seem like I still do. I just despise the position that was forced upon me, and I wish things were different. It can be a useful coping mechanism to make dark comments and jokes about it."

"I'm the same way. I battled depression after my mom died, and my therapist at the time encouraged me to make light of the thoughts going through my head instead of giving them weight."

"E-exactly." I hadn't been expecting him to understand that.

"Do you really think things would be different if people knew who you were?"

"When Mortals had to pay a toll to me, I was known around the world, and for the first time in my life, it felt like I was actually created for a reason. I was seen for the role I play in the universe. I no longer felt invisible. But that time has long since passed, and I've reverted back to invisibility. If it weren't for my family, I would still be in that dark place."

"It's the same with Eurydice."

We reach the gate, where four new souls await with Hermes, who gives me a large grin. "How's it going, you two?"

"I just told Orpheus my tragic little backstory."

Hermes sends a pout his way. "My condolences."

"Isn't there somewhere you need to be right now?" I ask in a not-so-subtle tone.

He tsks. "So testy. Yes, I do have somewhere to be, but picking on you is so much more fun."

"Hermes."

He rolls his eyes. "Fine, fine. I'll see you at dinner."

Once he disappears, I gear up to give my usual speech, but Orpheus shocks me by saying it first.

"In case you haven't figured it out yet, you are dead," he says, standing up in the boat. "As a soul in the Underworld, you will live out your afterlife in either the Asphodel Meadows, the Field of Mourning, Elysium, or Tartarus, depending on how you chose to live your Mortal or Immortal lives. The Judges of the Underworld will view your memories and decide where you belong, then they will escort you there. Please keep your hands inside the boat at all times and don't try to escape once we reach shore. Any questions?"

The gathered souls seem confused by Orpheus's presence, but since they recognize he's a Mortal, they come towards the boat of their own volition and don't hesitate to grab onto his hand in order to enter the boat.

I'll be damned.

Once everyone is settled, I start rowing again, and I stare at Orpheus in awe.

He sits down in the seat directly in front of me and catches my eye. "What?"

"You are without a doubt the strangest Mortal I have ever met."

He huffs a laugh. "I'll take that as a compliment."

Chapter Thirteen
Thanatos

I watch Eurydice as she writes in her notebook, her hand scribbling on the page at a speed that makes me wonder if her handwriting is even readable. She then returns to looking under the microscope for a few minutes before repeating the process again.

It's like watching an artist create a new painting or a musician composing a song. Her passion for her craft, her dedication to it, makes watching her enrapturing.

"Wait," Eurydice suddenly says, and I realize she's talking to herself, not me. She looks down at her microscope, flips a few pages in her notebook, and reads her notes.

"What is it?"

"Shh!" She waves me away, so I fall silent and let her work.

She scribbles, reads, and observes for another ten minutes before she speaks again, and this time she says in an awestruck tone, "Holy motherfucking shit."

I can't help but laugh at such an exclaim.

The look of excitement in her eyes reminds me of Hermes when he gets a present. "I know why the Fates wanted me to figure this out."

Now I feel like it's an appropriate time to ask, "What do you mean?"

She starts to pace around her makeshift lab table, which is two desks pressed together. I move over to her bed and sit on its edge, recognizing this is part of her process.

"The sample we took of the water—it's not water. Not at its genetic level. I double-checked it several times, comparing the samples of the water to the samples I took of your blood, and I'm certain of this: those rivers have the genetic components of a God. It has DDNA. In your blood sample, there are so many new and unrecognizable elements, but this river is closer to a non-primordial God. It reminds me of the samples I would see from Prometheus. No wonder the Fates said to treat the river as one of my subjects, it might as well be."

I don't know what to make of that, and I tell her as much. "That makes no sense."

She points a finger at me, a wide smile breaking over her face. "But it does. Remember what you told me at the riverbank? You said Cronus used to rule Olympus, the Mortal World, and the Underworld. When he was dethroned, his sons split those positions up, but for some reason, Hades was tied to the Underworld in a way his brothers weren't. But I've been thinking about it, and I have an idea as to why. Poseidon dealt with storms and chaotic seas, but you never mentioned he had problems coming into his abilities like Zeus and Hades. The Mortal World is the ethereal form of Gaia, a God. She's a self-sustaining entity. The Underworld and Olympus aren't. They're dimensions created by Gods, and therefore they derive their strength and power from Gods. Olympus has always had people living within it, all of whom are powerful Immortals, so Zeus not facing much resistance makes sense. But for Hades, he came to the Underworld when no one was here. Only the imprisoned Titans, Hecate, and Charon. The Underworld went from being a part of a closed circuit of energy between Gaia and Olympus to being on its own with only one main source of energy to fuel it."

Realization dawns on me. "Hades."

She points at me again, her eyes growing comically wide in excitement. I feel like I'm a schoolboy getting praised by my instructor.

"Yes. Hades. He's the only one tied to the Underworld. Not the

Titans. Not Hecate. Charon, yes, but he was made for a purpose within the Underworld, so his powers aren't supposed to fuel the realm. But Hades was bonded to it by the Fates themselves. The Underworld was relying completely on his power and strength for the first couple thousand years. It's why he couldn't leave. He became as dependent on the Underworld as it was on him, which brings me back to the river sample. You've told me that Hades can manipulate the Underworld itself, as well as every soul in this plane. But Zeus can't do that to Olympus or the Gods who live there. Nor can Poseidon. It's because Hades *is* the Underworld. You can't have one without the other. The Underworld has the power and essence of Hades, which means the rivers do too."

"Okay...but how does that keep the souls trapped beneath its surface?"

"If the dimension is essentially Hades, and the Underworld acts like an extension of him, doesn't it make sense that the Underworld holds the souls just like a body does? That would explain why souls can't leave this dimension. The souls can't escape the river because a soul can't leave their body without having their thread cut, but those souls are already dead. So they're stuck."

I nod along as she explains her theory, and I have to admit it makes complete sense. I don't know why we hadn't thought of this explanation before, but I think Hecate was right: it was a scientific solution, not a magical one.

"You're brilliant," I tell her in earnest.

She gives me a bashful, almost dismissive shrug. "I still haven't found a solution yet."

"You have made more progress in a day than all of us combined over the past ten thousand years. I reiterate my statement: you are brilliant."

"Thanks, Thanatos," she says softly.

I stand, closing the distance between us, leaving us only a half foot apart. "No, thank *you*. In the short time you've been here, you've managed to give hope to souls that have not known peace in thousands of years. Even though you're dead, you are still dedicating your time to helping others, both in the Underworld and in the Mortal World. I don't think you grasp how incredible that is. You're one of a kind, Doctor."

She lets out a nervous laugh, and I see her wringing her hands out of my peripheral vision. "There's nothing else I'd rather be doing."

"I know." I grab onto her hands, holding them still in my grasp. "I have encountered every soul in history, I have known many Immortals and Mortals, and no one has as pure a heart as you."

Her lips part in an 'O' shape, and I find my gaze drawn to it despite a voice in my head telling me not to. I know that developing feelings for someone whose heart is already spoken for is unwise, and that it will only end in my misery. But my mind has been occupied with her since her arrival, and my heart has been claimed since the moment I saw her smile. It's stupid, it's a recipe for disaster, but it's the truth.

Which is why I don't stop Eurydice from cupping my jaw and placing her lips on mine.

Though I have never shared a kiss with someone, instinct takes over and I pull her body against mine, placing my hands on the small of her back. I love the feel of her skin underneath my palm, and I especially love the sensation of her lips moving over mine. A heat spreads throughout my body that I've never experienced before, and when Eurydice licks the seam of my lips, seeking entry into my mouth, a small groan escapes me. Her tongue starts moving against mine, deepening a kiss that was already sending me to another plane of existence. As I bunch up the material of her shirt in my fist, Eurydice whimpers, and the sound has a profound effect on me.

I suddenly feel my cock start to harden in my pants, and I freeze up in shock.

Obviously, I'm well aware of how anatomy, arousal, and sex work. But in all my years of existence, I've never experienced emotions like desire or yearning before. Before I came to the Underworld, I barely felt like a person. When I was roaming the universe with my brother, Phobos, I was just death and nothing more. But my friends changed that. They taught me about companionship, love, respect, passion, and they gave me the words to describe what had been plaguing me for so long, and what plagues me to this day: loneliness.

But they could never show me what desire feels like. What it's like to yearn for someone, to want them, body and soul. I didn't even think I was capable of feeling such an emotion until I met Eurydice. I knew I was drawn to her, that I had come to care for her deeply, and in a way I'd never felt before. But this…this is something entirely new. She's awoken something in me.

And now I recognize another new emotion that has been building inside me for some time.

Fear.

EURYDICE

Thanatos ends the kiss abruptly, and I'm left in a complete daze in the absence of his mouth on mine.

That kiss…*holy shit*.

I've never had a kiss like that before, at least that I can remember. But even still.

"What is it?" I ask, noticing how frazzled he looks.

He shakes his head, turning his back on me. "We can't do this."

My heart deflates a little at that. "Because of who I left behind in the Mortal World?"

He nods, still not looking at me.

I grab onto his arm and twist him back towards me. "Then give me my memories back."

Now he looks at me. "You know I can't do that."

"Then bring me to Hecate, I'm sure she could figure it out."

"No, I mean we are forbidden from giving a healing soul their memories back before they're ready. It will stall your healing process; you'll be forced to stay in Mourning longer."

I roll my eyes. "I'm never going to heal properly when I feel this way for you and have this mystery lover dangling over our heads. The idea of spending years torturing myself over how I feel and what I can't remember makes me crazy. That would be a worse fate than to know everything and be able to decide what I want for myself."

Thanatos studies my expression for a second, then he shuts his eyes with a sigh. "After dinner, we'll talk to Hecate. If anyone can give you your memories back, it would be her."

Relief spreads through me. "Thank you."

He gives a shallow nod, then he starts towards the door. Before he can put too much distance between us, though, I grab onto his hand, linking my fingers with his.

"I will never regret kissing you, no matter what I do or don't remember."

The smile he gives me is weak, and it doesn't reach his eyes. "I hope that's true."

"This grilled chicken is incredible, Charon. I don't know how you do it," I compliment, wafting the smell from Hecate's plate.

Charon shrugs off my comment. "It's nothing."

"Eating and sleeping are things I miss so much. When I was a kid obsessed with *Twilight*, I wanted to be a vampire so bad because I thought never having to sleep or eat or use the toilet would be so cool. It's actually so boring. There's too many hours in the day."

Everyone chuckles at that, and Hecate gives me a sympathetic pat on the shoulder. "It takes some getting used to, but all of this spare time will allow you to pick up many new hobbies. Aristaeus, Persephone's father, learned French, studied British literature, and started yoga during his time in the Underworld. You have to discover what interests you."

"Thanatos gave me some books to read. I've been enjoying that."

Persephone perks up at that. "That's awesome! What books?"

"I just finished *The Metamorphosis* and I'm starting *Frankenstein*."

"Love that book," says Hades.

"Mary Shelley is an amazing writer. Great conversationalist too."

I gawk at the Goddess next to me. "You've talked to Mary Shelley?"

Hecate gives me a smug grin. "The number of famous Mortals we've met are abundant. Some of us at the table have even slept with them."

I glance around, wondering who she means, but Hermes spoils the search. "She means me and Hades, but mostly me."

"I hope you don't find it creepy when I say I would love to hear about your sex life in great detail."

Hermes laughs, winking at me. "All in due time."

"So how are your experiments with Acheron and Cocytus going?" Charon asks suddenly, leaning forward in his seat. He's asked this every night since I started my research.

"I discovered a great deal already." I proceed to tell them the same theory I told Thanatos earlier, and when I'm done, all eyes are on Hades, who looks ghastly pale.

"So I'm what's keeping those souls trapped in the rivers?" Hades sounds so distraught that I put this idea to rest immediately.

"No, Hades, it's not within your control. It's like having an extra arm or leg. You can't control if your arms get goosebumps or if they fall asleep, just like you can't control this."

"If what you say is true, how would we go about freeing them?" Hecate asks, swirling her wineglass while she thinks. "When the Fates cut their string, the soul enters a state between life and death, and that's what allows the soul to leave their confines. We need to find a way to put those souls in that same state."

"But they can't die again," Hermes points out. "So what options are there?"

"Resurrection," Charon says, as an offer and as a statement.

`My mind begins to whirl, my thoughts spinning in a loop at a rate that I can't even comprehend, but amongst the noise, one single idea sings louder than the rest. The answer, I suspect, will solve all our problems.

"Ambrosia," I breathe.

"What?" Hermes asks.

I burst up from my seat, making the plates and cups rattle. "Ambrosia! The fruit of the Gods. We briefly studied it, but Prometheus didn't think it was smart to start including it in medicines. If a Mortal ingests it, they become Immortal, and that wouldn't go unnoticed by Zeus. But before that decision was made, we tested it on a Mortal subject, and it is a death as well as a rebirth. Your Mortal body dies and an Immortal body is born. Like a vampire. I'm sure consuming it would put you in that in-between state."

"Would it bring the souls back to life?" Charon asks passively.

"I have no idea. It's possible, but I think it's worth the risk to try, don't you guys?"

There's a look in Charon's eyes I can't quite discern. "Absolutely."

CHARON

The second dinner is over, I teleport to my house, startling Orpheus, who had been dozing off on my couch.

"She figured it out!" I shout, laughing in disbelief.

"What?"

"Eurydice inadvertently figured out how to resurrect souls." I briefly explain to him what she told us at dinner, and I slowly watch as his eyes widen in hope.

"Oh my Gods, this is—"

A knock comes to my door, and my heart freezes in my chest.

I place my finger against my lips and gesture with my other hand for him to hide. Orpheus swiftly darts around my couch, using it as cover, and only when he's out of sight do I open the door and find Persephone standing there, her smile sweet and innocent.

"Is everything okay?" I ask, taking on the same look and tone of innocence.

"Can I come in?" Her voice is unusually calm.

I fight against the urge to glance over my shoulder, and I give a reluctant nod. She pushes past me, her eyes scanning around my living room and kitchen, and a sinking feeling begins in my stomach.

She knows.

This is confirmed moments later. "Orpheus, you can come out now."

The Mortal pokes his head up from behind the couch and gives her a little wave. "Hi there, Your Majesty."

She turns back towards me, crossing her arms over her chest. Then she waits.

I shut the door and lock it, releasing a sigh. "I can explain."

"Please do."

"I understand where you and Hades are coming from. I know there are high risks when it comes to resurrection, but I couldn't let him go home without trying. And now we have a chance to save Eurydice. You heard what she said—"

"Orpheus, could I have a second alone with Charon?" she asks, never looking at him. Without a word, he walks past us and slips outside, theoretically out of earshot.

"What the fuck were you thinking?" she hisses, her eyes filled with disappointment. "You have no idea how upset Hades was knowing one of his best friends lied to him, and here you go doing it again after promising you wouldn't. And what about Eurydice? You know she and Thanatos have feelings for each other—"

"You don't know that for a fact."

"Oh don't bullshit me. Eurydice is crafting an afterlife for herself down here with Thanatos, your best friend, who doesn't have a selfish bone in his body and has finally found a chance at love. And what do you go do? You actively work to destroy his and her chance at happiness."

"She doesn't remember Orpheus, but once she does, she'll want to leave with him. She loves him. Whatever she's doing or feeling now is a lie."

"It's no more a lie than her life with Orpheus, and you know it. It should be her decision on whether she wants to be with Thanatos or her husband. It should be *her* choice of what she does with her life or afterlife. You both have no right to meddle with something you don't understand and risk the safety and happiness of someone you are claiming to give a shit about. And why do you anyway? You hate people, especially strangers. Why are you helping someone you barely know, going as far as to defy your family to do so?"

Shame wells in my chest, and I hate that I can't give her a good answer. "I don't know."

She studies me for a moment, then she shakes her head. "Oh, Charon."

"What?"

"You like him."

I scoff at that. "I don't."

She pinches the bridge of her nose, squeezing her eyes shut. "I'll give you some time to talk amongst yourselves, but in an hour, I want you both in our office. You're going to tell Hades what you did, then we'll go from there."

"I never wanted to hurt him. Or you."

Persephone's gaze softens ever so slightly. "I know, but you did."

ORPHEUS

Persephone opens the door and stalks out, leaving Charon staring after her. She glances at me briefly, and I see pity in her gaze, which I'm absolutely sick of seeing at this point. I hope there will be a time when I never have to see it again.

Once she teleports away—after a few minutes of her trying and failing to do so—I get back inside and silently sit on the couch. Charon shuts his door and joins me.

"You heard all that didn't you?"

"I did."

There's a pause, a contest to see who will break the tension first, but neither of us seems willing to speak.

Finally, after a few minutes of racing thoughts, I ask a question I've been dreading the answer to since I met Phobos. "Eurydice and Thanatos have a relationship?"

Charon leans back against the cushions, staring up at the ceiling. "I don't know. Thanatos clearly has feelings for her, but I don't know if she returns them. Persephone seems to believe so."

Phobos's words echo in my head. *My brother and your wife have become very close in the last week. So close, in fact, that my brother dreads the day she will remember her life with you. He fears that, even if you don't succeed with your mission of retrieving Eurydice, that he will lose her regardless.*

"How dare Thanatos pretend to understand my pain and sympathize with me when he's trying to fuck my wife? Eurydice always defended him and would insist to anyone who listened that he was a man of honor and unconditional kindness, but maybe everyone is right about him."

I see anger spark in Charon's eyes. "Thanatos is a better man than either of us will ever be. He can't control how he feels, and I know he's doing everything in his power to make sure she's happy and doesn't have any regrets later."

"She's my *wife*. She—"

"She's not," he snaps. "Haven't you ever wondered why marriage vows say 'until death do us part'? Because marriages aren't supposed to last for eternity. I'm sure Zeus and Hera could attest to that. Most souls find love many times over throughout their afterlives, especially when they're in Mourning."

Anger flares in my own chest, and I snap back, "Once she remembers me, she'll forget about Thanatos. I know her, and I know she would never pick the Underworld and a winged freak over us and our life together."

Charon laughs, but there's no humor in it. "You know, you're a real hypocrite. You told me you're down here trying to save your wife because you don't want to become like your father, wallowing in his grief until it consumes you. But guess what? This—" He gestures to me and the entire room. "Is letting your grief consume you. Instead of accepting death as a natural part of life, you're here trying to break the laws of nature and rescue someone who may not even want to be saved, all because you won't grieve. You may not be numbing your pain with drinking, but you're still doing the same shit your father did."

"Oh yeah? What about you?" I lower my voice and proceed to mimic his perpetual frown. "Oh boo hoo me. I'm not famous like other Gods and no one appreciates me. I live in a palace with people I love and yet it will never be enough because I'm a self-centered asshole."

"That's rich coming from you. You say you love your wife and want her back, but all I'm hearing is that you want the person you were with her and the life you had with her back. That's not love; that's vanity." He sneers.

"If you really think those things about me, why the fuck are you helping me? Was Persephone right? Do you…" I trail off, unable to finish the question.

Pain mixes with the anger in his eyes. "You see me."

I want to be seen. Isn't that what anyone wants?

I shake my head. "No. I hardly know you, and it's clear you don't know me. Yes, I want myself back. I miss the person I was before this grief took hold of me, and I'm worried that if she never returns, I will be lost forever. But I want my wife back more than anything else, and fuck you for insinuating my motives are selfish."

Charon scoffs. "Your motives are fucking selfish. You are trying to disrupt the laws of nature to ruin the peaceful afterlife of your wife who if trying to move on, like you should be doing! That is the definition of being selfish."

"Okay, so I ask again, why the fuck are you helping me? Why haven't you thrown my ass in the fiery pits of Tartarus? Because *I see you*? You're right. I do see you. I see what a conceited asshole you are."

"And I see what an arrogant little prick you are. But yet, despite your glaring flaws and shitty attitude, I can't get you out of my mind. You haunt my every thought, and I find myself incapable of letting you go where I can no longer be near you, even if it goes against the rules I live by or the wishes of my family."

I don't know what overcomes me. I must have some kind of stroke or mental break. I feel like my limbs are being maneuvered like a puppet as I close the distance between us and kiss him. I cup his face in my hands, not allowing him to pull away, and consume his mouth like my life depends on it.

Charon is immobile at first, but then his hands grip onto my shoulders. At first I think he's going to push me away, but then his tongue strokes against mine, and a low rumble starts from the back of his throat, making me shiver.

Then it feels like I've come back to myself, and I break the kiss. The two of us stand panting, our foreheads pressed together, his shoulders still gripping mine.

"I'm sorry," I whisper, though I don't really know what I'm apologizing for.

He shakes his head, dropping his hands. "You're upset, you're not in your right mind. I get it."

His expression grows hard, maybe even a little cold, and I'm left standing dumbfounded as he stalks over to his room, slamming the door shut behind him.

Chapter Fourteen

Eurydice

"You want me to what?" Hecate asks.

"I want my memories back," I repeat.

Thanatos had to go retrieve a soul, so I decided to confront Hecate by myself. The two of us are in the library, where Hecate was combing for books on ambrosia and if there are any other known locations for it besides Olympus.

We figured Zeus would frown upon giving it to us, so we need to find other methods.

"You have no idea what that would entail. You'd—"

"Yes, I know I'd have to stay in Mourning longer and I would take longer to heal, but I have to do this. I'm falling in love with Thanatos, and he is keeping me at arm's length because I apparently have a significant other in the Mortal World who I don't remember. I want to have my memories back so I have all the facts and can make an informed decision. It's so frustrating feeling this way when some mysterious person is hanging over my head. Could I have really loved them if I don't even remember them? I mean, I remember all of my friends, my hobbies, my dreams. All things I loved."

"You don't remember him because you loved him so dearly. Thanatos mentioned you don't remember your parents either, and it's for the same reason. You're mourning the life you had with them, coming to terms with your regrets and guilt."

"But that guilt will only grow if I continue to be in the dark. I—wait a second, did you say *him*? You know who it is."

Hecate's eyes flare, and she stays silent, confirming what I just said.

"How do you know who I was with when I was alive? What aren't you telling me?"

She sighs, giving me a small nod. "Give me a few days to concoct a potion that will return your memories to you, then we will explain everything."

"*We*? Who's we?"

"Two days. Give me two days."

I guess I don't have much of a choice, so I nod. "Two days."

Thanatos

The minute I returned from cleaving the latest soul, I was summoned to Hades and Persephone's office, where I found Charon and Orpheus standing on the lavender carpet, and my stomach sank.

"What were you thinking?" Hades asks them, his voice hollow and cold. His anger, though subtle in his expression, is showing in his magic, which is practically pulsing in rage. Small tendrils of shadow curl off of his person, and I doubt he even realizes it. I know Charon can sense his power too, which is why he has his head bowed in submission. Orpheus is one step from cowering.

It's easy to forget that Hades is as powerful as he is, but make no mistake, he could take on every God in this room and still win. Including me.

"It's my fault." Charon keeps his eyes on the floor, his expression schooled. "Orpheus was more than willing to acquiesce to your order, but I forced him to stay. I convinced him we could discover a way to save Eurydice."

A twinge of anger flares within my chest, though I try to brush it off. I have no claim to Eurydice, so Charon trying to help her husband shouldn't bother me the way it does. As much as I wish it weren't true, her heart belongs to Orpheus, whether she remembers or not.

Hades jaw clenches. "Why?"

This time, Charon lifts his eyes. "Because I was stupid enough to develop feelings for him and I wanted to keep him close for as long as possible."

This confession shocks us all but Persephone, who casts her gaze down to her feet. Hades notices, and I see him slip his hand into hers. She must have guessed Charon's feelings already, though how, I have no idea.

"Eurydice plans to go see Hecate about getting her memories back. She may have done so already," I inform the room, trying my hardest not to look at Orpheus.

Hades shuts his eyes, his shoulders rising and falling as he sighs. "Once Eurydice has her memories back, she will be able to decide what she wants. If she desires to take ambrosia and return to the Mortal World, she can do so. If she chooses to stay, she can do that too. But it will be *her* choice, am I clear?"

Both Charon and Orpheus nod, and if I'm not mistaken, I hear a little quiver in the former's voice as he says, "I'm sorry, my friend. I never meant to betray your trust."

Hades's face stays as hard as stone. "Go. Stay away from the palace and Eurydice until I say otherwise."

Charon gives us a defeated look, then he teleports him and Orpheus away, leaving me alone with the very angry king and queen before me.

"Was anyone going to inform me and Persephone that you were working on getting Eurydice's memories back? Or is every member of my family determined to act behind my back?"

I place my scythe against their desk as I fall to my knees, my wings collapsing along with me. "I have not been in my right mind. Ever since

Eurydice came into my life, I have felt unfocused and out of control. I have experienced emotions I have never felt before, had physical reactions I never knew I could have. It's as terrifying as it is thrilling."

Hades and Persephone glance at one another, and I watch their anger and annoyance leak out of them, replaced with a tenderness I am unused to seeing, especially from Hades. It's the kind of tenderness that can only be shown once you have someone to share in it.

"Thanatos, that's what everyone feels like when they're in love," Persephone informs me, giving me a small smile.

"Really?"

She nods, cupping her husband's cheek gently. Hades's eyes flutter closed at the contact, his expression one of pure bliss, as if her touch alone is enough to make all woes fade away.

Love. I've felt it before, though in a very different way. I love my family, and I would do anything for them, but it's amplified with Eurydice. I know without a doubt in my mind that I would kill to protect her, that I would go to any length to ensure her safety and happiness. I feel the strangest combination of desire, fear, and joy whenever I'm around her, especially when I kissed her.

Feeling her lips on mine, feeling her body pressed against mine, is the closest I've ever felt to truly living.

My eyes begin to burn, and I stare down in horror as water falls down my cheeks in small droplets.

Tears.

I've never cried before—never felt so strongly about something or someone to shed tears over.

It becomes harder to breathe, and before I know it, my body heaves with the force of my tears, and a guttural sound escapes my throat of its own accord. My wings start to curl around me, as if to shield me from this new emotion I'm feeling, but it's futile. Even the arms of my two friends enveloping me into their embrace doesn't make the pain lessen. I don't think anything can.

"I'm going to lose her," I whisper, and a hand begins to stroke my hair in answer, trying to offer me comfort.

Persephone.

"You don't know that," she whispers, pressing her forehead to my temple.

"But I do know. I've always known."

Death is destined to be alone. Death is destined to be rejected by life. Death is destined to lose what few people he loves, no matter how long it takes.

"You told me once that my destiny is not set in stone, that I can make it whatever I want it to be," Hades whispers, cupping my nape. "The same goes for you. Maybe we all will be alone one day, left to face the ineffable void, but if that's the case, it matters what we do with the time we have. Even if you will be all alone in this world one day, don't you want to look back and remember the life you lived with the people you love?"

"Yes, but how can I do that after Eurydice chooses Orpheus? I will be left without a heart, which she has become an impalpable part of."

Hades tightens his grip on me. "Tell her that. Tell her how you feel so she has her eyes wide open once she makes her choice."

"Admit my love for her only to be rejected in a few days when she remembers her husband? I don't know if I could bear it."

"You'll never forgive yourself if you don't."

"How do you know?"

Hades's eyes lock with Persephone's, and I know he is no longer talking directly to me. "I pray that the last words out of my lips will be 'I love you,' and that the only regret I carry in my heart is that I couldn't say them to you a thousand times more."

Persephone's eyes cloud with tears of her own. "I'll hear those words echo in the darkness even after we're long gone."

"And you will." Hades grabs hold of her hand and places a tender kiss on her palm. *"Dopnek eht luxia heristas eht nielum ponrum."*

Until the light crests the sky again.

EURYDICE

After Hecate left to start on the memory potion, I dove into the books on ambrosia she found. There's only three, and two of them only mentioned ambrosia briefly. So any hope of new information rests on a book titled *The Heroes of Ages: Heracles, Jason, and Achilles*, but it's taken its sweet time getting to the topic. I've read two hundred pages about Heracles and Megara completing labors with the goal of getting their hands on ambrosia, and I'm only now getting to the point where that happens. They just finished defeating the Giants in Olympus during the Gigantomachy, and Heracles is being handed ambrosia by Prometheus—

Thanatos teleports into the library, scaring the ever-loving fuck out of me. I let out a little scream and drop my book, losing my page.

"I'm sorry, I didn't mean to frighten you." Thanatos sits down on the couch by my side, his hand briefly reaching towards me before he retracts it. His whole body is tense and kind of twitchy, like he's restraining himself. But why?

"Are you alright?" I ask, looking him over for any physical signs of distress.

He shakes his head, the feathers of his wings ruffling behind him. "I haven't been alright since you came into my life."

I'm not sure how to take that. "I'm sorry?"

"Don't be." He hesitantly brushes his knuckles against my jaw, his eyes glued to my parted lips. "As the God of Death, I have never really felt alive. I would feel flickers of joy, anger, and sorrow when among my family or when I would read, but I mostly felt hollow, cold. But ever since you came to the Underworld, every moment of my existence has been flooded with emotion. Happiness, fear, pain, jealousy, confusion, possessiveness, desire…and love. I did not know what it was truly to be alive until you. I'm no longer clouded by black and grey, but flooded with color. I know the feel of the sun instead of the cold of the moon."

What he's saying seems too good to be true, especially after how insistent he's been that my feelings for him will fade the second my memories return. "Why are you telling me this? You were clear that you didn't want to—"

"I need you to know how I feel. When you have your memories back, when you remember the love you left behind, if you decide to stop whatever is blossoming between us, I will understand. Above all, I want your happiness. But you need to know where my heart lies, and it's in your hands."

I don't care if he thinks I'll change my mind, or if he believes my heart belongs to another. All I care about is right here and right now, and I love him. I've always loved him. I can't remember a time when I didn't love him, and I don't think there will ever be a time when I won't.

So I launch myself at him, planting my lips on his and wrapping my arms around his neck. He lets out a grunt of surprise, but then his hands grab onto my hips, and he pulls me against his side, making me straddle his leg.

"I would make promises to you right now, but you wouldn't believe me."

Thanatos brings one hand up to cup the side of my face, his touch so gentle and light, like he's afraid I'll break if he's not too careful.

"I just don't want you to make any promises you can't keep. Or have any regrets."

"The only regret I could have is not being with you, even if it's for a few days."

"I hope it will be for more than a few days, which is why I have told you all this. When you get your memories back, if you still want me, you'll have me for as long as you do."

I place a kiss on his lips, then on both his cheeks, his nose, his forehead, and I make my way down towards his neck. He shivers when my mouth touches his Adam's apple, then again when I reach the hollow of his throat. His wings, which have been bunched up behind him this whole time, twitch and tense up, and my curiosity makes me pause my ministrations.

"Are your wings sensitive?" I ask, loving the dazed look of bliss in his eyes.

"I don't know," he admits, and his cheeks become rosy in embarrassment. "You must understand I'm not like other Immortals. I don't think or feel the same way they do, or as Mortals do. I've learned and experienced different emotions over time, but some have escaped me. Feelings like desire, attraction, yearning, lust…they are unfamiliar to me. I have never felt them until I met you. My body has never reacted this way before, a-and I'm not just talking about my wings." He shifts in his seat uncomfortably, and I glance down to find him hardening under his pants.

Is he telling me he's never gotten a boner before? "Never?"

"Never."

I feel like my brain is malfunctioning. "Are you a virgin?"

He gives me a shallow nod.

"Hey, look at me." I tilt his chin up so he's forced to do as I ask. "That's nothing to be ashamed of. I'm not disappointed or weirded out. If anything, I'm just shocked. You're fucking gorgeous; I just can't comprehend that *I'm* the only person you've ever felt attracted to."

He lets out an incredulous laugh. "There is no word in any language to describe your inner and outer beauty, Doctor. It is I who cannot comprehend your attraction towards me. In every way, you are exquisite."

I melt against his body, situating myself so I'm fully straddling his waist with my face resting in the crook of his neck. My hands start out grasping his shoulders, but I begin teasingly petting the base of his wings, wondering what his reaction will be. "If we weren't in a library where anyone could walk in, I would have my wicked way with you right now," I whisper into his ear.

He audibly gulps. "How so?"

I laugh, kissing just below his earlobe. "Now that I know this is all new to you, and I want to figure out what turns you on. I want to explore your body and discover what pleasure I can wring from you. Do you like things sensual? Do you like to take control? To give up control…" I lick at the chords of his neck, and I get a moan from him in reply.

I chuckle against his skin. "Do you like it when I talk to you like this?"

He nods, leaning his temple against the side of my head. "Yes."

"Do you like it when I touch your wings?" I stroke down towards his feathers, and he makes an unintelligible noise.

"Eurydice, m-maybe we should wait—" he begins, but I cut him off with another kiss.

"I don't want to wait. You just said that if we only have a few days together before I get my memories back, you want to be with me for whatever time you can."

"Yes, but—"

"I want to be with you, Thanatos. If I really am going to remember some love of my life from my past, then I also want to remember what it felt like for you to be mine and me to be yours. I want to have all of you, even if it's for a short while. Isn't that what we agreed to?"

He nods, and I get goosebumps at the heat that floods his gaze. He grips onto me tightly, then before I know it, we're in my bedroom, where Thanatos sets us gently on my bed, with me still straddling him.

"I know the mechanics of how sex works," Thanatos tells me, his gaze roaming over my body with an intensity that sends heat flaring through my veins. "But you'll have to tell me what you like, what will give you pleasure."

I chuckle, starting to slip out of my shirt. "If you hadn't noticed already, I like to be in control in the bedroom. I like to pleasure my partner and learn the different facets of their body until they're unable to think or speak. Then I take pleasure for myself."

By the way his cock twitches beneath me, I'd say he's down for that. "Where do you want me, Doctor?"

Ooo I like him calling me that with that look in his eyes. "I want you naked. I want to see all of you."

I get off of him in order to let him undress, and I have never seen anyone strip so fast. Within seconds, Thanatos is bare before me, and I'm left staring at how beautiful he is. His slender build but defined muscles remind me of the Renaissance paintings one would find in a museum. His skin, his face, his hair, his wings…I cannot even describe how attractive I find every part of him.

Then my eyes land on his cock, and it's of course perfect. Not too long and not too wide, just the right size to make it pleasurable without any discomfort.

"Your turn," he whispers, and I waste no time following orders.

I bare myself before him slowly, wanting to tease him. He eats up every portion of skin I uncover for him, and his attentiveness is fueling not just my lust, but my ego too. By the time I'm completely naked, Thanatos looks like Tantalus within arm's reach of the apple tree—tortured with how close yet far salvation is.

"What do you want me to do next?" he now asks.

Usually I would tease him more. I would make good on my promise of exploring his body and discovering all his pleasure points, but I want him far too much. There will be time for exploration later. I need him inside of me like I need air to breathe.

"Get on the bed on your back," I direct.

He does as I ask, expanding his wings out to their full length so they don't bunch up under him, lying on top of the blankets, waiting to see what I'll do next.

I don't leave him wondering long. I sink down to my knees, keeping my eyes locked on his face. I gently grab his cock, making him stiffen, and my lips curl in a cat-like grin as I lean forward, letting my breath fan his sensitive skin.

"Eurydice," Thanatos pants, his posture rigid and tense, like he doesn't know whether to run or stay.

I answer with a long lick up his shaft, and he gives me a full-body shudder. I lick him again and again, keeping the motion soft and delicate, like licking an ice cream cone. As much as I want to explore him, I don't want him coming prematurely. Hopefully there will be time for me to figure out what makes the ancient god tick, but tonight isn't about that.

"How are you doing?" I ask him, licking the head of his cock.

The God of Death lets out a whine. "You are…This is…"

"You poor baby," I croon. "Want me to put you out of your misery?"

I don't wait for him to respond, instead I once again straddle his hips, pressing my hands down on his chest to make him fully recline. I reach down and hold up his cock with one hand and gently sit myself down on him. I try to go slow since this is his first time, but it proves to be a challenge. As he fills me up, his face scrunches up in euphoric bliss, and he fists the blankets at his sides, trying to lie completely still.

When I'm fully seated on him, I lean forward and kiss his lips. "You can touch me. I promise I won't break."

He lets go of the blankets, tentatively placing his palms flat on my back, and something about my touch grounds him. He adjusts so that he's sitting himself up, leaning his forehead against my bare chest. I feel his panting breaths fan against the valley between my breasts.

"I'm afraid this might end quickly," he admits.

I cup the nape of his neck with one hand and trail my fingers down his back with the other, beginning to gyrate my hips. "It doesn't matter. Take as long or short as you want. This round is about you."

I move up and down him in a slow and steady beat, but you would think otherwise with how heavily Thanatos is panting and how tightly he holds onto my body. His hips begin bucking of their own accord, and then I feel warmth spread through me while the God in my arms groans. He comes for a couple minutes, and the entire time I hold onto him, stroking his wings. When he's gone through his aftershocks and seems to be coming down from his high, I feel wetness begin to gather on my chest. It takes me a second to realize Thanatos is crying, and worry begins to set in.

"Was that not good?"

Thanatos holds onto me tighter. "I-I never thought anyone would ever be willing to share themselves with me like that."

"Shh," I coo, hugging him just as tightly as he does me. "I know. "

When Thanatos's tears cease, he pulls back and frowns at me, gesturing to where he's still seated inside of me. "You didn't come, did you?"

I shake my head. "No, but like I said, it's okay—"

Thanatos flips us so now I'm the one on my back, and I watch mutely as he tucks his wings in towards his back and hardens his features with resolve.

He pulls out, his eyes trailing down my face to my chest, and after a second of pondering, he ducks his head down and kisses my chest, right where my silent heart is. He places another kiss between my two breasts, then another on my nipple, then another and another and another. He kisses every inch of my neck, chest, and stomach, his reverence and care so moving it makes my face screw up. He's so gentle, so loving. I hate that no one pays enough attention to see it.

Thanatos finally makes it down to my folds, and he stares at them in contemplation, as if my vagina is a fucking Rubik's Cube.

"Tell me what you need?" he asks sheepishly.

I reach down and begin circling my clit, and a hiss of pleasure slips through clenched teeth. "Rub this in circles. Hard."

Thanatos watches my fingers for a moment before nodding. "If I used my mouth, would it feel good? Like it did with me?"

His naivety is so endearing that I can't help but smile. "Yes, it would feel good."

He leans in and cautiously licks my clit, and my thighs clench around his head, making him let out an *oomph* in surprise. He takes my reaction as a good sign, and he experimentally locks his lips around the hood, sucking on it hard.

"Holy shit!" I squeak, grabbing onto his head, keeping him trapped between my legs. His hands grip onto my thighs in answer, and I watch as his wings unconsciously begin flexing behind him.

With my legs over his shoulders, my heel is right where the base of his wings are, so I gently press my foot into that spot, and Thanatos groans into my core, the vibrations from his voice adding another layer of pleasure to his ministrations. I continue rubbing my heel into where his wing meets his back, and I watch his feathers ruffle and twitch, like they have a mind of their own. My teasing becomes too much for him, apparently, because after a few minutes of both our ministrations, Thanatos rips himself away and flaps his wings, bringing himself from his knees to hovering over me within seconds.

He slides back inside of me, keeping his wings outstretched this time, and begins sawing in and out of me. He rubs my clit with one hand, cupping my cheek delicately in the other, and locks his eyes with mine. They're so entrancing, like gazing at snow as it begins sticking to the ground, but his stare is anything but cold. I see so much love there, and it fills me with a warmth I've never felt before. He leans forward and kisses me just as I reach my peak, and my walls clench around his cock as I wail against his mouth. A few more thrusts and he comes inside me again, his lips lingering on mine until we've both come down.

Thanatos pulls out and lies beside me, his expression dazed and eyes filled with wonder.

"*Quto stal nielumes,*" he whispers in the language of the Gods.

The first part meant "that was" but I don't recognize the third word. "What does that mean?"

He turns his head towards me, and then he smiles. "That was heavenly."

Chapter Fifteen

Charon

Orpheus and I don't speak for hours after we get back to my house. He immediately mumbles an excuse to go take a shower, so I retreat to my room and do what I always do when I'm stressed out: I play.

My fingers stroke over the piano keys of their own accord, and soon Franz Schubert's Piano Sonata No. 20 in A Major begins to flood the room. It's one of my favorite pieces of his, and it's just the right length for a composition. I hate pieces that only go on for two minutes, and I hate ones that go for fifteen just as much. The best pieces of music I've ever listened to are all no more than eight minutes and no less than five. Just like this one, which clocks in at seven and a half minutes.

"Do you always play pieces that are so depressing?" a voice asks from the doorway. Orpheus stands there with a towel wrapped around his neck and his hands in the pocket of a PJ set I gave him.

I don't take my eyes off the keys as I answer him. "I play a song that fits my mood in the moment."

I hear his footsteps softly approach my bench, but I still keep my eyes trained on the keys. He sits down beside me and begins strumming the keys himself, making this an impromptu duet.

"I'm sorry, Charon," he whispers after a moment.

"What for?"

"All of this. You were right, I'm just like my father despite trying my hardest not to be. He didn't care how his grief and destructive behavior affected anyone else around him, and here I am wrecking the lives of everyone around me because I can't accept the fact that my wife is gone." His voice breaks on the last word, and I catch his lip quivering in the moon's light peeking in through the window.

"I'm sorry I said all of that earlier, I was just angry."

"No, you were right to call me out. You're helping me, and all the while I'm jeopardizing your relationships with your friends, and until now I didn't really care. I didn't care about anyone or anything except Eurydice, and even then, I never stopped to think about what she wants. I just assumed she'd want to come back with me…I'm so stupid."

"You're not stupid." I place one of my hands over his, stopping him from playing any further. "You love her. You miss her. Of course you aren't thinking straight. Nobody blames you."

"But I blame myself." He lifts his eyes to mine and they're clouded with tears. "I'm sorry I kissed you. I shouldn't have done that, it was wrong."

My gut sours at that, but I try to brush it off. "It's fine."

"I don't mean like that. I mean…I'm attracted to you, Charon. And I'm drawn to you in a way I can't explain, but I still love my wife. I'm still not over her death—clearly—and I'm not ready to do anything with anyone yet. I won't be for a while."

I nod, squeezing his fingers. "I understand."

"I didn't mean the things I said to you either," he whispers shamefully.

"I know it seems foolish to care about being known or remembered," I begin, tapping random keys on the piano gently with my pointer finger. "But when you interact with people day in and day out for thousands upon thousands of years, and no one knows you exist? It makes me feel like I don't matter. And as fucked up as it is, I kind of miss when Zeus forced Mortals to pay a toll to me, because that was the only time anyone remembered me, even if they only did so out of self-preservation.

Hades is feared, Thanatos is hated…but I'm nothing. It's hard knowing that if you left, no one would give a shit."

"But that's not true. You have family who would do anything for you, who love you unconditionally. My mother is dead, I'm estranged from my father, I have no friends…all I had was Eurydice. I'm known around the world as a famous musician, but they don't really *know* me. Eurydice did though. She knew me inside and out, and I would take that over a million people knowing me by name and reputation alone."

Persephone had said the same thing not long ago, but I had dismissed what she was trying to say at the time.

But I don't dismiss it now.

"You're pretty wise for a Mortal," I say with a smirk.

He chuckles at that. "And you're pretty cool for a God."

"Not a God," I remind him.

"Well, whatever you may be, I have the sneaking suspicion that I like you. And I don't like most people."

"Something we have in common…but the sentiment is mutual."

THANATOS

I told Eurydice I had a soul to collect, but it was a lie.

Where I'm really going is to the Wall of Erebus, the ethereal form of my father, the primordial God of Darkness.

Over the thousands of years I've lived in the Underworld, my father has only spoken to me a handful of times, just to "check in on me," as he put it. My mother has spoken to me even less, though the couple times she has, she assured me that she watches over me from the night sky.

I don't believe her though. Nor do I believe my father wanted to check on me.

They're like flies caught in the web of a spider, constantly staying alert for when their predator will show up to eat its latest meal. You're safest when you know where the spider is at all times and can't sneak up on you.

When I reach the wall, black mist parts, morphing into the gate where I drop souls off, and where Cerberus lies sleeping in a cage.

"I'm not here to deliver souls. I'm here to speak with you."

The shadowy walls close together, forming the mystical wall once more, and out of its mist walks the projected form of my father.

When a primordial being takes on their ethereal form for good, they can create an astral projection of themselves that looks identical to their divine form. It can interact with the world as a normal God or Mortal can, but it can only be projected for hours at a time. My father's projected form is no different.

His projection is around my height, with the same feathered wings I carry, though his are white. His skin is a darker shade of brown than mine; his hair is black; his eyes are black without pupils, with little white irises in their center; his face and jaw are square; his nose short and wide; and his plump lips are surrounded by a goatee.

"Hello, son," my father's deep, echoing voice says. He has his hands locked behind his back, his expression guarded. Tendrils of the wall's shadow fall around where he and I stand, like his projection has cut a hole in his form and now the wall is bleeding from the loss of his spirit.

I give my father a stiff nod, clutching onto my scythe for support. "I have questions."

Erebus shows me his palms, giving me the cue to continue. After spending so many centuries in the Underworld, he smells strongly of poppies, the same scent the souls carry—the scent of death. Eurydice has that smell, and it grates on me to smell it on my father after what we shared tonight.

"Do you remember what you said to me before you took on this form for good?"

"No, but I'm assuming you do."

"You said that one day all will return to as it was. Olympus, the Underworld, the Gods, the Mortals...you said that one day they will all cease to exist, and beings like you and Mother will return to your previous states of unconsciousness. Even Phobos will disappear. But I will remain."

Erebus gives no reaction. "And?"

"How do you know that? Did the Fates tell you this? How do you know my fate is to be alone?"

Erebus shakes his head, looking down at me in pity. Erebus is the only person who has ever made me feel small, and it takes all my willpower not to let myself cave to his disappointment and hatred. "The Fates have never spoken to me the way they do you and your brother. I have received no prophecy or premonition. The reason I know you will one day be alone in this universe is because of your very existence. When you were born from your mother's night sky, I knew that Immortality was a fallacy. We all did. Everything dies eventually. Everything except you. And if that's the case, then one day everything will be gone, and you'll have finally completed your goal of destroying the happiness your mother and I helped create."

I was not ignorant to how my father viewed me, but the words are still painful regardless. They take me back to the time before I lived here in the Underworld, when I was by my brother's side and I felt as if I were alone in the universe.

"I had treated your words like an omen since they were spoken. But all this time your prediction was nothing more than your resentment and hatred towards me turned into a weapon. You wanted me to go about my days dreading the future."

"How do you think the five of us felt when you showed up? I've never known a day of peace since you were born, since the promise of bliss was ripped away from us."

"Did it never occur to you that your anger should be directed towards Chaos, who planted these ideas into your minds? Phobos and I never asked to be born. I cannot control what I'm, nor can he, and yet you punish us for it. We're the monster you brought to life and now curse the sight of."

Erebus rolls his eyes. "Did you really come here to lecture me over a conversation we had thousands of years ago?"

"No, I came here to put a rest to the doubts and fears you planted in my mind. Now that I have found someone who shows me the love and care you never did, I can look forward to the future instead of dreading it."

"Doesn't change what you are. You'll always be death."

I feel myself smile, but not in malice or satisfaction. I smile because I no longer feel like I'm carrying the burden of a fate I cannot alter. I smile because no matter what my father, or anyone else say, no one knows what my destiny shall be. And I'm blissfully happy living in that ignorance.

"Yes, but death is what gives life so much meaning. You may mourn the time when you thought nothing could alter your state of contentment, but you didn't appreciate the happiness you felt until you learned you could lose it."

Erebus does not seem to take in my words. He discards them and gives me a bored look. "Are we done?"

I nod my head, allowing him to start walking back towards the shadows which make up the wall.

"I hope one day you will be able to make peace with what you can't control," I tell him.

He pauses just before he touches the wispy surface.

"May the Fates cast their judgement justly," he says.

And then the projection of my father disappears, leaving me alone with those final haunting words.

CHAPTER SIXTEEN

EURYDICE

Thanatos had to leave around four in the morning to cleave a new soul, so I used my spare time to finish reading that book. Though I'm familiar with the story of Heracles—as most Mortals are—I completely forgot that he had been rewarded for his bravery during the Gigantomachy with ambrosia. I think that detail slipped my mind because it's famously known that Heracles and Megara died in each other's arms of old age, where they still rest in their tomb in Athens. But the book is very clear that Heracles was given ambrosia, and instead of taking it, he chose a Mortal life with Megara…and then nothing. No further mention of what happened to the ambrosia he was gifted.

I doubt he gave it back to the Gods. He would have been smart enough to know that returning a gift from them is a great offense. There have been people killed by the Gods for less.

So what did he do with it?

I raise this question to Thanatos when he returns, and he has no answer for me either.

"I agree with you that returning the ambrosia wasn't an option." Thanatos licks his lips, deep in thought. "Perhaps we should go ask him."

My brain short-circuits at that. "We're just going to casually knock on *Heracles's* door and talk to him?"

I'm going to meet *the* Heracles?

Thanatos smirks upon seeing my reaction. "A fan of his?"

I playfully roll my eyes, shoving his arm. "Every Mortal is a fan of his. Ask most people and they'll say Heracles was their first love."

"Was he yours?" Thanatos asks, and by the glimmer in his eyes, he already knows the answer.

I shake my head, wrapping my arms around his torso. "No, I much prefer the melancholic, tenderhearted underdogs."

He smiles, but it is a bit strained. Something tells me that description not only fits him, but the someone who hangs over our heads like an anvil.

"You are by far the strangest Mortal I have ever encountered." Thanatos places a soft kiss on my forehead.

I preen from the compliment. "When do you want to go?"

"After we tell Hades and Persephone about our plan. I'm sure Seph will want to tag along."

Indeed, after Thanatos teleports us to their office, the Queen of the Underworld insists on coming along, squealing in excitement, much to the amusement of her husband.

"Psyche is going to flip when I tell her about this," she says with a little skip.

"Psyche?" I inquire.

She nods. "My best friend. She has a huge crush on Heracles."

I chuckle, enjoying her reaction. "Doesn't everybody?"

I've never been to Elysium before, obviously, but I've read about it at length. When I was in school studying theology, Elysium was a central point of discussion. All of my teachers would skirt around discussions about the Underworld, but they spent weeks at a time talking about Elysium: who rests there, how it differs from other parts of the Underworld, and what it takes to get in there.

It's surreal to be going there in the flesh now.

After the king and queen share a kiss goodbye, Thanatos grabs onto both of our hands, teleporting us to Heracles and Megara's house—I say house but it's really a mansion—right next to the forest of brightly-colored trees. It appears to be three stories, with so many windows I can't even count them all. The walls look to be made of actual gold, and the windowpanes are silver. If you can imagine what a house in paradise would look like, this would be it.

Even the doorbell is fancy, engrained with the letters of their first and last names.

After ringing the doorbell twice, a familiar face opens up the door. She's very short, only about 5'1"; she has a slim figure and face, tawny skin, curly dark brown hair and small eyes, a long nose, and full lips. She's wearing a pair of jeans and a cream-colored sweater, and her hair is tied back in a messy bun.

Megara Remes.

"Can I help you?" she asks, her voice dripping in a thick Greek accent.

"Hi Megara Remes, I'm such a big fan," I breathe, unable to look away from her beautiful face. Out of the corner of my eye, I see Persephone gawking as well.

"And you are?"

"Oh, silly me." I slap my forehead like I'm in a fifties cartoon, shaking my head. "My name is Eurydice."

"I'm Persephone." The queen extends her hand out, and she blushes like a teenager when Megara takes it and places a kiss on her knuckles.

"An honor to finally meet you, my queen."

A nervous giggle leaves Persephone. "Oh please, none of that. Persephone is fine."

"Then I insist you both call me Meg."

Persephone and I share a look of excitement, but the moment is ruined by Thanatos, who not-so-subtly coughs.

"Oh right." I clear my throat and try to stop fangirling and lusting after the woman in front of me. "We need to talk to you and...Mr. Remes."

Meg chuckles, leaning her forehead against the doorframe. "Don't call him that to his face or else he'll go into rooster mode. No one needs to fan his ego."

She lets the three of us inside, and I audibly gasp at how beautiful it is. Chiseled pillars line the foyer, leading to a marble staircase at the end of the room. The second and third floors are visible from the bottom, with marble railings lining the edges of each floor and the stairs as they spiral up. The ceiling is high above, with gold accents surrounding a large painting of Heracles surrounded by the creatures he defeated in his labors. Every door is under a carved marble arch and made of thick red wood—maybe mahogany. The styles of the architecture are a clash of Ancient Greece and the Renaissance, classic and chic.

I remember visiting the palace of Versailles after I graduated university, and the décor and lavish style of this mansion rival that palace. Marie Antoinette would come on the spot if she saw the foyer alone.

"Herc! We have company," Meg shouts.

"In the library!" a deep, masculine voice replies.

Gods above, I'm becoming a puddle on this marble floor and I haven't even seen him yet.

Meg leads us past the staircase and down a long hallway lined with doors. Gold sconces lie against seemingly hand-painted walls, depicting a mural of Greece that's only disrupted by each door. About half way down the hall is where the library is, and it is straight out of that scene from *Beauty and the Beast*. The bookshelves go from the floor to the ceiling, the height reaching probably twenty feet. Chiseled pillars once again support the ornate room, resting between every shelf and the large windows on the north-facing wall. The ceiling depicts realistic clouds in various shades of pink, perfectly matching the blush walls. In the center of the ceiling is a large crystal chandelier, and it makes the whole room shine as the sun hits each individual gem.

In front of the giant bookshelves lies several couches the color of the dawn sky, with polished mahogany tables scattered around holding chess sets, books, and ash trays. Sitting on one of these couches, leaning over a chess board in thought, is Heracles Remes.

He's just as gorgeous as the paintings and statues I've seen of him. He's about average height, reaching just 5'8"; he's built like a God, with endless muscles on his golden tan skin, shortly cropped blonde hair, light blue eyes the same shade as Hades's and Hermes's, a square jaw covered in a neatly-trimmed beard, an angular nose, and a rugged smile that sends a flutter through my chest.

"My love, this is Queen Persephone, her friend Eurydice, and of course, Thanatos," Meg introduces, stepping aside to let her husband greet us.

Heracles does the same thing Meg did—raises her hand to his lips and kisses her knuckles, and I swear I hear Persephone whimper.

"I'm glad Lord Hades settled down. Despite public perception, he's a good man."

"Couldn't agree more," Persephone breathes, more flustered than she was when meeting Meg.

Heracles's eyes move to Thanatos, and he gives him a stern nod. "My lord."

Thanatos bows his head. "A pleasure to see you again, Heracles."

"Is it?"

I glance between the two, my brows furrowing. "Am I missing something?"

With a small sigh, Thanatos explains with reluctance, "Heracles tried to save his friend, Admetus, from death by brute force. The Furies ended up coming to claim his friend, who then spent months in Tartarus for trying to escape death."

"Why couldn't you do it?"

Thanatos rubs the back of his neck, and I see his wings ruffle behind him. "I was incapacitated."

"He means I kicked his ass," Heracles says with a smirk, pride oozing from his tone.

Any attraction I felt for him vanishes into anger. "He didn't want to harm your friend; he was just doing his job. If Thanatos had a choice, he wouldn't be doing this. If he had a choice, he wouldn't have subjected himself to the verbal and physical abuse thrown at him these past thousand years just because of who he was born to be. He didn't choose to be death."

Everyone stares at me in a mix of bewilderment and awe, with a little hostility coming from Meg. I'm half convinced she's about to come over and kick *my* ass when Heracles breaks the tension.

"It seems Hades isn't the only one settling down." He chuckles. "I'm assuming you have a reason for coming here today, Eurydice, besides trying to knock me down a peg."

I feel a bit sheepish at that, but I power through. "We need to know where you put the ambrosia given to you after the Gigantomachy."

Heracles starts to laugh, but when he sees the look in all our eyes, he sobers up. "You must have quite a story to tell."

Persephone shrugs. "You could say that."

Heracles grins. "I got nothing but time to kill. Lay it on me."

I quickly explain the situation we find ourselves in, and by the time I'm finished, Meg has her eyebrows raised and eyes wide, while Heracles chuckles, a deep rumble, almost like a lion's growl. "Just a couple weeks in the Underworld and you've caused quite the stir," Heracles comments, eyes trained on me.

I force myself to keep his eye contact, not wanting to show how embarrassed I feel. "I didn't intend to."

Heracles's expression, one of excitement and joy, puts me at ease. "The Underworld needed a stir. Things were getting a bit dull."

Thanatos tilts his head to the side, his eyebrows creased. "The Underworld isn't meant to be exciting."

Meg scoffs. "Of course you would say that."

I narrow my eyes her way. "Are you implying Thanatos is dull?"

"Eurydice—" Thanatos begins, placing his hand on my shoulder, but I cut him off.

"Thanatos is anything but dull." I sound like a teenager defending her boyfriend to her parents, but I don't really care. "He has a brilliant mind, an unending curiosity, a beautiful heart, and not to mention, he's *fantastic* in bed."

Thanatos makes a choking noise, and I see his wings bunch up behind his back. Persephone eyes him with a knowing smirk, only making him look more awkward.

Heracles bursts out laughing, pointing a finger my way. "I like this one. She's got spunk."

I cross my arms over my chest, mirroring Meg's stance. "Give us the information we came here for, please. I'm growing tired of your snide comments about Thanatos and I'd like to leave as soon as possible."

Heracles take a couple steps forward, bowing his head slightly. "If you want the ambrosia, you'll have to make a little trip."

"To where?" Persephone asks, voice filled with half curiosity and half dread.

CHAPTER SEVENTEEN
THANATOS

"Atlas. That's where the ambrosia is."

Hades, Persephone, Hermes, Hecate, Charon, and Orpheus are all gathered in the office so we can discuss our plan going forward. We left Eurydice in her room so she can continue looking over data from her findings. She wants to make sure there isn't another element we'll need to help free the souls in Acheron and Cocytus.

"Heracles said once he decided to stay Mortal with Meg, he buried the ambrosia in a box at the base of the Atlas Mountain, right beneath the Hesperides Garden," Persephone explains from where she sits on Hades's lap.

During the battle with the Titans, Atlas was Cronus's righthand man. He caused the most carnage and killed many Immortals during the fight, so he was given one of the harshest punishments of the Titans. He was tasked with spending eternity holding up the sky, preventing it from crushing the Mortal World, and him along with it. His seven daughters, called the Nymphs of Sunset, grew a garden at the base of his mountainous form, where a tree of golden apples grows that can cure nearly any illness or wound. These apples would go on to be eaten by the Golden Ram, whose wool was used to create the Golden Fleece. Heracles said the ambrosia is at the base of that tree.

So in order to get it, we have to get past Atlas's seven daughters. After Heracles's interactions with them—which included killing their serpent, Ladon, and stealing two of their apples—they are very protective of the apple tree and of each other. Heracles barely made it out alive when he hid the ambrosia there. Getting it won't be easy.

"The Nymphs of Sunset are skilled with illusions and the manipulation of the mind," Hecate warns. "They won't be easily defeated."

"Which is why I'm the best person to go retrieve the ambrosia," I reply. "They cannot kill me nor seriously injure me."

"You should still take someone with you. They can get the ambrosia while you distract the nymphs." Hecate sighs. "It cannot be me. I'm nearly done with Eurydice's potion and I need to be here to administer it."

"I would volunteer but I really don't want to," Hermes says with a smile.

Charon rolls his eyes. "And we are internally rejoicing for it."

Hermes pouts. "You're being more of a dick than usual. Is there something you want to share with the class?"

Before their bickering can escalate, Orpheus steps forward. "I'll go. The Nymphs won't perceive me as a threat, and it will allow me to get the ambrosia quickly."

"Are you sure?" asks Persephone. "It will be dangerous. You could—"

"I know, but this is the right thing to do. Those souls deserve peace, and I regret not prioritizing that over my own grief."

"And if you die?" Hermes asks, serious for once.

He looks to Charon. "Then you can throw my ass in Tartarus like you threatened from the start."

Charon opens his mouth, then shuts it, his jaw clenching. I can see the conflict in his eyes, the desire to keep Orpheus safe while also knowing that he's right. The Nymphs will never perceive him as a threat. He's the perfect person to get the ambrosia.

"I will keep him safe," I assure everyone, but mainly Charon. "You have my word."

He nods, his tense expression never fading.

"So when are we going?" Orpheus asks, repeatedly sneaking glances at Charon.

"The sooner the better."

"Then let's go now." Orpheus strides over to me and extends his hand, his expression wary but determined.

I grab onto his hand, pressing our palms together, then I nod to my friends. "We will return shortly."

"Be safe," Persephone orders in her regal, authoritative tone.

I smirk at that. "As my queen commands."

And then we vanish.

ORPHEUS

The Atlas Mountains are in northern Africa, capped with snow and surrounded by lush green trees and vegetation. It wasn't at all what I was expecting. Since Atlas is a Titan, I thought he would look more… person-like.

When I question Thanatos about this, he explains, "Prometheus asked Hecate to transform him into a mountain. Before the war, Atlas and Prometheus had been close, and he wanted to give him that small mercy for old times' sake."

"Is he still conscious?"

"Yes and no. He's not a primordial deity, so he has no ethereal form or the ability to form an astral projection of himself, so he is unable to speak or express himself. But now his punishment is less of a hardship, and he can find some semblance of peace."

Thanatos has teleported us about a mile away from the garden to give us time to prepare, which was smart. The grassy plains of the savanna gradually fade into lush fields of grass; the acacia trees morph into tall ones with golden leaves and reddish-brown trunks. It's as if we've stepped into a completely different world.

Despite the beautiful scenery though, all I can think of is Eurydice. So, I decide to address the elephant in the room.

"You love her."

Thanatos pauses mid-step, his feathers ruffling. "Yes."

"Does she love you?"

He hesitates, but then replies, "Anything she thinks she feels for me will disappear when she remembers her life with you."

As much as I hope things will go as he says, I know my wife, and I know how deeply she feels things. "Eurydice has a heart the size of these mountains, but she doesn't let just anyone into it. She is careful with who she trusts and loves. If she said she loves you, she means it. When she remembers me, she'll still love you, even if she loves me as well."

Thanatos says nothing to this, so I continue on.

"If she chooses to come back with me to the Mortal World, what will you do?"

Now he looks at me. "There is nothing to do. I want her happiness, no matter what that may entail."

I let out a sigh, letting my thoughts wander as I walk. "I think part of her has always loved you. At first it was probably a crush, built around fantasies she had conjured since her youth, but as she grew older? It was different. She would still get excited when she would hear about you, she would still try to learn any information about you. She saw a portrait someone had painted of you fighting Zeus on the street once, and she spent five thousand dollars on it. It hung in her office."

"We met once when she was a girl. I don't understand her fascination with me, even less so how enduring it was."

I shrug. "I saw one movie with Chris Evans and continued to crush on him throughout my teens and early twenties. It was the same for her.

But unlike me, she got to spend time with you and have her affections returned. It was a fantasy, a love built in a dream, but then it became real for her when she got to know you."

He stares at me for a long moment. "Why are you telling me this?"

"Because I want her happiness too. It's been selfish of me to not take into account what she would want, and that ends now. If she wants to stay in the Underworld, if she wants to be with you…I won't stand in the way."

He nods, his wings held rigidly against his back, his jaw tense.

Neither of us speak the rest of the walk there, but when the garden comes into view, Thanatos whispers to me, "Stay behind me."

I do as he says, hiding behind his now outstretched wings, and stay silent as he greets Atlas's daughters. "Hello there."

I sneak a peek through his feathers to get a look at them. One of the Nymphs slowly approaches Thanatos, but the others stay behind, taking a protective stance. As with all Immortals, each of them is devastatingly beautiful. I think they all had different mothers, because each one has unique skin tones, hair color, and facial features. They all have their hair up in some sort of fashion, either a braid or bun, and they wear long dresses of ivory silk. The one that stands in front of Thanatos has tawny skin, blonde hair knotted in a braid, and red eyes. She reminds me of the vampires from *Twilight*, though she obviously doesn't sparkle.

"Have you come for another one of my sisters, God of Death?"

"No, I come on behalf of Lord Hades and Lady Persephone. They seeks your assistance, Anastacia."

The Nymph huffs a laugh. "Don't tell me Hades took a wife?"

"He did, very recently. Queen Persephone is the Goddess of Spring, the long-awaited final member of the Horae, and the daughter of Demeter."

I can tell this is shocking news. "I did not know Demeter had a daughter."

"Neither did any of us."

"What does she want?"

"She and Hades request the ambrosia Heracles and Megara buried underneath your garden. They want to free the souls trapped in the rivers of the Underworld, the ones who did not pay the toll to the Ferrymen eons ago."

"What's in it for me and my sisters?" Her voice gets harder, laced with disgust. "What do you and yours have to offer other than death and misery? How can we trust you with something as valuable as ambrosia?"

It may be stupid, but I step out from behind Thanatos and into Anastacia's line of sight.

She takes a step back upon seeing me, her eyes wide. "Why have you brought a Mortal with you?"

"My name is Orpheus Martin," I tell her. "I journeyed into the Underworld to save my wife, and I thought I would be met with all of the cruelty and terror that has been rumored to dwell there for thousands of years. But what I found instead were people that dedicate their whole lives to making sure the souls of the dead stay safe and happy. I found people that, despite all the laws I had broken with my trespassing, tried to help me. Thanatos has been nothing but kind to me, even though he has every reason to hate me. Hades could have hung me by my balls in Tartarus, but he listened to what I had to say and cried when I showed him the depths of my grief. Hecate, Charon, Hermes, Persephone—they've all treated me as their equal, not talking down to me or around me like so many Gods do. They're a family founded through sorrow, and despite all they've been through, they try to ease the sorrow of others."

I dare to take a step forward, and this time, she doesn't back away. "I know you want to protect the people you love, and I know how hard it is to believe people surrounded by so much darkness can produce any kind of light. But there is no one more worthy of trust than the Gods of the Underworld, no matter what anyone thinks to the contrary."

She studies me for a second, then her eyes narrow. "And why should I trust your opinion, Mortal?"

"I've given you no reason to, but I'd be willing to prove my trustworthiness."

She glances over her shoulder at the garden, and I take the opportunity to admire its immense beauty. Lush grass morphing into a patch of glowing flowers that surround a large tree of gold, glistening in the sunlight.

She notices my awe and smirks, amused. "Is that so? Alright, I propose a test then. I want you to walk through the garden without looking back. If you make it to the end without looking behind you, I will give you the ambrosia. If you fail, you will meet a swift end by the blades of my sisters."

No pressure then. "I accept."

A hand lands on my shoulder, and I'm turned towards a very concerned-looking Thanatos. "Are you out of your mind?"

I shrug. "Probably, but it's worth a shot."

"You seem oddly calm facing your own mortality."

"I've felt dead ever since Eurydice died," I whisper, my throat growing raw. "And I've been so focused on bringing her back because I was afraid of feeling so hopeless, of drowning in that feeling. But I can't escape it. In trying to do so, I have complicated all of your lives and put Eurydice in a position she never should have been in. I should have just let her be at peace, but I was selfish. Let me be selfless for once, Thanatos."

He looks conflicted, but he ultimately nods, letting me go. "Eurydice would be proud of you."

That statement gives me a little extra courage to go through with this. "If I fail, can you promise me something?"

He nods once.

"Promise me you will spend every single day of your life making her happy."

The smile he gives me is laced with pain, and it's just a testament to Thanatos's loving soul that he feels sorrowful for the husband of the woman he loves. "I promise."

"Okay." I turn towards the garden, where our Nymph friend awaits. "I'm ready."

EURYDICE

"This is it?" I ask, grabbing onto the test tube Hecate hands me. If I didn't know any better, I would think this is just filled with water. I was expecting a potion to be glowing with sparkles and color.

Hecate nods, assuring me "Yes, that is it."

She and Persephone are sitting beside me in the palace library, on the couch across from the fireplace. Hecate says she needs to be here in case anything goes wrong, and Persephone said that my well-being is her responsibility as queen, so she should be here for support. Hades said he would have been here too if it weren't for the prayers and soul inquiries he had to take care of.

I'm honestly glad he's not here, it's already nerve-racking having two people staring at me while I'm about to remember everything from my past.

"Okay, here goes nothing." I take a deep breath, then I down the contents of the test tube in one large gulp.

I wait a second, then two, then the memories start flooding in, like water rushing out of a broken dam.

My mothers, Cara and Agnes. I remember days spent at the beach with them, afternoons playing dress-up and watching movies together. I remember being given my first microscope for my tenth birthday by them; I remember winning every science fair throughout primary school, and I remember how proud it made them. They always supported my dreams, even when they didn't understand them. They never understood my fascination with Thanatos or the Underworld, but they never told me it was wrong. When I would come home after getting into fights with my peers over him, they would hold me while I cried, insisting that Thanatos was good.

And then, when I was fifteen, I met a boy at school. He's beautiful, brilliant, and so so sad. I find him sitting alone in the library, his cheeks stained with tears, and when I ask him why, he whispers, "I miss my life before my mother died."

I sit down beside him and say, "We can't change our pasts, but our futures are still unwritten, and we do have a say in what it holds. The question is, what do you want to do with it?"

From there, we became friends. Then we dated, both in close proximity and long-distance. He proposed to me, we got married, and we were blissfully happy for many years. He became a world-renowned musician while I did my work with Prometheus.

And then it all comes crashing to a halt when we take a trip to England for one of his concerts. The storm conjured by Demeter covers the ground in ice and snow, and one reckless driver chose to speed on a road that was still frozen. He wasn't watching when I was crossing the street, and he drove away when his car hit me.

My husband held my broken body in his arms until he couldn't anymore, then Thanatos carried me into the afterlife. He let me cry into his chest when I feared that I would forget my life and my love, but he assured me that if I do forget, it won't be forever. And those words gave me the strength I needed to drink from Lethe.

When the memories finally stop entering my brain, and I feel all those missing puzzle pieces slip into place, all I feel is sorrow, not relief. I thought regaining my memories would ease my confusion, but I've never felt more lost.

"Do you remember?" Hecate asks softly.

I nod, unable to form words.

"Good, because there are some things you should know."

I look to her with dread. "Like what?"

"Like the idiotic quest of a certain Mortal."

Chapter Eighteen

Eurydice

I've never missed being able to eat or drink more than I do right now. I want nothing other than to bathe myself in tequila.

But alas, I'm dead, so I have to deal with my problems like a normal, healthy individual. It sucks.

Thankfully, Hermes offered to keep me company while *he* drowned himself in tequila.

Silver linings, I guess.

"I don't know what to do," I admit quietly, feeling my eyes burn even though I have no ability to form tears. I feel so many emotions—sadness, anger, confusion, guilt—but it all seems less intense than it used to. I feel like I should be sobbing and freaking out, but I'm not. My human instincts are fighting with my soul instincts. It's bizarre.

Hermes takes another shot, then he focuses his attention on me. "Has anyone ever told you that I was a lover of Queen Penelope of Ithica?"

"Umm, Odysseus's wife?" *I don't really see what this has to do with anything.*

He nods, pouring himself another shot. "I had been sleeping with Aeacus, one of the Judges of the Underworld, for some time. I was incredibly happy with him, and even now I can't think of a single problem with our relationship. But one day, years after the Trojan War, I heard from my brother Ares that Odysseus had been staying on Calypso's island for years, leaving Penelope to wonder if he was alive or dead. Ares thought it was hilarious that a Mortal queen was sitting in her palace all alone, but I didn't. I know how suffocating and all-consuming loneliness can be. So I paid her a visit."

He takes a shot, then he continues. "Pen and I quickly became friends, and even quicker, we became more. But I was still with Aeacus. I loved him, but I also loved her. I confessed this to her one night, and she said to me, 'I thought I loved Odysseus until he left, until I saw what my life was like without him. I know I love you because the idea of being without you for even a moment fills me with misery. If you don't feel the same about me, then this will never work.' So I asked myself, 'Who can I not imagine my life without?' And the answer was Penelope. I broke things off with Aeacus, and I spent the rest of Pen's life with her on Ithaca."

"Did you ever regret your decision?" I whisper.

Hermes is usually a jovial, childish person, and it sometimes makes me forget how old he actually is. He's been alive for thousands of years, and right now, his wilted expression highlights that.

"Not for one second. Pen died of cancer when she was eighty-three. Leukemia. It came quickly; by the time we realized what was happening, it was too late. She died, was chosen to go to Asphodel, and she's been there ever since. I kept visiting her for the first few years she was here, but she cut things off. She didn't want me to spend my immortal life in love with a ghost."

I reach out and touch his hand, which was just about to reach for the tequila bottle. I grip it tightly, clasping both my hands around his. "I'm so sorry, Hermes."

He smiles, though it doesn't reach his eyes. "Ask yourself who you can't imagine being parted from. Does the idea of Orpheus going back to the Mortal World for several decades fill you with dread? Or does the idea of leaving here with him and abandoning Thanatos make you feel that misery?"

I open my mouth to answer his question, but it doesn't feel that simple. "I love Orpheus. I can feel my love for him...but it's different. It's like I'm feeling someone else's emotions, not my own. There's a disconnect. But with Thanatos...I feel my love for him stronger than I feel anything else. I know being dead mutes my emotions, but it's like my feelings for him are the only ones that are on full blast. But what if it feels that way because I just got my memories back? What if it will get better over time? I don't want to make a choice only to regret it later."

"I've spoken with many souls in the past, and even souls who live in Asphodel feel a disconnect from their former lives. It's normal. You died, Eurydice. You drank from Lethe and allowed your soul to heal from the regrets and missed chances from your life. You have moved on from your life."

"If that was true, why didn't my memories come back sooner?"

"Probably because you are in love with two people, and your soul knew you would grow more distressed if you knew about Orpheus, and the job of Lethe is to prevent those kinds of feelings. I don't think your memories would have come back unless you had Hecate's help."

"Maybe." I look away from Hermes and stare at the bottle in front of him, trying to digest all he has said. This isn't a decision that I can make lightly, nor is it one I can make easily. I feel caught between my love for Orpheus, which is steeped in history, loyalty, and dedication—and my love for Thanatos, which is steeped in passion, understanding, and endurance. I'm also caught between life and death, both of which are irrevocably tied to the men I love. Picking Orpheus means picking life, giving me a second chance to live out the life that was cut short. And picking Thanatos means picking death, which is inevitable and everlasting.

Can I see myself putting aside my feelings for Thanatos while I live out my life with Orpheus, then continue to do so when I'm back in the Underworld? Can I go about my second afterlife knowing Thanatos's sad smiles and delicate touches were so close by? But can I stay here knowing that Orpheus is in the Mortal World all alone, without the wife that swore to love him come hell or high water?

That sounds like obligation, not love.

I think a large part of me does feel obligation towards Orpheus, especially since he risked his safety to come rescue me. It's not that I don't love him, because I know I do, but it feels disconnected, like I told Hermes. History, loyalty, dedication, obligation—all words I've used to describe my feelings for Orpheus, and all words that lack the spark I once felt. My love for Orpheus feels like something that ended that I'm contemplating starting up again. There's a finality to it. But with Thanatos, it's different. Even now that I have all my memories back, what I thought before still holds true: I never stopped loving him. I buried those feelings down when I met Orpheus, writing them off as a dream that would never come true, but they were still there. My love for him has endured for most of my life, and I don't see that changing. How can I go back to reality when the dream of my heart has come true? How can I bury those feelings again and return to being a dedicated wife? I can't.

For life, there is a beginning and an end. You follow the steps, you stumble and fall, but you stop dancing when the music ceases to play. But death is a dance that never ends. The dance of death is forever.

Thanatos is forever.

Orpheus

I take my first step into the Garden of Hesperides, feeling the intense stares of the Nymphs boring into me as I enter their sacred space. The second I step over the threshold, which is marked by a gateway of roots and golden leaves, the scene before me changes. Gone are the ethereal flowers I don't know the name of, gone is the golden tree that promises safety and healing, and gone are the ancient Nymphs staring me down.

Like water washing away chalk off of concrete, the garden becomes the tunnel to the Underworld, the secret entrance I used in Greece. I have to squeeze my eyes shut a couple times and rub my closed lids, thinking that when I open them that everything will return to normal, but the tunnel is still there.

Was it all in my head? Did I just snap under my grief and imagine the last several days? Have I been stuck inside this godsforsaken tunnel this whole time?

No, it can't be. I refuse to believe it. Didn't Hecate say the Nymphs were experts at illusions? This has to be one of them.

It just looks so real...

One foot in front of the other, I tell myself. *Keep your head straight ahead and put one foot in front of the other.*

I take another step, then a third, then a fourth.

And that's when I hear a voice.

"Orpheus."

I freeze, shaking off the instinct to answer the call, then I take another step forward.

"Orpheus, I need you," a voice wails.

Eurydice.

It's not real, I tell myself. *This is what the Nymphs want. They want you to look. It's all an illusion.*

"Orpheus, where are you? Why won't you come to me?"

What if it's not an illusion? Maybe this is real. Maybe I am actually walking towards the Underworld's exit, with Eurydice running after me, screaming to me. She sounds so scared, so sad. It tears at my very soul to hear her like that. All I want to do is comfort her, hold her.

No. No this isn't real. It isn't real. Even as I say this to myself, it doesn't ring true in my heart.

Keep your head straight ahead and put one foot in front of the other.

I clench my hands into fists at my side, my grip so tight I feel my nails digging into my palm.

"Orpheus! Orpheus, please!"

One foot in front of the other. One foot in front of the other. One foot in front of the other.

A hand suddenly touches my shoulder, stopping me. A small hand, with a delicate, gentle touch. Soon a female body presses against my back, and arms wrap around my waist. The smell of poppies fills my nose. A soft voice whispers my name once more.

"Orpheus."

My chest heaves on a sob, and I let the tears flow freely down my cheeks. I let all of the pain, sorrow, anger, and guilt hit me all at once, and I weep in the arms of my wife. I curse the Gods, I curse the Fates, I curse her, I even curse myself. I rage against the world for taking away everyone I love. I beg the world for a reason behind all of the pain I carry in my heart. But as always, my questions go unanswered.

"I'm so sorry," I whisper, believing, just for one moment, that Eurydice is really here, that it is her touch I feel.

"Look at me, my love," Eurydice whispers, and I so desperately want to. I want to lose myself in her loving stare, to feel her lips pressed against mine again, to feel her embrace me for real.

Because this is just an illusion.

This isn't real.

I take hold of her hands and pull them off my skin, stepping out of reach from her. Doing so feels like pulling two magnets apart, and I struggle with every step I take. Eurydice continues to call my name, but I keep walking towards the end of the tunnel, towards where the gloomy Underworld becomes the bright liveliness of Greece. I walk and I walk and I walk until I reach that opening. I walk until the shadows of the tunnel fade and sunlight falls over me, warming my skin.

Only then do I collapse, tears overtaking me again, and this time, when someone touches my shoulder, I know it's Thanatos. He pulls me into his embrace and holds me as I cry, staying silent while I let my grief finally consume me.

I don't know how long he and I kneel on the ground, but when I pull myself together and look behind me, there stands Anastacia, and in her hands is a bundle of something wrapped in a beautiful silk identical to her dress.

She unravels it, revealing a grape-like cluster of round, glowing, rouge-colored fruit the size of clementines.

Ambrosia.

Chapter Nineteen

Eurydice

"Believe me, Frankenstein, I was benevolent; my soul glowed with love and humanity; but am I not alone, miserably alone? You, my creator, abhor me; what hope can I gather from your fellow creatures, who owe me nothing? They spurn and hate me."

My eyes fly across the pages of the book, and I become more enthralled with every word I consume. I can see why Thanatos and Hades love this book so much, especially the latter. Just like I saw Thanatos's soul in the pages of *The Metamorphosis*, I see Hades's in *Frankenstein*.

After my talk with Hermes, I felt so restless I needed to get out of my head. I needed a distraction, and books are the perfect method of escape. While I'm sitting on my bed, curled up with the book in my lap, I can forget that Thanatos and Orpheus will be back any minute and that I'll have to tell them my decision. And on top of that, I have to see if my theory on how to free the souls in Acheron and Cocytus will work, putting the afterlives of dozens of souls in my hands.

No pressure or anything.

A knock sounds at my door, followed by Hecate's voice. "Can I come in?"

"Of course." I set my book aside and mentally prepare myself for the news I know she'll bring.

She lingers in the doorway, leaning against the frame. "They're back. They have the ambrosia with them in Hades and Persephone's office."

"Did you tell them I have my memories back?"

"Yes. But it's your choice whether you want to talk to either of them right now or not."

"I can't focus on them until we help the souls."

"Oh don't worry about that. Hades, Persephone, and I can take care of it. As the rulers of the Underworld, it's probably best for them to take the reins. But if you want to come, you're more than welcome to."

I probably should go with them…but I need to rip the Band-Aid off. It's not fair to keep Thanatos and Orpheus waiting when I have made my choice. I've never been one for confrontation, but this isn't something I can procrastinate like I would my taxes.

"Can you send Thanatos up here?"

Hecate gives a single nod. "Of course."

She leaves without another word, and a few minutes later, Thanatos appears in the middle of my room, his drooping wings the only indicator of how he's feeling. The rest of his body is closed off and hard, as is his expression.

"You were wrong," I tell him.

I feel his eyes bore into me, but I can't meet his gaze. Not yet.

"About what?"

"Remembering Orpheus didn't make me forget the love I feel for you. In fact, regaining all of my memories only reinforced what I felt. I've loved you since I was eight, and even when I gave my heart to Orpheus, part of it still belonged to you. And now, after all we've shared together, I could never forget you and what we have. And I don't want to."

Now I lift my gaze to his, and tears line his eyes.

"What are you saying?" he whispers.

I push myself off my bed and walk over to him. His eyes trail me the entire time, and his body trembles in his effort to stay in control.

"I love Orpheus. Part of me always will. But my place isn't in the Mortal World anymore. My place is here with you."

"You can't mean that."

"Of course I can."

He shakes his head, trying to back away from me. "You could have a second chance at life. You could go back to the job you love, where you could discover how to cure any Mortal illness. You could see your friends and parents again. You could be with your husband again. How could you want *me*?"

"Because I do." I reach out and cup his cheek, and his eyes flutter shut at the touch. "I want you more than I've ever wanted anything in my life."

Slowly, the black skin beneath my palm becomes bone, the white eyes I love so much fade into nothing, and his feathered wings seem to turn inside out, now showing nothing but a reddish membrane. Like a bat's wings.

Standing before me now is a skeleton, and I know what has happened without having to ask. This is his ethereal form. He's showing me what he truly looks like. I don't know whether he's doing this to push me away or as an act of trust, but I'm glad regardless.

"I'm death." He says it in such a quiet, guttural voice. He says it like the very fact he's death is reason enough to not choose him, to not love him. It breaks my heart.

"You told me that if I still wanted you after I got my memories back, that I would have you as long as I did. Well I'm telling you that I want you as long as the Fates will allow."

"Even like this?" His mouth doesn't move, and I can't see a facial expression from him, but he sounds ashamed.

"I want you in every way."

I lean up on the tips of my toes, using his head as an anchor, and place a kiss on his mouth—or where his mouth should be. All I feel under me is smooth, cold bone, but if I'm not mistaken, I hear a whimper coming from him.

"You can have me in every way I can offer."

His ethereal form fades away, and those beautiful white eyes are once again staring into mine, and I feel complete.

"Orpheus and Charon are down in Hades's office. Do you want me to tell them you're not ready? You don't have to—"

"It's okay. He doesn't deserve to be kept waiting and...I want to see him."

Thanatos nods, his hands gliding up and down my arms. "Want me there with you?"

"No, this is something I need to do alone. Besides, you should go to Tartarus with the others. Those souls will be scared and confused once they're freed. They'll need help."

"I'm not sure that's a good idea. My presence would only unsettle them."

"They're already unsettled. Hecate, Hades, and Persephone can't handle them all on their own. You and Charon would both help a great deal, I know it."

He considers my words for a moment, then he nods once more, leaning down to press a kiss on my forehead. "We won't be long."

"Take all the time you need, I'll be fine."

"I know." He smiles, pride glowing in his eyes. "In all my years, I have never known a more resilient, braver soul than yours."

I feel like I'm glowing from his praise. "I love you."

He smiles wide and true. "I love you too."

ORPHEUS

She looks as beautiful as she did before she died.

Eurydice slips inside the office, wearing her hair tied back in a low ponytail, dressed in jeans and a white ruffled blouse. She seems pretty calm as she faces me, I would almost say indifferent. But then she gives me a small smile and says, "Hi."

And all is right with the world again.

I rush over to her and crush her in an embrace, burying my neck into her shoulder, breathing her in. She still smells the same. She looks the same. She feels the same.

For a beautiful, blissful second, it's like I have my wife back. I clutch onto her, knowing this will probably be the last time I'm able to do so, and I don't stop myself from kissing her. Her soft lips part under mine, and she enthusiastically kisses me back. We both move with the intensity and passion of two people at the end of the world, and even though our lives will go on after this, the world she and I built together will end here.

She doesn't have to say anything. I know where her heart lies now.

I break the kiss and lean my forehead against hers, still holding her body close to mine. I try to breathe her in, to commit her entire being to memory, but there are things I cannot ignore even if I tried: her cold skin, her calm demeanor, her everlasting scent of poppies completely absent…

All these weeks, and it's only now sinking in that she's dead.

"Does he make you happy?"

She nods. "Yes. But so did you, and I don't want you to think that you were some placeholder in my life, or that our love wasn't real. I loved you so much. I still do."

"But…" I whisper.

"But my place is here now. My life is over. I can't go back to it."

"What am I supposed to do without you?" Tears fall down my cheeks, and I don't bother wiping them away. "How am I supposed to accept that your life is over but mine still goes on?"

"It will take time," she whispers, brushing my nose with hers. "And it won't be easy. But you'll find joy in life again. You'll be able to enjoy a world without me in it, and I hope, one day, you'll find someone to enjoy it with you."

Charon pops into my mind then—the feel of his kiss, his urgent touch. I push these thoughts and feelings aside though. It's too soon.

She uses her fingers to brush away my tears. "Remember what I said to you the day I met you?"

I lean into her soft touch. "That I can't change the past, but I can decide what to do with my future."

She nods, extracting her hand from my face. "Don't hold onto the past, Orpheus. Learn to let it go. You did so once. Find the strength to do it again."

"I only did because of you. *You* have been my strength since we were fifteen."

"That's the thing." Her lip slightly quivers, and her expression grows anguished. "You love with your whole soul, Orpheus. Your life revolves around the people you care about, and when they leave, you're left spinning off course. You have to learn to be your own strength. You have to learn to live life for *yourself*. Promise me."

I nod, feeling another tear fall down my cheek. "I promise."

She leans forward and place a gentle, brief kiss on my lips. "Make no mistake. I will always love you, Orpheus Martin. There was no one else I would have rather spent my life with."

"I love you," I whisper, fully weeping. "I don't want to let you go."

She gives me a melancholic smile. "I'm already gone."

CHARON

With delicacy and precision, Thanatos drops one clump of ambrosia into the water, right where the Rivers Acheron and Cocytus meet. The souls underneath look as anguished and starved as ever, husks where they used to be flesh.

Thanatos takes a step back, lowering his scythe until it pierces the water's surface. Almost immediately, the river seems to turn to vapor. Pink mist rises into the air like a geyser, making my friend and I stumble back, shielding our faces in case they get splashed. When the mist dissipates, all that's left in the now dry river are the eternally anguished souls, free at last.

And alive.

We were right. Ambrosia can bring a soul back to life.

Thanatos instinctively moves to help the souls—or Mortals, I guess—out of the dry ditch, but they shrink away from him. A few Mortals even scream, clutching onto each other as if he's about to attack them. Their reaction to me is no different. I reach out to them and all I get are glares and looks of disgust.

I did put them in the river, so I guess their animosity makes sense. Part of me thought I would feel something about it, about my hand in their pain. Whether it was shame and guilt, or satisfaction of finally being remembered for something...but I feel nothing. Their anger, disgust, and recognition makes me feel hollow.

Since Thanatos and I aren't wanted by these traumatized Mortals, Hecate and Persephone focus on calming the souls down, with Hades cautiously trying to lend a hand. He is the one to suggest Thanatos and I alert the families of the newly free Mortals return. We're as welcomed with these souls as we were with their freed relatives, but when they hear the news that their loved ones have returned from their once permanent fate, all caution and apprehension is forgotten. Thanatos is hugged and thanked, and *I'm* kissed on the cheek and cried onto.

I'm not good with the touchy-feely stuff, and neither is Thanatos, though my friend is marginally better than I am; he actually hugs these grieving souls while I just awkwardly pat them on the shoulder. The souls don't seem to mind though. They're far too happy to learn that their loved ones are no longer trapped to care about our stiff reactions.

In small groups, we teleport them to Tartarus, where tearful and heartwarming reunions commence. Everywhere around me there are hugs, kisses, praises to the Fates, and declarations of love. Such a sight once would have made me deeply uncomfortable, but now a new sensation fills its place.

Longing.

Hades steps away from Persephone and Hecate and goes to stand by my side, gripping onto my shoulder gently. "If it weren't for your meddling, these souls would still be trapped."

"Eurydice is the true hero, and Orpheus," I argue, stumbling a bit over his name.

Hades stares me down for a moment, then he informs me, "Seph and I have decided to allow these freed Mortals to live with their families in Mourning until their eventual deaths. Making them go to the Mortal World will only raise suspicion. After all, the last time they were there was thousands of years ago. It will be an impossible transition that won't go unnoticed. Besides, even though they're no longer dead, their souls still need to heal."

"I think that's for the best," I agree, watching two Mortal men run into each other's embrace, laughing into each other's shoulders, raining kisses down wherever they can reach.

"We have this handled," Hades murmurs, nodding over his shoulder. "Go. Be where your heart calls you to be."

I give my friend a small smile. Even after my betrayal, my breach of trust, he still wants my happiness. His friendship and grace is far more than I will ever deserve.

With a deep bow of my head, one of gratitude and humbleness, I teleport away from Tartarus to the gate of the Underworld, where Orpheus stands near Cerberus, his eyes plastered to the path that leads to the hidden tunnel, to the passage that will take him back to the Mortal World.

"Glad I caught you," I say as way of announcing my presence. Orpheus turns around and gives me a smile, though the action is flimsy and weak, like it took strength to do so.

"So am I. I was worried I wouldn't get the chance to thank you, Charon." He lifts his weepy eyes to mine, and a sharp pain pierces my chest. "For everything you did for me, for the support you lent me...I will never forget any of it."

"You shouldn't thank me. I didn't have altruistic reasons for helping you. I was being entirely selfish," I mutter, half smiling.

He chuckles, wiping his nose with his sleeve. "That makes two of us."

I reach into the pocket of his jacket and take out his phone. "If you ever need anything, anything at all, just contact me. I'll be there."

I hand him back his phone, now with my contact in it, and he accepts it with a smile. "I will take you up on that."

The two of us stare at each other for a moment, and I don't try to hide the swirling emotions that build in my chest. Orpheus is the only person besides my family that didn't annoy the shit out of me—the only one that doesn't make me want to tear my ears out whenever I hear them speak. I've never been the most social, friendly person, and that's usually something that turns people away. But not Orpheus. He's just as anti-social and surly as I am. He's unlike anyone—Mortal or Immortal—I've ever met.

But his heart belongs to someone else.

Just my luck.

"I will keep in contact, Charon," Orpheus promises. "You just need to give me some time."

I laugh, but it's short and feels like it was yanked out of my chest. "I'm Immortal, I have all the time in the world."

Orpheus nods, a small smile forming on his lips. "I'm counting on it."

Chapter Twenty

Orpheus

There's a march happening in the streets of Greece.

The roads, still slick with ice, are crowded with angry Mortals—and some Divine Creatures—all holding signs that have the same general idea.

The Gods hate us. The Gods only care about themselves. Why worship them if they don't care about our lives?

I agree with the sentiment, but the last thing I want to do right now is be around people. I want to go into my shitty hotel room and sulk, which is exactly what I do. Once I slip inside and shut the door behind me, I slump against it, sliding down to the floor.

My eyes burn, but no tears come. My chest aches, but no sounds come out. I think I'm beyond that now. I've expelled as much of the pain as I can, and now I'm stuck with the leftovers, which I will have to carry with me the rest of my life. I'll just get better and better at ignoring it.

But all I can do right now is feel it, which is what I should have done weeks ago.

I press my palms against my eyes and rub them, now feeling the price of my adventure in the Underworld. I'm fucking exhausted. I feel like I could sleep for a week straight without waking, and right now there's nothing I'd rather do.

But as I'm getting up to do just that, a chill races down my spine, and the hairs on the back of my neck stand at attention. My whole body is alerting me to danger, but there's no one here.

At least that I can see.

Phobos glides out of the shadows of my window blinds, his expression cold and menacing. Gone is the mask of warmth and friendliness I was met with last time. Now all I see is a very pissed off God.

"Orpheus Orpheus Orpheus…" Phobos tsks, shaking his head. "I had such faith in you, and yet here you are, having completely failed at the *one* thing I wanted of you. I asked you to get your wife back. You'd think you would move the heavens to do that, but you surrendered quicker than Paris did fighting Menelaus. I should have known better than to trust a Mortal. You're all weak."

"Why do you care?" I don't dare move, even as he prowls closer to me, like a wolf about to attack a fleeing deer. "Do you hate your brother so much that you feel the need to ruin the joy he's found?"

"Yes," Phobos hisses, reaching out to grasp my neck. He shoves me back against the wall, keeping me locked there with only one hand.

I feel his fingers tightening around my jugular, and it's becoming harder and harder to breathe by the second. I know fighting him would be pointless. He's a God. So I do the only thing I can think of: I rip my phone from my pocket and attempt to call Charon, though my hands are shaking so much it's hard to press any buttons.

When the phone's ring ends and I hear Charon's voice on the other end, I manage to rasp out, *"Help. Phobos."*

And then the world goes black.

CHARON

"Help. Phobos."

"Orpheus? *Orpheus!*"

No answer. The call gets dropped, and my heart stops dead in my chest.

Without wasting a second, I teleport to Eurydice's room, where I find Thanatos watching her inspect ambrosia under a microscope.

"Orpheus is in danger!" I shout, startling Eurydice, who lets out a little squeal.

Thanatos is at my side in an instant. "What's happened?"

"He called me and said 'help' and 'Phobos.' He didn't sound right. He sounded like he was choking."

"Why would Orpheus say my brother's name?" Thanatos demands, his tone clipped and tense.

I'm about to say that I don't know, but then something occurs to me. "The third time he tried to sneak into the Underworld, he had something on to mask his scent. He was able to go undetected by Cerberus. I've been wondering how he got his hands on something like that, but what if it was your brother?"

"But why would he—" Thanatos's eyes grow wide. "I started to think maybe he would forget his grudge against me, but he's been biding his time, waiting for the moment to strike at me like a viper would a mouse."

"Thanatos, you have to go get him," Eurydice pleads, her hands shaking as she reaches for his arm. "I know he's your brother, but please. I can't bear to have him hurt."

Thanatos places a kiss on her cheek. "Of course I will. Do you know where he is?" He directs the question towards me.

"His hotel is the same one where that Centaur bachelor party happened that killed five Mortals. I knew it instantly by his description of the cheap chandelier and ugly olive paint."

Thanatos nods. "Stay with Eurydice. If Phobos comes for her—"

"I will protect her with my life. I promise you."

He clasps my shoulder, showing his gratitude with a single look.

"Take the others with you," Eurydice says. "Hecate or—"

"This is something I must do on my own." He unhooks her hands from his arm, then he places several kisses on her knuckles, like he's trying to soak up as much of her as possible.

"Good luck, my friend," I say in farewell.

Thanatos's only answer is a smile, and then he's gone.

Thanatos

It takes me a few tries to find the right hotel room, but when I do, I stand face-to-face with my twin brother for the first time in thousands of years. He's looming over a passed-out Orpheus, and even though the shades cover most of the sunlight bleeding in from the window, his black T-shirt, leather pants, thick boots, and tattoo sleeves are visible. It only takes a glance at the tattoos to know that they're words from our language, though I'm too far away to read them.

Despite the tattoos and the new wardrobe, my brother is unchanged. He's still just as angry, hateful, and cruel as he was ten thousand years ago. Even the smile he throws my way is the same.

"It's been a long time, brother," he greets, stepping over Orpheus's body and starting to walk towards me.

"Indeed it has." I look him up and down, realizing just how long. "After all this time, why do you appear now? Why meddle in this Mortal's affairs?"

Phobos rolls his eyes. "Because by meddling with his affairs, I finally had a chance to meddle with yours. Believe me, this isn't impulsive. I've been planning this for a very long time—watching you from a distance, lying in wait for an opportunity to make you feel a shred of the torment you forced me to endure."

"What torment?"

Phobos scoffs, his body vibrating in his anger. "I have been scorned by everyone ever since my birth. Our own parents can't stand the very sight of me—"

"You aren't the only one they despise—"

"But they fucking speak to you, don't they? I've seen Father appear in his astral form to you a number of times, and even Mother has come to visit you a couple of times. Do you think they do the same for me? The last time I spoke to either of them was when we were told we weren't welcome among the other primordial Gods. When we were forced to wander the ether alone, with only each other to depend on. But then you *abandoned me*."

The anguish in his tone pierces my heart, but I refuse to enable him. I spent centuries doing so, and all it brought me was misery. "You grew too hateful, Phobos. You became exactly what our peers thought you always were."

"Why shouldn't I have grown hateful? If I instill fear in everyone, whether by my powers or my very presence, then what's the point in trying to get approval from them? You always cared too much about what others thought of you, Thanatos. So fucking what if everyone hates you? Instead of whining about it like a beaten dog, you could have—"

"What? Traveled the ether, filling anyone we came across with misery?"

"They will never expect us to be any different, so why try?"

"Because then you'll always be alone, which you and I felt long before we parted ways. You can't tell me your life was fulfilled back then."

"No, but imagine how fulfilled I was when my brother disappeared? How do you think I felt when I showed up in the Underworld only to be kicked out the second my presence was known? How fucking fulfilled do you think it made me to watch you find love and friendship in strangers when you couldn't find any in your own flesh and blood?"

I observe my brother for a moment. "How long did you watch us?"

"On and off since you left. No matter what your precious king does, he can't stop fear from entering the Underworld. I can remain there in my ethereal form without being detected. Obviously my days are busy now that there are Mortals, but before them? I was there. Up until a few days ago, it had been some time, maybe a few centuries, since I had last visited. It was your fear of losing Eurydice that drew me back. In eons, you've never experienced an ounce of fear, but along comes this Mortal woman, and you feel a fear so poignant I could sense it from lightyears away. I saw a golden opportunity to make you miserable, but I overestimated this Mortal's resolve."

We both look down at Orpheus, who still lies unconscious on the ground, his chest rising and falling unevenly.

"I thought he could win his wife's heart back, leaving you heartbroken for the rest of your existence, but it was a mistake to be so indirect, and it would have been far less satisfying. Now, you'll know who marked your future with pain, and you'll know you could have prevented it if you had only accepted who you are instead of hiding from it."

And with that, he teleports away, leaving dread sitting dead in my chest.

Eurydice.

CHARON

I am so focused on my phone, waiting for any messages from Orpheus or Thanatos, that I don't notice right away when a new presence enters the room, nor do I comprehend the dread that fills my gut.

What catches my attention is a gasp from Eurydice, and I turn to find her in the arms of Phobos, who has a large grin on his face as he gazes down upon her.

"How nice to finally meet the woman who stole my brother's heart. You're even more beautiful in person."

She struggles in his grip, but his hold is far too tight. His eyes then fall to me, and he narrows them. "Charon, last time I saw you was when you threw me to Cerberus after I snuck in under your nose. How is that furry little fuck doing these days?"

"He'd be excited to see you again, and if you don't let her go, I'll arrange that."

"Sorry, I wish I could, but Eurydice and I here are late for a little reunion."

With another grin, he teleports away. I take out my phone, cursing under my breath as I fumble through the contacts, but just as I press on the call button, Thanatos appears before me, carrying an unconscious Orpheus in his arms.

I rush over towards him, unable to stop myself from touching his face, his neck that's a little swollen, and those beautiful hands of his.

He's okay. Thank all the Gods.

"He took her," I whisper, still keeping my eyes on Orpheus.

"Where?" Thanatos demands, handing the sleeping Mortal over to my arms.

"I can't sense things like Hades can, I don't—"

A buzzing noise fills the room, and I look down at the ground to find my discarded phone receiving a call from the man himself. Now that his hands are empty, Thanatos bends down to grab the phone, and he's kind enough to put it on speaker.

"Thanatos won't answer his phone, do you—"

"I'm here, Hades."

"Phobos—"

"Yes, we know he's here. He just took Eurydice. Can you sense where they are in the Underworld?"

He pauses, then he says, "The Pit of Fire."

Thanatos and I share a horrified look, then my friend vanishes without a trace. The line goes dead on the phone, so I assume Hades did the same.

I hear a groan from my arms, and I'm relieved to see Orpheus blinking up at me, his gaze narrowed in confusion. "What the fuck…did— oh shit, Phobos!"

He moves to get up, but I keep a firm grip on him. "The others will take care of him. You need rest."

He tries to swallow, but it seems to be too painful. "Why aren't you going with them?"

"Because I can't focus on anything else while you're injured," I admit honestly, and my response seems to take him aback.

To be honest, it takes me aback as well. I'm not used to being in touch with my emotions.

It fucking sucks.

"I'm sorry," he whispers, his voice weak and hoarse.

I shake my head, holding onto him a little tighter. "We all do stupid things for the people we love."

"Even you?"

Especially me.

The door to Eurydice's room opens to reveal Hermes, who looks as frazzled as I currently feel. "Uncle called me and told me what happened. I didn't know how badly Orpheus was injured, so I brought some help just in case."

Hermes tugs on the arm of someone, and a very reluctant-looking Apollo comes into view. I haven't seen the God since he last came to visit Hades with his twin sister, which was some time ago. He looks just as handsome and seems to be just as much of an asshole as he was back then. I swear it comes with living in Olympus. They're all a bunch of pricks.

"Phobos strangled Orpheus; I think something might be wrong with his throat. He can hardly talk."

"And why does this pertain to me?" Apollo asks, narrowing his eyes at Orpheus.

Hermes punches his arm, glaring at his brother. "He's our friend, can you please heal him?"

"What's in it for me?"

Hermes rolls his eyes. "Aside from the satisfaction you're a decent being?"

Apollo ignores that comment, looking nowhere but the injured Mortal in my arms. "You're a musician, yes?"

Orpheus nods.

"I'll heal you on the condition I get a box seat at the Sydney Opera House. Hermes said you're the concertmaster."

"Deal," Orpheus croaks.

Apollo bends down and places his palm over Orpheus's neck, which begins to glow as he uses his powers. After a few seconds, the glowing fades, and when Apollo takes his hand away, Orpheus's neck is no longer swollen, and he has no trouble saying, "Thank you, my lord."

Apollo shrugs. "Just don't put me in the nosebleed section. I'm expecting a box close to the stage."

Hermes wraps Apollo in a large hug, making the latter *oomph* in surprise. "Thank you, brother."

Apollo pats Hermes arm. "Yes, yes, can I go now?"

Hermes lets him go with a grin, and just before Apollo vanishes, he glances between me and Orpheus, a smirk playing on his lips.

Smug bastard.

EURYDICE

Wherever Phobos took us, it's fucking hot.

We're obviously in Tartarus, but the exact location is a mystery to me. It was nowhere near this hot when I was examining Acheron and Cocytus. Judging by the dark, scary-looking river to my right, I would venture to guess I'm somewhere entirely different. If I remember correctly, this is the River Phlegethon, which fuels the Pit of Fire—the prison holding the fallen Titans and Giants.

I remember seeing it when Thanatos took me flying, but it is far scarier up close than from up above. My knowledge on the Pit of Fire is very limited from my time in school, but from what I do know, if you are locked inside, you can never be released again.

When I look down, I see a hole in the ground the size of a meteor crater, which the river's water falls into. There's miles upon miles of depth in this prison, where all I can see are bright flames swirling like a coil down the pit. There's a vague outline of a flaming circle with bars in its center, and I can swear there's a pair of eyes staring back up at me.

I have a pretty good guess why Phobos would bring us here and I'm really hoping I'm wrong.

I look away from the flaming pit and towards my captor. "You don't have to do this, Phobos."

He rolls his eyes. "Save it, Mortal. Nothing you could say will make me forget the thousands of years of vengeance in the making."

Gods, he's nothing like Thanatos. It's strange seeing the face of the man I love but not recognizing a single part of it. There is no warmth in Phobos's eyes. No quiet, calm nature to how he carries himself. No humble outlook on life, no love of the written word, and no compassion for anyone around him.

It's strange to think about what could have been. If things had gone differently, Thanatos would be just like his brother.

As if summoned from my thoughts, Thanatos appears a couple feet away from us. Hades, Persephone, and Hecate appear soon after. I have no idea where Charon or Hermes are, but I hope they're taking care of Orpheus. I have no idea what state Phobos left him in, and I can't stop myself from worrying that the worst happened, that next time I see him will be as a soul.

I can't think about this right now. I have to get out of this situation.

Yeah, no shit, but how?

"Let her go, brother!" Thanatos roars, his wings spread out to their full length and his scythe clenched tightly in both hands. I've never seen him look so angry before, so unkempt. Thanatos is usually reserved and sophisticated, but right now, with the rage burning in his eyes and the promise of blood in his snarl, he looks more like his brother.

He looks like how everyone in the Mortal World views him as.

A monster.

This is what Phobos wants, I realize. If he throws me into the Pit of Fire, I'll be trapped there for eternity, and it will send Thanatos into a spiral. No doubt he'll kill his brother, and even if he doesn't, his rage and grief will consume him. He could lose everything. His family, his friends, *himself*.

I can't let that happen.

But what can I do? When Phobos grabbed me, I tried to swipe something from my experiment table to defend myself with, but the only thing I could manage to grab was one of my test tubes from Lethe. I highly doubt a stupid glass test tube will do much against this man.

But the water will.

If I can get Phobos to drink it, he'll lose his memories. He won't remember his hatred for Thanatos and his desire for revenge.

At least, I hope so. Thanatos told me how many memories a person loses depends on their life and their death, and while Phobos's life has been tragic, he's not dead. So who's to say this will even work?

And what if I don't have enough water?

"Why do you deserve to be happy with her after what you did to me? Don't I deserve happiness? Don't I deserve all that you've gained?"

"Let. Her. Go," Thanatos commands. From beside him, I see Hades emitting black tendrils of his power, Hecate's palms glowing a bright green, and Persephone with vines covered in thorns at her feet.

He must know he can't win against all four of them, but maybe he's beyond caring. I guess if you've spent thousands of years planning to take vengeance on someone, holding that much hate in your heart, you're willing to die to achieve it.

This is proven when his arms loosen around me and I begin to fall.

I hear several shouts from above, then I see Thanatos diving after me, his wings tucked in so he can catch me before I reach the flaming gate that holds the Titans and Giants. I feel his hands wrap around me, then there's some pushback as he flexes his wings, stopping us mid-air.

I bury my face into his chest and hug him like I can tattoo myself to his body if I try hard enough. He holds me like he would allow me to if I could.

"You need to get me close to him, Thanatos." I'm not even sure he heard me since my face is still covered by his body.

"What?" Thanatos grabs the side of my head and tugs back so he can see me fully.

"I have a flask from the water in Lethe. If you get me close to him, I can give him the water and he'll forget about all this." I hold up the test tube I snagged, and my hands shake a little.

Thanatos looks conflicted, so I gently murmur to him, "Don't let him turn you into something you're not."

His jaw clenches, and anguish fills his eyes. I know exactly what he's thinking. He's worried if he doesn't take care of Phobos for good, that I'll always be in danger.

"He's your brother."

His breathing starts to slow, and his gaze softens. "I know. But if we're going to do this, we'll need more water than that." He nods to the test tube.

"So what do we do?"

Without answering, Thanatos flaps his wings and we soar into the air, far above where Phobos and the others stand near the Pit of Fire's edge. I expected to see a battle raging on between our friends and the God of Fear, but that's not what we see at all. Hades, Persephone, and Hecate are kneeling on the ground, their eyes wide in terror and their bodies convulsing in an effort to breathe.

"What's happening to them?"

"He knows he can't take them in a fight, so he's using the only weapon he has in his arsenal: fear."

I can't imagine what they must be feeling and or seeing if three of the most powerful Gods alive are brought to their knees in terror by Phobos's powers.

Suddenly, Thanatos dives towards the ground, like he did in his attempt to save me, and grabs onto Phobos by his shirt. The God of Fear yells out in confusion, but the noise is soon swallowed up when Thanatos teleports the three of us to the River Lethe and Phobos is dropped into it. He penetrates the river with a splash, then in a few seconds, he breaks the surface, coughing and spitting out its water.

Thanatos and I circle around the river for a few seconds before we land at the riverbank, and right away I know my plan worked. Everything from Phobos's expression to how he carries himself has changed. As he swims to the bank and collapses on the ground, soaking wet and panting, he seems frightened. He looks up at us like strangers, and it makes me wonder just how much of his memories are gone.

Hades, Persephone, and Hecate show up behind us, and the three of them still look terrible. Hades and Persephone clutch onto each other like they'll die if they separate, and Hecate seems to be counting her breaths with her hand on her chest.

Thanatos sets me down on the ground and kneels to inspect his brother. Phobos flinches away from him when he offers his hand, and he begins shivering, though I'm not sure if that's from terror or the cold river.

"Do you know your name?" Thanatos asks.

He gives a shaky nod. "Phobos. The God of Fear."

"Do you know my name?"

Phobos stares at Thanatos for a second, then he shakes his head. "Should I?"

Thanatos offers his hand again, and this time, Phobos takes it. Together they both stand, with Thanatos supporting most of his brother's weight.

"I'm Thanatos, your twin brother. You have no memory of me?"

Phobos once again shakes his head, and I swear he looks apologetic.

"I betrayed you a long time ago," Thanatos explains, his voice growing hoarse. "I left you when I should have stayed by your side and helped you. But I will not do that again. I will stay by your side while you heal, and you will have the home you and I were robbed of for so long."

Thanatos looks over his shoulder at Hades and Persephone, seeking permission, and they both give it more readily than I would have expected.

"Welcome to the Underworld, Phobos," Persephone greets with a shaky smile.

Chapter Twenty-One

Charon

"You're sure he'll be okay?" Eurydice asks, her nervous gaze trained on Orpheus, who's asleep in one of our many vacant guest rooms.

Hermes, who is on her other side, gives her shoulder a squeeze. "My brother may be a prick, but he would never back down from a deal. He assured us that he would be fine, and I believe him."

"I can't believe Phobos was manipulating him like that," she whispers.

"Fear is a very powerful weapon," I say. "It can be an excellent motivator."

I can feel both of their eyes on me, but I can't tear my gaze away from the sleeping Mortal in front of me. My eyes flicker up and down as his chest rises and falls.

Suddenly, I feel a hand slip into mine, and I look away for a second to find Eurydice there. "Thank you for looking after him while he was here. It means a lot to me."

"You shouldn't thank me. My motives weren't altruistic."

She looks back at Orpheus, and she begins to smile. "Even so. Thank you."

I squeeze her hand. "It was my pleasure."

She steps away from Hermes and me and goes to Orpheus's bedside.

She leans forward, places a kiss on his forehead, then whispers something in his ear that I can't discern. She then turns her attention on Hermes. "Do you fancy a walk? You owe me a detailed backstory on your past lovers."

Hermes chuckles at that, offering her his arm, which she takes gladly. "I thought you'd never ask."

The two of them teleport away, leaving me alone with Orpheus.

I copy what Eurydice did and go over to his bedside, but I don't interact with him. I just pull up her desk chair and sit down, watching over him while he sleeps. I feel like a fucking hypocrite calling Thanatos a stalker when Eurydice first came down here. A couple interactions with a hot guy and I turn into a psycho.

"Charon?"

My eyes lock with Orpheus's, and I feel like a kid caught with their hand in a cookie jar.

"How are you feeling?"

His throat bobs as he swallows, then his eyes lift to the ceiling. "I should have told you about Phobos."

"Why didn't you?"

He refuses to meet my gaze. "He gave me that potion to sneak in, and all he said he wanted in return was for me to bring Eurydice back to life. I knew he wanted something from me, but I was so desperate to get to her, I didn't care what it was. To be honest, I didn't really care what he planned as long as I got her back."

"I get it."

Orpheus closes his eyes, and I see tears collecting on his lashes. "This was such a big mistake. I never should have come down here."

My stomach feels like it's plummeted to the floor. "Don't say that."

He begins to cry, and I so badly want to reach out for him, but I feel like I've been glued in place. "I've wrecked up everyone's lives. Because of me, your relationship with your family is rocky, Eurydice and Thanatos were put under unnecessary stress and heartache, and Phobos was let loose on the Underworld. You should have thrown me in Tartarus the second I showed up. I wouldn't blame you if you did so now."

Without thought, I reach forward and grab onto his hand, and I hold it as tight as I can without breaking any bones. "As far as my family goes, we're going to be okay. Family fight, but they're still family. For all the rest, it would have happened no matter what. And for what it's worth, I don't regret my choices. If I could go back, I would still choose not to throw you into Tartarus."

He sneaks a peek at me through tear-shut eyes. "Yeah?"

I nod in affirmation. "You're the most tolerable Mortal I've met."

He laughs at that, wiping his eyes. "Just tolerable?"

I pretend to consider this. "You're a couple steps away from becoming pleasant, but you still have a ways to go."

"Finding someone tolerable for you is basically the same as liking them, so I'll take that."

I let out a deep breath, looking over that beautiful face of his, committing it to memory. "I do like you. Gods help me, but I do."

He squeezes my hand. "You're pretty tolerable as well."

Thanatos

"I want Phobos to stay in the palace." Persephone is sitting on the edge of Hades's desk, and the man himself is sitting in his chair, holding a glass of whisky in one hand. It's her who speaks to me now, with a tone that leaves no room for disagreement. "I want him right where we can keep an eye on him."

"I figured as much. With your blessing, Eurydice would like to continue to live in the palace, and I thought Phobos could take the room across from hers. That way I'll always be close by."

Persephone and Hades share a look, then the former gives me a nod. "That's fine."

"Thank you for allowing this. I know who he was and what he did, but I have to believe that he can find redemption here in the Underworld. He is what I would have ended up becoming had I not come to live here. Without his memories and with all our guidance, he can find peace. I know it."

Persephone's eyes shine with welling tears. "It will just take us a while to get used to the idea of him being here."

I take a hesitant step forward, not knowing whether my question will be received well. "What did he show you?"

Persephone falls silent, and it's Hades that gives me my answer. "I saw her die by his hands. He slit her throat, and I was forced to watch her bleed out in front of me, while your brother laughed in the background."

Seph licks her lips and clears her throat, then she says in a hoarse whisper,. "I saw the same, but it was him who died by your brother's hand."

"I'm so sorry." I don't know what else to say. It's all I can offer.

Hades sets down his glass and stands, his jaw tightening. "Your sins are your brother's, not yours. You are in no way responsible for his actions because you chose to live here. He made his decisions, and now all we can hope is that he'll repent for them and become better."

"Thank you."

His expression lightens a bit. "I told you when I first offered you a home here, we're all misfits in our own way. We all began life here at our lowest, in our darkest states of mind, but we grew stronger together. As a family. You're a brother to me in ways Zeus and Poseidon will never be, so I will support you, come what may."

I close the distance between us and gather him in for an embrace, which he readily returns with a tight grip on my waist and shoulders.

"I jest gratzieny, Bratner."

I'm grateful, Brother.

Hades grips me tighter. "*Sempsze, mej bratner.*"

Always, my brother.

EURYDICE

How are the new residents handling their transition?" I ask Persephone and Hades, who are sitting to my right. The lot of us are gathered for dinner—with Phobos being an exception. He's in his room, where he has stayed for several days.

Around the rim of her wine goblet, Persephone answers, "They're still very confused. We offered to bring them to Lethe so they can forget their pain, and only about half took us up on the offer. The others didn't want to risk not remembering their families. Those memories were all that they had when they were trapped."

"We've been checking on them every day," Hades adds, slipping a hand around his wife's. "It will take a long time for them to find any sort of peace."

"Could I come with you to visit them sometime this week?"

Seph brightens at that. "Of course you can. I bet many of them would love to meet the woman responsible for freeing them."

I give a bashful shake of my head. "It wasn't just me, I had all of your help."

"It's okay to own your accomplishments," Hecate says, plopping a bite of green beans in her mouth. "You've earned it."

Thanatos, who's sitting on my left, raises his glass. "To Eurydice."

The others follow suit. "To Eurydice."

I glance over at Charon, who stares down at his plate, his eyes unfocused.

"Charon?" I ask, snapping him out of his trance. "You okay?"

Charon's throat bobs as he swallows, then his eyes lift to mine. "No. I'm really not okay."

He doesn't say it with the malice or sarcasm he usually does. He sounds sad. Defeated.

"I know I fucked up." He looks around the table, at his family. "I know I betrayed your trust again and again, and I wish I could look you all in the eye and tell you I'm sorry, but I'm not. I would do it all again for him. Selfishly, I wanted to spend time with a grieving widower whom I have no chances with; even more selfishly, I want the support and comfort of the people I betrayed the trust of; and perhaps the most selfish thing of all is the perpetual shitty attitude I've sported because I didn't have what I felt entitled to, and it took until Orpheus to see how naïve and childish my wants have been. I know I don't deserve it, but could you all ever forgive me?"

Hades stands from his seat, slowly walking around the table, then his arms reach out and he pulls Charon into his embrace.

The Ferryman is stunned at first, but he quickly grips onto Hades like he's the only thing keeping him upright.

"You're forgiven," Hades whispers, cupping Charon's nape. "Whether you're known by ten people or ten thousand, we see you and we love you. And we always will."

Charon's lip wobbles at that, but he sucks in a deep breath and schools his features. "Thank you."

Persephone joins in on the hug, then Hermes, Thanatos, and Hecate do too, and now the Charon we all know and love comes out. "If one more person hugs me, I'm going to scratch their eyes out."

Hermes squeezes Charon tighter. "Eurydice, get in here."

I hold my hands up, shaking my head. "I'm not going to piss him off."

Hermes gives me a defeated look. "But pissing off Charon is so much fun."

"One of my favorite pastimes," Hecate adds.

"You all suck," Charon grumbles.

Persephone smiles. "We love you too."

THANATOS

"I brought you some dinner." I place the plate on Phobos's nightstand, and my brother continues to stare out his window silently, his knees pulled up to his chest where he sits on his bedroom couch.

"You could've came down and joined us," I tell him.

"I'm not welcome."

"Of course you're welcome."

Phobos swallows hard. "They fear me. I don't like it."

Hearing that is music to my ears. I feel like I've been transported back millions of years, when Phobos and I were young and the cruel universe had not yet tainted his heart.

"They do fear you. They fear you because of the person you used to be, but he's gone. You have a second chance, brother. You can change your life and change the way you live it. Don't worry about what anyone thinks of you, Phobos. It's a lesson I've had to learn time and time again. Be true to yourself and those you love, because that's all that matters."

Phobos looks away from the window and stares at me, but he still says nothing.

I turn to leave, but just as I take a step, Phobos says, "Would you like to eat with me?"

I look back at him, finding a glimmer of hope in his eyes.

"I'd love to."

Chapter Twenty-Two

Eurydice

"Are you adjusting well? I hope I didn't leave the house too messy." I start wracking my brain, trying to remember if I ever cleaned up the kitchen from my experiments or cleaned the towels, but my spiraling mind is cut off.

"The house is wonderful, I assure you," he says.

Sebastian, one of the souls freed from Acheron, didn't have any family when he died and therefore has no place to stay as he heals from the trauma of his imprisonment. From now on, I will be living in the palace with Thanatos, so my house in the Field of Mourning is free for someone like Sebastian to take over.

I beam at him from where we stand on Lethe's riverbank. He, as well as many others who are now freed, have been drinking Lethe's water to aid in their healing journey. Usually one drink works, but for these poor souls, they have needed several. Hecate, Persephone, and I have been coming down to the river to help out where we can, finding homes for those who have none and giving directions to those who aren't familiar with the Underworld's layout.

I've also started taking blood samples from willing participants in order to study how their biology has shifted due to coming back to life. I've gotten ten samples so far, Sebastian being one of them. More and more people have offered their blood or updates on their overall being, and I doubt their willingness to be subjected to study has anything to do with concerns or curiosity after their well-being. I think they do it for me.

Hecate let it slip that their freedom is due to my efforts, so when I make an appearance, I'm swarmed by the Mortals and their families of souls, thanking me and hugging me for what I did for them. When I worked at the IMRA, I never interacted with the people our research was helping, so being able to talk to the people I aided, being able to see what my training has allowed me to achieve…it's wonderful.

Every scientist dreams of making their mark, of being remembered for their achievements. I don't know if I will be remembered by the scientific community or by history, but the people I helped, both living and dead, will remember. To me, that's better than any Nobel Prize or acclaim.

"How are you feeling physically? Any trouble sleeping, eating, or doing activities?" I inquire, whipping out my notepad to take notes. I ask these questions each time I visit the victims, and I feel like a pediatric doctor trying to question a child who hates being here.

Sebastian shakes his head, awkwardly stuffing his hands in his pockets. "No, I'm alright."

I eye him suspiciously. "Are you sure about that?"

He avoids eye contact as he shrugs. "I'm eating and sleeping a lot. It's honestly all I've been doing."

That seems to be a common reaction. "From what I've seen from the samples, your bodies are starved. You were dead for thousands of years, and now you're alive. Your body is trying to replenish itself. If this is becoming a bother, I can ask Hecate if there is a potion you could take to lessen the intensity of your symptoms. I would recommend just letting things ride out, though. You need to allow yourself to heal."

Sebastian nods, giving me a small smile. "Thank you, Doctor James."

I've started using my maiden name again. It felt wrong continuing to use Martin now that I'm with Thanatos.

"Of course. Don't hesitate to reach out if you have questions, new symptoms show themselves, or if you need something, such as more clothes or food."

He dips his head in thanks, then he excuses himself, claiming to be tired. I'm sure that's true, but I could tell being under my magnifying glass is the last place he wants to be right now.

Maybe someone else wouldn't mind.

"Even in death you are a busybody," a familiar voice says from behind me.

I whirl around and nearly drop my notebook when I see Prometheus standing a couple feet from me. He's wearing a suit, like usual, with a burnt orange tie that makes his ember eyes pop. He's smiling big and wide, his arms outspread. I don't leave him waiting, running into his arms and laughing gleefully into his chest.

"I've missed you," I whisper, basking in his warm embrace.

He pulls back from our hug, cupping my jaw in one hand while gripping my shoulder with the other. "As have I. I've been meaning to come see you, but work at the IMRA has been made difficult by the storm's lingering effects and the protests from Mortals. Not to mention, I have yet to find a replacement for your position."

"I know, I'm impossible to live up to," I tease.

A smile spreads across his cheeks. "You are indeed. Hesione has been filling in for you, but we both know her skills lie in gene therapy."

Very true. "You know, I could always continue my work from here," I suggest with a leading tone, leaning my head towards my shoulder in a half shrug.

Prometheus gives me a disapproving look. "You're dead, Eurydice. You should be enjoying your afterlife, not working."

"We both know that without my work I get bored," I protest, trying not to sound whiny. "I tried the whole 'resting in peace' thing and it lasted only a week before I was testing samples from Lethe. I've been dead a month and I figured out a way to free souls that have been trapped for eons and discovered the secret to bringing souls back from the dead!"

Prometheus's brows rise, his body stilling. "What?"

I guess no one caught him up on what's been going on down here. "Boy, do I have a story to tell you." I chuckle.

Still looking dumbfounded, he nods. "Yes, I believe you do."

"Say that I can continue working, and I'll spill every detail."

Prometheus's lips twitch and amusement crosses his features. "You haven't changed."

"Is that a yes?" I scrunch my mouth up, batting my lashes at him like a child begging for a new toy.

He rolls his eyes, but he doesn't look annoyed. "Yes, fine. You can continue working."

I let out a squeal of excitement, my hands clutching tightly onto his arm. "Thank you! Thank you!"

He waves me off, still trying not to show his own joy. He wants to pretend I coerced him and that he wasn't begging for me to work again, but I know the truth behind his admonishing expression and amused gaze.

"Now." He finally gives me a small smile, confirming my previous thoughts. "Tell me what in the name of all the Gods you meant by *resurrecting the dead*."

I link my arm through his, nodding towards the palace looming in the distance. "How about you stay for some dinner and get the full story? Then I can give you my notes and research from the last month."

"It's good to have you back, Doctor Martin."

"Doctor James," I correct gently.

Prometheus tilts his head, confused. "Doctor James?"

I pat his arm sympathetically with my free hand. "Buckle up, my friend. You're in for quite the tale."

While Prometheus is discussing my visions from the Fates with Hecate over grilled chicken and steamed vegetables, I step out from the dining room to gather my research together for him to take back to the IMRA. He's used to reading my jumbled reports and stacks of notes, but usually

I'm able to unload some of them onto his lap every day, and this is an entire month's worth of observations, testing, and analysis.

He might need a few people to help him deliver it all. When I brought up this concern to Hades and Persephone before I left the dining room, they assured me it wouldn't be an issue.

They haven't seen how disorganized I am though.

When I open up my bedroom door, my steps come to a halt before I even cross the threshold. Standing over my workstation is Phobos, his eye pressed into the microscope, his expression curious.

I feel a chill race down my spine, and that's when Phobos looks up, giving me an apologetic look. "I'm sorry. I can't always help it."

"Help what?"

He looks back down at the microscope, and I swear I see shame flash in his white eyes. "The fear. The unease. Sometimes I can rein it in, but most of the time, it just happens."

I nod, trying to ignore the bone-chilling dread coursing through me. "What are you doing in here?"

"I've heard the others discuss your experiments. I was curious," he explains, taking a step back from my equipment. "My apologies for intruding."

After Phobos lost all of his memories, his countenance has been far calmer and more laid back. Maybe even a little timid. According to Thanatos, this is how he was when they were first born, and it makes me angry knowing the hatred and rejection he received created such an angry, cruel person. Even now, without the knowledge of his past, he's still burdened with the fear and unease he instills in those around him.

"It's no problem," I assure, gesturing to the microscope. "What do you think?"

"Of what?" He hesitantly leans back down to peer into the lens.

"That's what your blood looks like. Well, your brother's, but I would venture to guess yours would look identical."

Phobos lets out a disbelieving laugh, tenderly holding onto the side of the device like it's a priceless treasure. "It looks like a cluster of stars."

"Your mother is the Goddess of the Night and your father is the God of Darkness. You and your brother were born from the night sky, from the stars themselves."

Phobos lifts his head to look at me, and in his eyes I see a whirl of emotions. Confusion, sorrow, shame. He wears his them plain on his face, and that was the case before he lost his memories too. He is raw emotion, whereas Thanatos is all stoicism.

"I don't remember them," Phobos admits. "All I have is a vague sense of awareness for what is true or false. When Thanatos told me my name and our relation, I knew it was true. You telling me of my parentage, I can feel the truth in your words."

I know exactly what he means. "You need time to heal. Once you have, your memories will return and everything will make sense."

His head drops towards the ground, his fingers stroking the neck of the microscope absentmindedly. "Something tells me I won't like what I remember."

Not knowing how to ease his apprehension, I decide to change the subject. "Are you interested in science?"

He looks around at my makeshift lab of desks, papers, and beakers, then he gives me a shrug.

"I could always use an assistant for my studies," I begin, smiling. "You interested?"

He flinches, as if I just insulted him. "You want me to help you?"

I nod firmly, trying to show him through my body language how serious I am.

"Everyone else is too afraid to be around me," he states as a fact, not as a question.

I close the distance between us, and as I expected, the dread in my stomach intensifies, but I try my best to ignore it. "You're Thanatos's brother, so that makes you family, and family stick together."

His lips part and his eyes widen, like the idea of family is lost on him. "In that case, I think I would like that. Thank you."

In a spur-of-the-moment decision, I reach forward and hug him. A shudder goes down my spine, my anxiety and dread so intense I somehow feel nauseous despite being dead. Phobos stands completely still, and I can tell by his rigid stature that he's debating whether to flee from my embrace or not. But I hold tight, and eventually, Phobos pats my back. It will have to do.

I pull away from his embrace, secretly thankful to put some distance between us. "For your first task as my assistant, can you help me gather all these papers?"

Phobos gives me a small, timid, brief smile, and that alone feels like a win. "I would love to."

CHAPTER TWENTY-THREE

EURYDICE

ONE MONTH LATER…

"Now, you see this border? What's that called?" I question in a soft tone.

Phobos, his eyes on the lens, gives a little excited gasp. "Is that the cell wall?"

I giggle at his enthusiasm. "Yes, it is. And that circle in the center?"

"The nucleus?"

"Excellent!" I tell my assistant/star pupil.

Ever since Phobos started working with me on my experiments, he's become a lot more comfortable around us all, settling into life in the Underworld. I've come to truly enjoy his company, and despite our rocky introduction, I believe the two of us have become friends. I can definitively say that about everyone in the Underworld. Two months into my death, and these Gods from legend are now family to me. I think this is part of why Phobos and I have been able to bond: we're both newcomers into an established unit. We get to navigate a new experience with new people together.

I glance over at Thanatos, who is reclined on our bed with *Prose and Poetry of Mikail Lermontov* in his hands and his scythe resting on my pillow. When he's not cleaving a soul, he's here with us, observing my work and listening to the lessons I teach his brother, occasionally reading like he is today. I think his presence puts Phobos at ease; he certainly has that effect on me.

Somehow he senses my gaze, and when his lifts his eyes to mine, the warmth and love I see there brings me complete peace.

He and I have been taking things slow ever since I got my memories back, and he's been incredibly patient and supportive while I sort out all my feelings. I am confident that I made the right choice in staying here, but I am still grieving my life with Orpheus, our marriage and our love. Part of me will always love him; he was my husband, after all…still is, I suppose. I can't say I'm completely moved on from him, or that I'm no longer in love with him, but my very being calls to Thanatos in a way I can't explain. He's the missing piece to a puzzle I didn't realize was unfinished. My very soul belongs to him, and his to mine. It's that simple.

I think Orpheus, in time, will find his own missing piece. Or realize that he already has.

With his eyes still locked with mine, Thanatos says to Phobos, "Mind if I steal her away, brother?"

Phobos shakes his head, never once glancing up from the microscope. "I'll be here."

I step away from my working area as Thanatos slips off our bed. He meets me in the center of the room, with his hand outstretched towards mine, and I take it without hesitation. I'm unsurprised when he teleports us away to the library, where the book he was reading me last night lies on the couch, right in front of the crackling fireplace. The book is a first-edition copy of John Keats poems.

I've come to learn that Thanatos is a big fan of Romantic Era poetry, and since I'd never read anything from that era before, Thanatos has made it his mission to introduce me to every poet.

"Are we picking up where we left off last night?" I ask, eyeing the well-loved hardback.

Thanatos cups my face in his hands, wrapping his wings around my shoulders. "I don't care what we do. I just wanted to be alone with you."

An incredulous, joyous laugh bubbles out of me. "You say that like we didn't spend all night and morning alone."

He pecks me on the nose. "I crave your company like a flower craves the sun's light. As much as I appreciate you dedicating time to teaching my brother, I anxiously await for the moment each day when I have you all to myself."

John Keats has nothing on my man. "Sounds to me like you're jealous of your brother."

He shakes his head, his thumbs brushing my cheekbones. "Not jealous. Just addicted to your attention."

I lick my lips, running my hands down the buttons of his shirt. "Addicted, huh?"

His white eyes grow heated. "Yes."

I give him a mischievous grin, brushing my index finger against the sliver of skin available on his collar. "I like having this much power over you. Millions of years old, an immortal god that personifies the end of life…and you quiver at my touch."

Thanatos's hands slide down to my jaw, tilting my face up towards his. "You are the only one who ever has and ever will have power over me. My heart, my soul, my life, they are all yours."

I slide my hands down his sides, gripping onto his belt to pull him closer to me. "When you say things like that, it takes all my willpower not to jump your bones."

His head tilts at that. "Is this a Mortal phrase for copulation?"

"Don't say copulation. It's too clinical."

"Apologies. Is this a Mortal phrase for fornication?"

I let out a half laugh and half groan. "That's even worse!"

Thanatos smiles down at me teasingly. "Anytime you wish to 'jump my bones,' you are free to do so. I only ask you not do so where any books can come to harm. I've heard of couples having intercourse against bookshelves and I couldn't handle that."

Gods is he adorable. "Do you have any objections to sex in the vicinity of books? Like a library perhaps?"

His eyes widen in disbelief. "But anyone could walk in."

I giggle, beginning to undo his belt. "I know, that's half the fun. Are you feeling up to a little fornication?"

"I didn't think you were ready to restart out physical relationship yet."

I pause at that, feeling the need to explain. "This whole situation is very unorthodox and I was trying to give myself some time to process and move on, but I don't think it's that simple. Healing isn't a line only going up. There's loops and curves along the way, and instead of leaving you to wait for me at the finish line, I want to traverse all those twists and turns with you. I may have good and bad days, I may want to take things slow or fast, but I'm not going to stop being with you."

Thanatos leans down so our foreheads connect, then he gently brushes his lips with mine. "If you only want me to hold you and reaffirm my love for you, I will do so. If you want me to worship your body again and again, so be it. I am no Mortal man driven by my desires instead of my heart. I can be by your side as you heal without sex. I don't want you to do something solely to appease me."

I tug on his belt and walk backwards towards the couch, dragging him along with me. "I love you, that's why I want to be with you physically. I appreciate what you said, though. I find your respectfulness and chivalry very attractive."

I fall back onto the couch with Thanatos looming over me, his wings outstretched like a hawk about ready to dive towards its prey. "I am happy to use my mouth to reassure you of my feelings and intentions whenever you wish, though right now I would like to use my mouth to please you in other ways."

I don't think I've ever heard Thanatos flirt before. I like it. "I could get used to an eternity of this."

He kneels down in front of me, with my legs on either side of his torso. "Trace thy footsteps on with me, we're wed to one eternity," he whispers, trailing his mouth down my neck and chest.

I arch into his touch, smiling at his words. "I'm guessing that's a poem."

He nods, slipping off my shirt and bra while reciting, "Say maiden wilt thou go with me in this strange death of life to be."

With my upper body now bare, Thanatos leans forward and kisses the valley of my breasts, murmuring against my skin, "To live in death and be the same, without this life, or home, or name. At once to be, and not to be that was, and is not—yet to see."

His mouth trails kisses over to my left breast, then to my right, his hands undoing the fastenings of my jeans. "Things pass like shadows—and the sky above, below, around us lie. The land of shadows wilt thou trace and look—nor know each other's face."

The timbre of his voice is low and sultry, adding an eroticism to the beautiful words he quotes. "The present mixed with reasons gone and past and present all as one. Say maiden can thy life be led to join the living to the dead."

He pulls down my pants and underwear together, leaving me naked before him, and his white eyes trail me over from head to toe as he finishes with, "Then trace thy footsteps on with me, we're wed to one eternity."

Indeed we are.

CHARON

My fingers play across the keys of their own accord, without me even having to think. I've played this song so many times in my life, especially as of late.

Rachmaninoff has always been one of my favorite, if not my most favorite, composers. His songs always have a melancholic edge to them, and I feel like that's how I can best be described. No matter how happy I may be, there's always a bit of sadness laced within the joy.

It used to be because I felt insignificant to the world. No one gave a shit about me, no one knew me, and it would always be that way. But after Orpheus, I don't care about that anymore. I hate most people, so why do I want the praise and acknowledgment of people? I'm finally understanding what he meant by being known by all but not being *known*.

Everyone can know your name, but they don't know you. That's what Hades and Thanatos have been saying. No one understands the real them but our family, and they have to battle internally against others' perceptions of who they are. With me, I can just be myself.

And that was never truer than when I was with Orpheus.

He's returned to his life now. He's back in the Mortal World where he belongs, and I'm down here like always, rowing my stupid little boat and harboring feelings for someone still in love with his dead wife, who's now a permanent part of my best friend's life, and by extension, my life.

So here I am, playing "Vocalise" by Rachmaninoff, draining a bottle of red wine that's been aging for five centuries.

I'm just reaching the climax of the song when my phone starts to ring. It's sitting on top of the piano, buzzing obnoxiously as it alerts me to an incoming call.

I pick it up without looking to see who it is. "Can you fuck off, I'm trying to wallow."

"Hope that's not because of me."

Orpheus.

"W-why are you calling? I thought—"

"I've been writing a piece that I'm going to present to my orchestra tomorrow. It will be my first original piece. I was wondering if I could play it for you?"

"Like right now?"

"No. In person."

"You know I can't leave the Underworld."

"I'm not talking about at the opera house. I want to come visit you and play you my song. I also…I really want to see you again."

"Really?"

"Really."

I feel myself smile for the first time in weeks. "When?"

"Maybe you should go check the gate. I don't know how long the bone I got for Cerberus will last."

I've never run for the door so fast in my life.

EPILOGUE

DIONYSUS

Two Months later:
One week before the annual Creation Day celebration…

I take another swig from my flask, wishing for once I could actually get intoxicated.

"You have no idea how horrible the conditions in the Mortal World are," Hephaestus argues to our father.

Zeus waves off his concerns. "According to Hermes, most of the ice and snow from Demeter's storm have melted."

I roll my eyes, deciding it's my time to chime in on the discussion. "We don't mean the fucking snow. Everyone is pissed off at the Gods, and rightfully so. We never take accountability for the mistakes we make, some of which come at the cost of Mortal lives. They no longer want to worship Gods who don't give a shit if they live or die."

Zeus scoffs at the very notion. "Impossible."

"Oh really? Gotten many prayers lately?"

Now Zeus pauses.

"Exactly."

With a shake of his head, Zeus looks around at the other Gods attending this meeting, including my uncle Hades and his new wife, Persephone, whose seats in the Hall of Gods have just been crafted by Hephaestus.

"What do you propose we do then?" Zeus asks no one in particular.

"Mortals are fickle. They'll get over it," Areas argues.

"I agree. So what if they're not sending prayers? Now I no longer have to worry about meddling with their miserable lives," Apollo adds.

"Oh you poor thing. A sick mother begs you to heal her dying child and your free time is encroached upon. Tragic," I bite.

"Watch it, brother," Artemis warns.

"No, you all need to wake up to reality." I stand up from my seat, directing an angry glare to the entire room. "Yes, the storm may be over, but people are still starving, people are still sick, and people are still dying. The tides have turned against our favor and now the Mortals are demanding change or else there will be retribution. We can start by canceling Creation Day. No one will appreciate all the Gods parading themselves around like nothing is amiss."

My mother, Hera, shakes her head. "As much as I hate to agree with your father, we can't cancel Creation Day. It's been tradition for thousands of years. It's what keeps us connected to the Mortals."

"No, it's a chance for all of you to prance around like peacocks," Persephone says with disgust.

I send my new aunt a grateful look, then I return my attention to my father. "If we continue to treat the Mortals like they're nothing, then their anger will only increase."

"So what? What will they do against all of us?" Poseidon asks.

"We may be powerful, but there are few of us. There are maybe a couple hundred Immortals? Well there are billions of Mortals. And those billion Mortals are cunning, strategic, and have something we don't—something to lose. You can bet your ass they'll fight for the lives of their loved ones and for themselves."

Zeus narrows his eyes. "This was Ariadne's idea, wasn't it? She told you to come here and say all this."

"No, she had nothing to do with this. I just have the ability to self-reflect and empathize."

"Don't you think it's time we let go of this archaic notion that because we created the Mortals it means we're above them? Cronus created us, but did that stop us from overthrowing him and taking power? Did we stay subservient to our creator? Does any child submit to the will of their parent for all time?" Hades asks.

"You're comparing apples to oranges, Uncle," Ares insists.

"Am I? I agree with Dionysus; if we don't change our ways, the Mortals will turn on us."

"Let them try." Ares gives a booming laugh. "I haven't taken part in a war in a long time, and I can sense one brewing."

Aphrodite rolls her eyes but says nothing.

Hestia looks at Zeus with pleading eyes. "Brother, maybe we should—"

"No." Zeus's voice silences the room. "We will not submit to the anger of Mortals, nor will we cancel a celebration of the day they were fucking created, a decision I'm regretting more and more each year. You tell your wife and in-laws that they can expect us at the Spartan palace in one week, where we will formally introduce Hades and Persephone as part of the Olympian council."

His tone leaves no room for argument, so I do the only thing I can do. I nod. "Yes, Father."

Zeus turns his attention back to the rest of the council. "All of you should rest up and prepare for the week ahead. On the 7th of July, we will celebrate and party alongside our subjects. This year's festivities will be like nothing we've ever seen before."

On that, he and I agree.

ACKNOWLEDGMENTS

I once again want to thank my family: mom, dad, my brother, and Allison. You are still my entire world. I love you very much.

I want to thank Sydney Thaxton, Kennedy Grubb, NelRae Toler, Samantha Ianarelli, John Ianarelli, Zoey Mistalski, Michaela Murphy, Stephanie Lattanzio, Jeremy Perdue, Andrea Bosco, AJ Bosco, Fred Rapp, Maddie Laine, Elizabeth Harris, Dae Todd, Cliff Todd, Aryanna Domorod, and Alyza Domorod for your love, joy, and support. I am lucky to have each of you in my life.

Thank you, Karen Bagley and Kaylee Moore, for making me able to function and always supporting me.

Thank you, Jamie Schlosser, Katherine Macdonald, and Renee Rocco for your support, guidance, and friendship. Thank you to Sam Hall for her help as well.

Thank you to Rebecca Scharpf, my editor, Rena Violet, for making beautiful covers for my books, and Stacey Blake, my formatter.

Thank you to my beta and sensitivity readers: Zoey, Annie, Tori, Mika, Cassie, Elizabeth, West, Samantha, and Maile. Diversity in literature means nothing if the author is not representing people accurately and does harm to those the characters are based on, so thank you all for helping me ensure I do right by the communities I write about. Special thank you to Janelle for making sure I wrote two Australians accurately.

Thank you to my ARC team; Abbie, Alyssa, Mar, Ash, Elle, Jess, Marissa, Meghan, Nikki, Nola, Roosa, Sarah, Varshni, Annie, Shauna, and Victoria. I couldn't do this without your help.

I want to thank the creators of the *Writing with Color* Tumblr page for helping me and other writers bring accurate representation to the books we write.

I want to give a very special thank you to the nurses, doctors, surgeons, and staff of Novant Hospital in Wilmington, North Carolina. You saved my dad's life. I will never be able to repay you for that.

FROM THE AUTHOR

This book was a labor of love. I have always implemented my own life struggles into my characters, but I've never had a situation where I was experiencing something alongside my them. A big theme in this book is grief, and while I have felt it before, I had never known the all-consuming nature it can create until I nearly lost my dad. He had a freak occurrence, one in a million, involving an infection that led to a corroded heart valve and an abscess on his stem. He had two open heart surgeries, was hooked up to an ECMO machine, and induced into a coma for 8 days. All the doctors said he was the sickest person in the hospital and nearly died. I've lost loved ones before, but the very concept of losing my dad consumed every fiber of my being while he was sick. I had already finished The Dance of Death and was in the middle of editing it at the time, and this experience connected me to the story in a way it never did before. My dad was lucky, and thankfully he's recovering fine, but the fear, helplessness, anger, and grief still lingers. I poured these emotions into the journeys taken by Orpheus, Eurydice, Thanatos, and Charon, and it has turned into the book I am most proud of. There is something about death that reminds you how beautiful and precious life is, and that is the whole point of The Dance of Death. Without death, we cannot appreciate life, and without love, what's the point of life?

If you don't know already, there is a novella called The Souls We Mend that wraps up the storyline of Orpheus and Charon. It will be out March 31st 2024, available exclusively on Kindle and Kindle Unlimited. There will be no physical version (Eventually I will publish a physical bind up of all novellas in the series, because there will be a few).

The next book in the series is *The Labyrinth of Lies*, which follows Ariadne and Dionysus. It will be out early 2025.

Whether you loved this book or not, I would appreciate if you rated my book and gave it a review. I value all of your opinions and would love to know what you think I did well and what I can improve on!

ABOUT THE AUTHOR

 Savannah James grew up in Northern Virginia before moving to North Carolina for college. She lives with her parents and brother while she works on getting her degree in anthropology. When she's not at school or writing stories, she can be found reading with her two dogs by her side, probably with Gilmore Girls in the background.

Find her at these links:
Linktr.ee/authorsavannahjames
You can also visit my website where you can find extra content from my books and my blog.

Made in the USA
Columbia, SC
30 March 2024

2559181d-ff5a-496a-89b1-19c11c492b6dR01